The Uprising

A. Davis

Chapter 1

This is a story about when everything changed. I changed, the world changed. You may not have known what was happening back then, but it had all started years ago. Not all the details may be here, but these are the events that occurred as best as I could recollect them.

The thunder was almost deafening- at least that's what I thought it was at first. Perhaps it was the proximity of dozens of stampeding feet to my ear. I always thought it was corny to liken the sound of a herd of elephants to thunder, but I have to admit it was rather spot on. At that point, I didn't know if it was better to pray that they miss my head or just get it over with already.

I felt a tugging and then a burning sensation in my left shoulder.

"Heads up! I don't want to lose you here, Dr. Wake!" My associate was yelling as he pulled me from under an oncoming foot. It was all happening so fast. There was a whirl of dust and an overwhelming taste of salt and sand in my mouth, making it hard to breathe.

"I think they're safe now."

"THEY'RE safe now?" I choked out as I found my breath. I couldn't help but laugh a bit as I wiped the tears from my eyes. The savanna can be a rough environment for the uninitiated, and I was barely out of the starting gate.

"I'm not sure this is what I signed up for! At least, it's not what was in my contract!" I tried to sound more confident than I was, but I could tell he knew I was just short of peeing my pants.

"I'm surprised you read it!" Jaffey said back. It's true, the contract was over 30 pages, and I admit that we were in a rush to get moving on the operation. I MAY have missed a few items as I looked over the document before signing it. OK, maybe more than a few, but if you can't trust a non-profit animal welfare group, who can you trust?

I looked around before getting to my feet. You can't be too careful out here. After all, my major nemesis comes equipped with enough fire power to take out what passes for a small village around here. These two poachers were on the hunt for a while and wouldn't take too kindly to someone interfering with their work.

"I think Nkiru took care of that last one. The second poacher was reaching for his rifle that last time I saw him, and now he seems to be missing his arm, and his leg, and his head," I heard from my left. It was Marcus, Jaffey's second in command. Marcus was in charge of vehicles and our own fire power, as well as being our only body guard- we travel light, no entourage here.

"I love Nkiru!" I chuckled and couldn't hold back a big grin. Nkiru was one of the females of the elephant clan. I wasn't sure which family she belonged to, as they were already joined together into one consolidated clan when we tracked them down. She was probably at least forty-five, as they said they didn't think she was still fertile. The aggregate of scars on her legs and hind end told her tale of near misses and escapes. Loxodonta africana africana, the savanna subspecies of African elephants, were quite large and majestic. It was a shame that their value was reduced to nothing more than what their tusks were worth on the black market.

"She'll be kicking butt when she's 70!" Jaffey said with a big grin of his own.

"We can only hope," Marcus said with a sigh. The optimism seemed to leak out fast from this little victory.

I didn't usually relish another person's demise, in fact, I would much rather see them pay for their actions through the court system. But, hey, I didn't shoot the guy. Nkiru did her thing. It was her revenge to take. I played by the rules, and it just so happened to work out- this time. Jaffey had warned me that poachers would do whatever they could and whatever they needed to get their bounty, and I needed to be alright with our protocols-- or lack thereof. A training period would have been nice. You know, get to know your co-workers, learn the rules and regulations, and that the coffee maker was in the break room- things like that.

"So this is on-the-job training, eh?" I said to Jaffey. He just smiled. Did he lose a tooth in this throw down or has it been missing the whole time? Maybe I just never saw him smile. Jaffey was originally from London, but has spent more than a decade on the plains of Kenya and Tanzania. I would put him around fifty-ish, but he could be a bit younger with a weathered face. The sun could do some serious damage out here. It didn't help him any that he used to be a smoker, either- two whammies for the complexion. But that was part of his character, right?

"We need to pick up the bodies...or parts as they are," Marcus was coordinating. Another part of his job, I guessed.

"I'm pretty sure that's not my responsibility!" I chimed in.

"Normally, no. But, it is just the three of us, and it would go faster..." Jaffey could be convincing when he needed to be. Still, not my cup-o-tea.

"Animals are MY thing, not human body parts. I went to vet school, not med school, remember? Mostly because I'm not a fan of people – especially these ones." I tried to reason with them.

"Well, they're dead. I don't think you have to socialize with them."

"Probably better conversation than I've had in the last day.....D'oh!" Usually I don't joke around so personally with people I just met, but we did almost die together.

"Wise-ass. I think I will like working with you. Now grab that arm."

We headed back to base camp with our oh-so special cargo in the back seat next to Jaffey. I just hoped they had some place to keep the bodies when we got there. There were more than enough wild animals out here looking for a good meal, especially an already tenderized bloody mess previously known as 'the poachers'. Oh, and don't get me started on the smell. Part of me felt bad for these hunters, though. They were just looking for ways to support their families, like most people. I just wished that they would find alternate forms of employment.

"So, Doc, looks like your expertise helped us in the end after all," Jaffey said to me as he leaned in from the back seat to the front where I was lucky enough to be sitting.

"Did you doubt it?" I asked him, thinking that he was against my participation from the start. Forensic medicine was something to get used to, I supposed. You really could tell a lot from the direction and size of blood spatter. Now, we could tell what family a piece of ivory came from, as we had DNA databanks on several known elephant families in and around the Mara National Reserve, as well as other places.

"I had my doubts, yes. When headquarters insisted on sending you out in the field so quickly, well, I had my reservations." Jaffey looked worried, like he was holding something back.

"Well, I agree with you, I really didn't need to do it in person. We had everything mapped out for you, the DNA told us where most of the poaching was coming from. You could have handled the take down without my help." I was wondering why I was here as well.

"Dr. Ceta, the one in charge wanted it this way," he said.

I didn't know much about the organization that I had just signed up with, my only contact before that point was with Jaffey. I had helped with the DNA analysis of the recovered ivory, something that was a little more in line with my work, not this cops and robbers stuff.

"What are we going to do with the bodies, I mean, body parts?" Not that I needed to know, it was starting to gross me out.

"Marcus and I will take care of everything. You don't need to worry about the details."

I was happy about that, but intrigued as well. What were they planning on doing with the bodies? I assumed they would be shipped to the government department that was in charge of taking care of poachers, and then probably to the remaining family, if there were any. Jaffey was making it sound like something nefarious was going down.

The ride wasn't too long, but we spent the rest of it in silence. I was preoccupied with thoughts of my new job and what exactly I was getting myself into. Jaffey was probably wondering if I was the right fit for the organization. It was going to be an adventure, for sure.

Base camp never looked so good. It wasn't much, but it had tents and sleeping bags, and that was what my aching body was calling out for. I let the men handle the body parts from there- I was pretty sure that it wasn't in my contract, besides there weren't that many to move.

All in all there were five of us. I never did catch the names of the other two men that stayed back at camp during that last attack. I wasn't even sure if they spoke English. Marcus was sparse with his words, so that left Jaffey if I wanted conversation, which I didn't at that point- I needed some sleep.

I awoke several hours later to relative silence. The rest of the group must have been asleep, I figured. I needed to stretch my legs and use the bathroom, so I got up to walk around. The others were indeed sleeping, and my morbid side started to show when my thoughts went to the bodies we had just brought back. I wondered where they put them. After using the facilities- think hole in the ground- I rummaged around the campsite.

I couldn't find the body parts anywhere. Perhaps they had sent them along ahead of us, but all of our vehicles were accounted for. Did someone come to pick them up? Jaffey could have radioed in to the game warden to have them removed. Still, I think that I would have woken up by all the commotion.

The fire had been dying out, so I stoked it back up into action and made some coffee. I would just have to wait until the others woke up to get some answers. It gave me time to think about the day's events, and wonder if I really wanted the answers to those questions. I was to head back to the States later that night, to start the 'real' part of my new job, the part that was far away from the deserts of Africa.

In my previous jobs as a forensic veterinarian, this would have been the time for documenting the evidence, compiling statements, and preparing for press releases and other media involvement. I was good at what I did, but it had its burn out levels. Emotions could get extreme when dealing with animals and welfare issues, and the turnover rate in these jobs was high. I had recently taken a break from all that, questioning if this is what I was really meant to do. I had hit my limit several times. I wasn't sure if it was time to jump back in- it felt too soon- but Jaffey had convinced me otherwise.

When the others awoke, I pulled Jaffey aside to ask him about the bodies. He brushed the topic aside as if it was about the weather, and that's when I started to get that ominous feeling. It was OK, I didn't really need to know what happened to the remains, but it made me wonder what kind of organization I was now a part of.

Further questioning had yielded little more than a grunt and a shrug.

"What about the press release?" I was certain there would at least be one of those. A non-profit group that worked in animal welfare lived for press releases; it was their mainstay, their livelihood.

"It may take a while, things out here move slowly...red tape, government issues, you know. I will let you know if I need your input when it's time." He didn't make eye contact with that statement. I knew he was blowing smoke, but I didn't know why. It would take several weeks before I knew what was going on with him, with the organization. If I was aware of the events to follow at that point, I think it all would have gone down differently.

Chapter 2

"Welcome back." It was my new partner-in-crime, or should I say partner-against-crime, Martin. He went by 'Martini'. Yes, he was a James Bond freak, among other things. We met just before I was sent abroad on the poaching ring case.

"That's not much of a tan. I thought Africa was hot and sunny."

"Did you ever hear of sunscreen? And we didn't get to spend much time by the pool, you know," I quipped. "And, yes, I'm OK."

"I didn't know you wouldn't be."

I went into the long story of the poachers and the shotguns and the elephant stampede. Martin was rather pale by the time I recounted the large foot within inches of my face. I think that I may have been close to the same shade myself, as I felt my heart racing from just the memory alone.

"Holy crap, batman! I had no idea that you'd be in the middle of the action! I wish I went with you!" Martin was getting worked up with the concept. "I could have taken out those poachers- pow, pow, pow!" He mimed an action hero- or the power rangers (that was maybe more his speed).

"Jaffey did fine with the whole 'taking care of the perp' thing. I have to admit that I was a bit preoccupied with the pachyderms. There were at least two dozen in the combined group by the time it all went down," I was explaining to Martin. "It was weird. If I didn't know better, I would swear that the elephants knew what was going on."

"What do you mean?"

"I mean it was like they knew who the good guys were. Like they knew we were there to help." I tried to explain what I saw. Or rather, what I felt. "Maybe it was just my emotional state at the time. I really felt like we were all a team. I mean us AND the elephants."

"Mmmm-hmmm. What did you say your background was?" Martin was looking at me with a raised eyebrow.

"Ha. Well, whatever. It's just what I felt in the moment. And you know my background. I told you all about myself when we met." I concluded by sticking out my tongue at him. I could be juvenile, too.

"Nice. Well you are back just in time."

"Just in time for what? Do we have a case here?"

"Yes, Dr. Ceta just sent over a fax." Martin reached over the desk behind him.

"A fax?? Are we in the stone ages? Even Charlie's Angels got a speaker phone message!"

"Who? Um, that's just how it's done here, a lot of faceless direction. Didn't they tell you when you signed up for this gig?"

"Uh, no." I admitted that I didn't get the whole tour. In fact, I didn't even meet Dr. Ceta. It was a bit of a whirlwind, as I recall.

"Well, HQ sends a fax, we process the crime scene, then you do your thang with whatever animal bodies we find- alive or dead," Martin went on as if I didn't know ANYTHING about the job.

"I know WHAT we do; I just figured our boss would be a bit more hands on. Like actual contact of some sort."

"To quote you, 'Ha'. Not here, honey, we are on our own."

"OK then. Where are we headed and what's the situation?" I took the fax from Marty's hand and read it for myself. "West Virginia. Dog fighting. Wow, they are big on details, prolific writers, even." I got a chuckle out of my partner.

We packed up the evidence collection kit. Most of what we needed was already in the car. The agency, STAFE, kept a fully stocked vehicle for spur of the moment exits, if needed.

"Are we the first ones going in to secure the scene? What about search warrants?" There were too many details that were not filled in for my liking.

"It goes like this- we assume there is a warrant already in progress. We usually have it by the time we arrive on scene. The agency is very thorough with the legal details," he filled me in.

"This is not how I'm used to operating. Usually, there are steps taken, like securing a warrant before we leave, and we are all kept in the loop. You know we can't use any evidence collected without proper procedure in place," I worried out loud.

"You'll get used to the procedure here. I've only been working for STAFE for two years- almost, anyway- and I got into the groove quickly."

We finished grabbing the few things that we needed- several bottles of water, protein bars, the backup camera (the main one stays in the vehicle at all times), and extra evidence bags.

"Is there..."

"It's in the car." Marty jumped in before I could finish my question.

"How about..."

"Yup, in the car. Trust me, EVERYTHING we need is in the car. The agency is very thorough."

"So, I'm just supposed to believe that an agency that won't even communicate face to face and uses a fax machine is on the ball with stocking a forensic investigation vehicle?" I got another chuckle. Well at least I was amusing my sidekick. Never the less, I did my due diligence and took stock of the vehicle's contents.

It was a six hour ride to the site in West Virginia from our office on the outskirts of DC, and a back-road trek for the last 45 minutes of it. I was always amazed by how much the GPS knew about the most hidden places. Or at least it thought it knew. My mind was drifting in and out as Martin told me about his last roommate, Jonathan.

9

"And you can't call him John. Oh no, no, no. Never. Have you ever seen a grown man have a hissy fit? I mean full-blown, slapping with both hands up and down with head tilted back, hissy fit?"

"Uhm, I don't think so, no. I take it he wasn't the easiest person to live with?" I was thinking of all the traveling and small talk we would be engaging in, or should I say, enduring, in the future. I really hoped we got along well in the long run. So far, so good, at least.

Martin gave me the eye and continued, "You would think he was a neat freak or something with all his rules. But no, he was a slob. Jonathan the slob."

"So not Felix, but Oscar?"

"What?" It seemed I lost him on that one. I forgot how much younger he was than me.

"It was a TV show in the 70's. The Odd Couple?"

"Oh yeah, with Mathew Perry? I never watched it, but I saw a few commercials for it."

I forgot they made a remake of it. Not that I watched many of the original episodes- in rerun, of course, I was only in my thirties. I let it go, and my gaze drifted out the side window to the scenery going by.

Awkward silence started to settle in. It was only a matter of time. We had to find our rhythm. Usually, this was where someone commented about the weather or other overly generalized topics. But since this was, theoretically, a long term relationship, I let it play out. Awkward silence was only awkward if you thought of it that way. This was a new chapter, and I wanted to do it right from the start, whatever that meant.

The terrain was getting more rural as we approached the town listed on the fax. My stomach started to flutter a bit. I usually got nervous when I was getting closer to the crime scene. You never know what you will come across in these situations and you never know what you'll see. And, coming off of an elephant stampede, I think I was a bit anxious.

I started to think about the last scene I processed in my previous job. It was last year, June, if I was recalling correctly, I was knee-deep in a body dump. Florida was known for its heat and humidity, but throw in a half dozen greyhound cadavers, and you had a smelly and bug-infested situation. That was when I was working with the Humane Society, investigating a dog breeder with less than honorable practices. The dog's ears had been cut off to hide any evidence of ownership on the bodies (US racing greyhounds had tattoos in their ears. The right ear had a birth date and the left had a registration number.) I was brought in to identify and document the cause of their deaths. It didn't take my expertise to see the cause. Starvation and dehydration were common occurrences in animal abuse cases. None of it was pretty, and none of it was painless. It was a hard situation to witness, but my role was to try to help catch the scoundrels who did these things and keep them from ever doing it again. I constantly reconsidered my choice in careers, and I had to remind myself that someone was needed to do this job, to take the perps to justice, to stand up and speak for those without voices. Why not me? I wished it wasn't needed, that I could put myself out of a job. If only.

A large pothole shook me back to the present. "We must be getting close by now," I said to Marty.

A strange humming sound came from the back of the vehicle. "What's that?" I said concerned that the last dip in the road jostled something loose.

"The fax. Should be conformation of our search warrant. The police should be there already with their own, though. This is just to confirm what we can look at and take as evidence."

"Another fax?" This was going to take a bit to get used to, I thought. "Even I'm a bit more progressed with technology than that!"

We arrived at a partial clearing on the left side of the road. A rudimentary dirt road, at best, curved around into a partial thicket. We followed it around the bend and parked next to an old trailer up on blocks. One police cruiser was up a little further on the right, and a solitary deputy was leaning up against the driver's side looking down at his feet.

11

"He looks bored. I hope he hasn't been waiting there too long. I mean, not the whole six hours by himself," I said to my partner.

"I worked a case a few towns from here but never met this guy before. Probably just a local. I wonder if they are volunteer here." Martin thought that all the towns around here were devoid of individual police forces, or any town officials for that matter.

We walked over to the twenty-something looking man in blue. "Hey there. I'm Dr. Alexandra Wake, the forensic veterinarian with STAFE. I understand there's a crime scene here." I offered my hand to him.

"Uh, yes, ma'am. It's been secured and we started to process it when we got a call from you all to stop what we were doing. So we stopped and waited for you to get here, like you said."

I was a little confused. We called? We had the power to stop the locals from conducting their own investigation? I wasn't aware of where we fit into the hierarchy of jurisdiction. And did he just 'ma'am' me??

"Yes, thank you," I just went with it, winked at Martin and turned back to the deputy for more details. "Did you touch any of the evidence?"

"Nope. Just a couple of boards. Oh, and the stand thing," the officer said proudly.

"Uh huh." So, in other words, everything. Great, OK, well I was used to that. Apparently everyone thought that the TV version of CSI was how things really happened. It was hard to explain how evidence could be destroyed and rendered inadmissible if someone walked even near the scene due to possible transfer, much less if random people touched everything.

"I hope you at least wore gloves and documented all the people on the scene."

"Well, it was just me and my boss, sheriff Tinely. We don't usually carry gloves in the car, sorry."

"Awesome." I tried to not sound upset. He was the local we had to work with, and full cooperation was needed to get my job done. Unhappy deputies usually translated into a lack of cooperation if not outright hostility. I motioned for Martin to start photographing the area as we approached.

"How 'bout showing us around the property and give us the details as you know them," I asked the deputy.

"Well, I reckon you know a bunch already, from what I heard about the phone call," he said.

"Let's pretend that I don't know any details. Start from the beginning so we don't miss anything," I told him as I looked over my shoulder to Martin with a questioning look. Martin was no help, he just responded with a shrug.

"We got a phone call last night from a neighbor, way over on the north side. Seems he heard some screaming. Like a woman being murdered, ya know?" The deputy looked at me for confirmation. I nodded, more to prod him along in the story. "Well, so, he called to tell us that and then we rushed out this way. We must have spent over an hour driving around these parts and looking, but we didn't find anything."

"Please continue," I prodded again. Now we were making our way around an old barn that was missing a few of its wall panels as well as most of its windows.

"At that point we saw a vehicle flying through the intersection back there," he nodded in the direction of the way we came in. "We gave chase, but we lost him around Billy's uncle's old place. It's just a foundation now, maybe you all saw it coming in? Anyway, we decided to back-trace his steps and find out where he was coming from." The deputy again looked proud.

"Sounds reasonable deputy.....," realizing that I never asked him his name.

"It's Deputy Freeman, Howard Freeman, ma'am." Again with the 'ma'am'!

"Nice to meet you Deputy Freeman," I faked a smile, but at that point I was rather tired and losing patience.

"Nice to meet you, too. Anyway, so then, we were able to see the tire tracks leading up to the barn. Looks like he was in a hurry and peeled out over there." Again he nodded his head

13

to indicate where they found the tracks. "So then we investigated this barn for illegal activity."

"What evidence did you find...and please just point from here. We need to preserve as much evidence as we can," I said in as kindly a fashion as I could muster.

"We first saw the blood stains on the walls in there, and we thought someone was murdered. But upon further investigation we found boards that they must have used as walls for a dog fighting pit and a gouged up break stick with blood." The deputy looked a little queasy at that and motioned us to go ahead and see for ourselves.

Martin continued to photograph the outside of the barn as we made our way to the door. I knocked and called in to announce our presence as a matter of habit, even though the deputy sounded sure the place was secured. An overwhelming odor of dog urine, feces, and decay hit us when I opened the door. Martin turned on his flashlight and aimed it around the inside, taking pictures before we entered. Inside to the right was a stack of old boards with some dark stained areas on them. To the left looked to be a bunch of random junk that collected over the years- car parts, old tires, rusted out farm equipment, and old cans. Martin took pictures of all of it. You never know what can turn into evidence as you worked a case, and you didn't get to go back unless you could get another search warrant. You only got one chance to do it right the first time.

"The deputy said he saw a break stick somewhere," I thought out loud.

"Over here against the wall," Martin was straight back and to the right nearing where they probably had the pit set up. I pulled on a pair of gloves and picked up the wooden stick after it had been properly documented by Martin. A break stick was a tapered object that got inserted into the mouth of one of the dogs to separate them when they were fighting. One or two were usually found around dog fighting scenes, usually close to the pit area, where the actual fight took place. This one was gnarled up with some dried blood on the side.

"I don't see any bodies. Do you see any signs of burial in here? We are going to have to scout the area for fresh dig sites and mounds." I didn't hear anything back from my partner; he seemed to be engrossed in sample collection from the pile of wood panels. "Martin? Marty? Martini? Oh good," I continued as if he responded, "maybe we can get a canine lineage from the DNA in the blood on the boards." Many of the professionals use known and proven lineages for their dog fighting. Some of these dogs could then be traced back through their roots, and known associations could be tracked down and interrogated.

As Martin swung around with the flashlight, I caught a glimpse of something through an old tire on the left. I approached it slowly, not knowing what, if anything was there. I heard Martin come up from behind me, intrigued by my movements. An old can reflected the light and illuminated a brownish object. I noticed the teeth right away- long canines with a few incisors missing. It was a canine skull, possibly a fighting dog. As I got closer, a second skull was visible.

"Trophies or just a dump?" I heard Martin ask.

"Not sure yet, we need to check for more body parts. Could be someone was collecting the skulls for show."

We spent the next hour going over the pile of junk in the surrounding area.

"It looks like just the skulls. If you look through the tire from this point you can see them clearly." I was standing back about ten feet to the right, approximately where the pit looked to have been set up. "I think he did it to intimidate or brag to his opponent. You can't really see them from any other vantage point." We documented and bagged and tagged the evidence.

"Let's document the surrounding area. I need a break from the smell in here," Martin said with a sigh. I knew exactly how he felt.

We vacated the barn and started to look around for evidence of a burial. Fresh graves could be easier to find when there were obvious disturbances to the ground, but older sites could be harder to identify. Sometimes mounds with new vegetative growth could indicate a site, as plants thrived on the nitrogen source of the decaying body.

"Over here," I heard Martin say after what seemed an eternity of looking around. I made my way to his location. He had already photographed everything and was starting to remove the thin layer of dirt covering what looked to be some clothing. After digging just a little way down, a human hand was unearthed surrounded by what appeared to be a sweatshirt.

"This is no longer our scene. The medical examiner will have to come out for this. Better call the deputy over."

I drove the way back to our office. Martin needed a rest, and I needed to go through the details in my head. Most dog fighting rings were closely associated with drugs, child pornography, and even human trafficking. Was this the case here? Or perhaps this was a case of someone who abused animals and then escalated into abusing people and ultimately murder? We had collected a good amount of evidence but proving dog fighting could be difficult. All of the evidence could be explained away as a random dog fight, even saying it's a rescue group. If it is a dog fighting location- and I was sure it was- it certainly wasn't the place where the dogs were trained. We didn't find any chains or O-rings where the dogs get tied out much less any conditioning equipment. That meant that there was another location that needed to be sought out, and it could lead to the killer of the person in the shallow grave.

"Hey, what do we tell Dr. Ceta about the case? Martin? Marty?" He was out cold. How could he sleep at a time like that? I tried to nudge him a bit, but he just rolled to his side and fogged up the window with his breath.

Six hours was a long time to spend in a car, especially when your sidekick was non-responsive. My adrenaline was still rushing from the discovery of a human body. I had been to many crime scenes for animal abuse, and I had heard of many of those perps who went on to killing people, but that was my first discovery of a body. I mean, I saw a few along the way when I arrived on scene, but there were medical examiners, police, and occasional FBI agents already there processing that part of things.

My mind started to wander to all the faces of the dead I had seen in my line of work- humans and animals.

Chapter 3

Thunder- that's all I remembered as I awoke from a dream. I was damp with sweat, and the sheets looked like they were pulled from every corner of the bed. A sense of sadness fell across me. Did I make the right decision taking this job? It was a struggle that I fought most days of my career. And like most days, I had to put it out of my mind, focus on helping the innocent, and fight the fight. "Let's do this!" I said out loud, to no one but myself.

I jumped to my feet and started getting ready for the day. It was a rainy April morning in Virginia, and I tried to focus on the green grass and flowers. The whole springtime thing should be more uplifting, but this time of the year usually made me sad. Perhaps ennui was a better term. I thought moving here and taking the new job would have been enough of a distraction to keep me going. Maybe I should just focus on work.

I made my way into the office on the third floor of an old building on the outskirts of the city. I heard some rustling from the back as I walked over to raise the curtains on the front windows.

"Hey Marty!" I shouted with as much enthusiasm as I could find. "Why is the office out here in this part of town when HQ is downtown, anyway?"

"They got the bucks, that's why!" He chimed in from behind the door. "Maybe they don't like associating with us hands-on working types."

"Well, I don't like it. Share the wealth, I say. At least when it's their wealth to share. What do they do over there at HQ anyway that they don't want us to be part of?" I asked not really expecting an answer.

"They're very private. I've only been there once, myself. I think they have a hidden room where they develop the latest spyware and stuff," Martin said with a smirk.

"Is that your official James Bond opinion, Martini?"

"How else do you think they know everything before it happens?"

"What do you mean?"

"Check out the fax on the machine," he said with a raised eyebrow. He did have the James Bond look down- at least as far as facial expressions went. I walked over to the machine and looked through the small pile of papers in front of it. One sheet had the headstock of STAFE that was addressed to me.

"How did they know what we found at the crime scene? I didn't file our report yet. Did you send them anything?" I was a bit annoyed. Any communication from our end should go through me, or at least cc'd to me.

"Nope. That's how it goes here. I've checked for bugs in the car and the office before with no luck. It's as if there's a mole, but no one else works here."

"Maybe it was the sheriff. They did talk on the phone before we were even notified of the case," I posed.

"Could be, but this happens all the time. They have secret ways of getting things done," Martin said followed by his version of ghostly sound effects and the wiggling of his fingers in my direction.

"You're a goober," I replied and shook my head. "So do I even bother with my report?" I mused, but mostly to myself, as I sat down at the computer to write it up. We had a lot to get done today, Most importantly: seeing if any of our evidence leads us to where the perp trained and kept his dogs. "Did the evidence get over to the lab?"

"Yes, it was the first thing I did this morning. I wasn't sure if you wanted the skulls first or let the lab do their thang first, so I left them at the lab. I hope that was OK," Marty said as he went through some paperwork of his own.

"Yes that's fine," I replied only half paying attention to him. I wasn't sure how to word my report, much less know if we should be pursuing our case given that a homicide would be taking precedence. I reached for the pile from the fax machine again to see if any other instructions came in for us from the agency. As I was turning away with the stack the machine went off, startling me.

"Looks like HQ can read minds, too!" I joked to my partner and grabbed the paper from under the machine as it was finishing. "Nope, false alarm. It's from the lab to let us know the results before they put it into the system- wow, they are quick in this town, contrary to popular opinion."

"What?"

"A joke about Congress...you know....sloooooooow....," I exaggerated the word. He still looked lost, so I moved on. "So the lab found traces of soot and wax on the handle of the break stick, the skulls, and on the boards. The canine DNA will take a couple of days to process."

"Soot and wax? Hmmmm." He looked like he was trying to put the pieces together, but as far as I knew, he could have been pondering what he was going to have for dinner. "Hmmmmmmm...."

"There's going to be smoke pouring out of your ears soon if you think any harder," I said as I winked at him. He still looked a bit confused. Maybe that was just his normal appearance, what did I know. "Anyway, you need to get over to the lab and get the skulls for me. I need to document any deformities and wounds present on the bones."

"Right-O. Need anything while I'm out?" Martin started gathering a few things together as if he was off for an expedition.

"Um, no, but thank you. You know you're just going to the lab, right? Do you usually pack that much?"

"It's just some paperwork for HQ. One of the techs at the lab said this morning that she was headed over there later. I figured she could drop off some stuff for me." He flashed a half grin at me as he went out the door.

Soot and wax. Wax and soot. It was on all the items that the person involved in dog fighting would have touched. So why would it be on someone's hands? The guitar riff to "Smoke On The Water" drifted into my head. Dun dun dun, dun dun du-nun, dun dun dun, dun dun dun. I started tapping it out on the desk and bobbing my head. Dun dun dun, dun dun du-nun, dun dun dun, dun dun dun. OK, clearly I was distracted. Smoke on the water- smoke was coming from Martin's ears when he thought too hard...sometimes I liked to trace back the reason for the songs in my head. I didn't always find the link, but sometimes I did. Of course I got a little proud of myself for finding it. I could be a goober, too.

As if on cue, Martin walked through the door with the box of skulls. "One box of skulls, just as ordered," he cheekily said as he placed the box on the long table running half the length of the far wall of the office. "Box of skulls- that should be the name of a band!"

"It probably is, somewhere," I told him as I walked over to the table. "I think at this point, every name has been used, whether it's a signed band or backyard get-together. Any new news from the lab...or HQ, while you were there?"

"No, but I got the feeling that they weren't in a rush to process anything else. And they seemed quick to get me out of there, like I was in their way. Sometimes I'm not so sure they love me there," he said as he winked in my direction.

"They could just be waiting for the machines to sequence the DNA, sometimes it's just a waiting game. Don't know why they'd rush you out of there, though. Did you shower today?" My turn to wink back.

I turned on the magnifying light that was on a flex arm attached to the wall over the table, and put on a pair of disposable gloves. Taking out the first skull from the box, I asked Marty to grab a ruler for me. There was an obvious laceration to the lateral aspect or the left eye orbit. I noted the depth and length of the wound in the bone. The orbit itself

21

had micro-fractures on the ventral rim all the way up to the wound.

"Looks like some deep gouging- probably from the opponent dog. Could have lost function of the eye with that blow," I said. Martin grunted in agreement. I glanced over his way for a second to gauge his mind-set. He had a sort of scowl on his face, and I asked if he was alright.

"I can't believe people find this entertaining- animals forced to fight each other, until death sometimes. Why don't they just fight each other, I'm sure no one would miss them if one of THEM died." He did have a point. But, unfortunately, our job was to process and document and collect whatever we could to stop them, not to take justice into our own hands.

"You never get used to it. Let's just see what else we can get to track down this loser." I was trying to keep myself motivated as much as I was trying to keep him focused on our jobs. "Here's some of the soot the lab was talking about." I backed my head out of the way so Martin could see for himself.

"What do you think that's all about," he asked while exploring the surface of the left temporal bone.

"Not sure, but I would guess maybe it's from his line of work?" I offered up my opinion as I noted everything I found on the skull. "What job has someone working with soot and wax? I can't think of anything having to do with dog fighting. What about a location? Maybe there's soot and wax where he held the person from the grave we found. I didn't see anything in the barn that could have been the source." I kept spit balling theories out into the open, more for myself to find a thread than anything else.

"I didn't see anything either. What does soot have to do with wax, was he a candlestick maker? Hahaha!" Martin amused himself.

"Can you call over to the lab? I want to know if the wax and soot were mixed together, or in layers, or what," I asked him.

"Sure. Do you have a theory?" He asked while walking over to the desk. I just gave him a questioning look. I was beginning to feel like that was my go-to look around here.

I pulled out the second skull to document any defects on it. The mandible was missing as well as the first molar from the right maxilla. Some soot was grossly visible on the left orbit and frontal bone. I looked further for any traces of wax. Under the magnifier I could see a few ridges of what appeared to be a waxy substance. No other defects were found anywhere on this skull.

"Georgie over at the lab said there were ridges of soot and ridges of wax. So I guess not mixed, but next to each other?" Marty said as he strolled over to the table.

"Ridges like fingerprints?" I wondered what it meant. Then I wondered if the lab lifted usable prints. "So were they able to run the prints through the system? Do we already have a suspect?"

"If we do, they aren't telling us anything about it. I got the feeling we are now out of the loop."

"I can't just let it drop. At least not until I'm officially told to do so. We need to figure out who this guy is because you know it's part of a bigger dog fighting ring. I mean, it's not an isolated incident."

"I agree. Where do we go from here?"

"Soot and wax."

I set out on an internet search and had Martin do the same- the keywords being soot and wax. If we could put together some facts to go with our evidence, we might be able to put a working theory together.

"Should I skip the candle making entries?" Martin joked.

"No, we better keep them in the mix, just in case. Who knows what this guy was into. Maybe he was starting his own wax museum for all we know." I waited for a chuckle or even a raised eyebrow, but got nothing. Well, at least he was taking things seriously.

"I got a furnace repairman? Soot but no wax. What about a mason- pointing chimneys?" Martin sounded like he might be on to something.

"Chimneys. What about a chimney sweep? Do they still do that?" I asked out loud as I looked for more search engine results. "Yes, they do still exist."

"Seriously? Do they wear top hats and tails like the movie?" That was the biggest grin I had seen on Martin's face since I met him.

"One of the logos seems to indicate so. But we still don't have wax. Focus." I told myself, but Martin gave me a weird look.

I started skimming websites and ads, testimonials and reviews. Martin busied himself with the furnace repair lead, searching through the same type of information that the search engines spewed out. After I thought I had exhausted that idea, I stumbled on a blog about tough stains.

"It looks like baking soda, dish detergent, and hydrogen peroxide gets out anything from any substance. I wonder if it really works." I mused.

"What does that have to do with anything?" Martin sounded tired.

"Nothing. I ran out of chimney facts. It apparently gets out soot."

"We still don't have wax." He yawned and dropped his head to the table.

"Borax, Lava, Ajax....all help get soot off your hands." I yawned now, too- was yawning contagious? "Wearing gloves, covering your hands with lotion, and chalking up prevent soot from getting into the grooves in your hands." I sank back into my chair and looked at the clock. Three hours had past. Only three hours? It felt like at least five. I watched the clock tick for a minute, then two.

"Hand lotion. Some hand lotions have wax. Wait." I said as I jumped back on the keyboard. I punched in a few more key terms and an obscure blog popped up referencing a type of lotion that was mostly wax- used by many chimney sweepers to prevent soot from embedding into the grooves of their hands and fingers.

"Got it! Now we need to find a chimney sweep that's involved in dog fighting!" I found new energy and started searching chimney sweeping companies in the area of the crime scene. "Marty, start calling these places. See what kind of information we can get out of them."

A handful of calls and a few white lies later, we were on the road following a lead.

"Shouldn't we call the police to do this?" Martin asked as he turned onto the beltway. It was a valid question.

"I just want to do a drive-by. And maybe a stakeout. And maybe canvas the area, questioning his neighbors. We need something more than soot and wax to get a search warrant," I explained to him and to myself. This was the right thing to do, right? The sane thing? Not that I was an expert on what's sane. Marty flashed me a half grin, and I could see something devious in his eyes. I was thinking that we will be getting along just fine.

After about the first four hours of the ride back to West Virginia, I started to doubt my decision. Road trips always sounded so cool at the beginning. I fumbled with the radio, finally landing on some older Portishead, and got the raised eyebrow from my partner. I flashed him a big grin while cranking the volume. A little "Sour Times" never hurt anyone.

"A bit depressing, don't you think?" He tried to reach for the buttons, but I intercepted.

"No, but you can change the station when the song is over." I turned to look out the window and took a deep breath. At least the rain had stopped.

"What do we do when we get there?" Martin considered our game plan as we neared the address he conned out of the secretary on the phone.

"I won't know until we get there. We're just winging it." I barely got the words out when Martin swerved violently to the right to avoid a Lincoln veering into our lane from the fast lane. My hand was clenching the door handle so tight that it was blanched white.

25

Tegan and Sara's "Walking With a Ghost" came on the radio, as I pried my hand loose.

"I hope that's not an omen," I mused, trying to make light of our near accident. We continued on in silence.

We were within half an hour of our destination when the fax machine went off. I slowly looked over at Martin and then back to the machine. Martin's words were in my head as I reached back to grab the fax. Does the agency know what we are doing all the time?

"Did you tell them where we were headed?" I asked Martin.

"No. Didn't even think of it. Dr. Ceta must be wondering where we are. Or...they...already...know," Martin tried his best to sound scary, but not so much.

"Says we should head back to the lab. Case closed. What's up with that? Case closed? We are just getting started. I wonder if it has to do with the DB."

"DB? Are we talking in acronyms now? And we are almost there. What do you want to do?" Marty said as he slowed down to pull over.

"DB- dead body, and let's keep going to at least see the place. There might be something in plain view we could use to get a warrant and keep going. STAFE might not know that we tracked down an address for the perpetrator."

"A DB, as you say, wouldn't be enough to pull us from the case, unless it's a federal thing and they are pulling rank, but as long as I've been working here, they've never admitted that's happened, but I have had my suspicions," he replied and sped back up.

"Well something is going on. I wouldn't think the agency would just drop the whole thing. I know we didn't get a lot of evidence, but it was a good start. And, I'm pretty sure they got fingerprints from the break stick. We definitely have to keep going and at least see the place."

The traffic lightened up quite a bit by the time we hit Brownsburg, a few towns from our destination. GPS seemed to want to take us down a road that wasn't there. Awesome. Grabbing my cell phone from my back pocket (yes, I know, a no-no if one wants to avoid the original form of butt-dialing, but I was in a hurry), I did a Google map, a MapQuest, and a Yahoo maps search to figure out another way to go. They all suggested another side street a few miles down that backtracks to the cross road we needed to take. At least I was able to get cell service to look that up- things must be going our way!

The sun was setting as we pulled onto the perp's road. "101 Hampton Rd. That should be toward the end on the left." I told Martin as I squirmed a bit in my seat.

"Antsy, or is your butt asleep?"

"Both. I hope no one is home to see us stalking about."

We were starting to get into 'creeper' mode when a police car pulled out of the driveway up ahead.

"That might be the address," I said. "What do you think is going on?" I craned my neck around as we passed by to get a glimpse of the commotion. "Looks like a hearse. Try to turn around and pull over, I want to see what's going on."

Two men were just loading a body bag into the back of the vehicle when we got positioned. Another police officer was headed over to his car to leave as well.

"There's a scanner in the back, maybe we can hear what happened." Martin offered. I quickly rifled through some equipment and pulled out the scanner. Martin grabbed it and shuffled through some settings just in time to catch the end of the officer's call into the department.

"...homeowner's body....apparent suicide, over," was all we heard through the static.

Chapter 4

It was another long drive back to the office on the outskirts of DC. I took to the wheel somewhere outside of Sutton, when we pulled over to regroup. A lot of questioning looks and very little conversation was exchanged between Martin and myself, and I spent most of the ride in deep thought about the agency, STAFE, and its director, Dr. Ceta.

"I know two things for sure," I said out loud even though I knew that Martin was in la-la land. "One: Every perp I've come across so far has died and two: This agency has serious communication issues!" I tried not to say that too loud. "That's not a great track record so far."

The next morning was hard to face. There were too many questions and what seemed like loose ends to allow any sleep. My first order of business was to find out a little more about the agency I was working for. What did I really know about them? I felt kind of foolish not being fully cognizant about them. I did my research for the interview, mind you, but it was slim pickings on the internet in regards to their background and history. I mainly went by the few articles that referenced them as sources of information and as legal aids in prosecution cases against animal abusers. There really wasn't much in the way of information on their organization.

I made my way to the office, about seven blocks from my new apartment. Martin wasn't there yet, so I went about starting up the computers and going through the mail. I kept drifting back to questions I had surrounding STAFE. I found myself browsing the internet for any new links to the agency that I didn't yet see, all while one hand was gripped tightly around a large mug of coffee. I'm not sure why this all gave me the willies.

Their short-but-sweet website didn't offer much. 'STAFE-Save The Animals From Exploitation'- not the greatest title, or acronym for that matter. 'Mission statement- To stop the exploitation of wild animal populations around the world and to protect the balance of nature.' Well, that's a little non-specific, and inauspicious. 'Director- Dr. Ceta, PhD.' Then there was a smattering of cases referenced that STAFE had a hand in bringing to justice. I needed more.

Martin stumbled in as I was Googling 'Dr. Ceta'. "Hey, I was wondering when you were going to get here. How did you sleep?" He just gave me a look with half opened eyes and made his way to the coffee pot. "That's about how I slept, too."

"Mwoeenhsdfdj," is what I think he said with a mouth full of coffee. Maybe it was 'morning'.

I was getting sucked back into the computer. There had to be something about our good doctor- like what was his degree in? Where was he from? What was his first name? The foolish feeling started to come back over me, and I felt my face getting flush.

"Whatcha doing? I thought we didn't have a case anymore?" Martin managed to get out finally after chugging several mouthfuls of hot brew.

"Don't you burn your mouth doing that? And I'm just looking into our employer, getting to know him a little better," I said with a grin.

"Dr. Ceta is a her. At least that's what I heard." Martin was doing his best to stay awake, but he was mumbling half of his words.

"Dr. Ceta is a woman? Huh. Guess I never pictured that for some reason. OK, well, do you know anything about her?" I tried not to sound too misinformed, but clearly I knew even less than I thought.

"I've never met her. For some reason, I thought you had. Who did you meet when you signed your contract?" He looked concerned now.

29

"Jaffey's secretary. Jaffey was already in Kenya when I was rushed through the whole 'new hire' process. The flight was already booked and I had less than a couple of hours to pack my stuff up and fly out. If most of my things weren't already packed from the move, I would've been in trouble for time." I thought back on that day, on the details of what took place. It started at the headquarters, downtown, where I assumed I would be working. I guess I made more than one erroneous assumption that day. I remember marveling at the ornate decor of the crown moldings as I walked down the entryway. I never made it into an office, the secretary informed me of the urgency of my first case.

I had been in contact with Jaffey for a few weeks prior to that point. My name had been associated with a few cases dealing with DNA extraction from illegal elephant ivory poaching. We used it to trace back the origin of the ivory to certain regions in Africa. Jaffey asked about the accuracy of this kind of 'mapping' and how it was done. I had explained how genetic markers from DNA found in elephant dung were mapped out, and the markers from the ivory were matched. He spoke of leads he was following to track down the poachers. I had no idea at that time that I would be joining him when he took them down.

"Who hired you?" I asked Martin.

"I met the head of HR. At least that's what I assumed her title was. She's the only one I saw there when I went to HQ."

I started to wonder just how big this organization was. "Huh, I wonder if the people at the lab met with HR as well. Do you know?"

"No, but I can call over and talk to Georgie if you want. What's this all about, anyway? Do you think there's some secret agenda?" This was followed up by Martin's now-famous spooky sound effects and wiggling of the fingers.

"Ha. Maybe I am making too much out of this. Let's take a trip over to the lab, I want to meet Georgie and get a look around the place- see all the high tech stuff," I said and closed all the browser windows. "It's been a year since I've set foot in a lab. I wonder what gadgets they have. Guessing by the quick turn-around of our evidence, they must do all the work in-house, that's a lot of expensive toys!"

"I haven't even seen all the equipment there, and I've worked here for almost two years. Georgie said I'd have to put on one of those protective gowns and booties to go into the back rooms, so I've never bothered," Martin said as he put his jacket back on. "It's a short drive over on paper, but the traffic will set us back a bit. I'm going to need the bathroom before we head over."

I smiled and drank the rest of my coffee. I thought back to Jaffey and the last time I saw him at base camp. I thought about the ride back from the site of the stampede with the two poacher's bodies- or parts- were stacked in the vehicle next to him. Maybe I was just looking for a reason for all of it- letting my mind jump to all kinds of conclusions. I'm sure a nice visit to the lab, to see familiar settings will bring me back to reality.

Traffic was bad, just as Martin said. Sometimes I forget that we are even in DC, being on the outskirts of the city. A good thirty minutes later for what should have been a ten minute at the most drive, we parked on the street down from the lab. Although they were not located at HQ either, they were a bit closer with a nicer address than us, in the northwest corner near the National Zoo. I tried not to be too jealous.

"Which building is it?" I asked as we exited the car and tried our best to avoid walking into other pedestrians.

"It's the shorter one, two buildings down. The lab is on the top floor."

"What else is in the building?"

"There's some media group, I forget their name. I think they own the building," he said dodging out of the way of someone looking down at their phone as they walked. "Annoying."

I agreed, dodging another one as well. "They're everywhere. Sometimes I think the planet could be overtaken by aliens and no one would notice."

31

We continued on to the building and entered the lobby. It was pretty nondescript, rather empty, really. One elevator, a fire exit, and a couple of mailboxes.

"What, no doorman?" I amused myself, knowing that Marty was still too asleep to register my comment, much less respond. "I guess we take the elevator up." Marty had already pushed the button. It looked like the elevator was currently at the fourth floor. I wondered if the lab techs were the only ones that come and go in here.

We got into the elevator and I asked Martin if he ever pushed any other buttons, looked around on the other floors, but he just looked at me like I was weird. Maybe so, so I pushed all the other buttons.

Immediately the lights started flashing in the elevator, and we lurched to a sudden stop. The car started in what felt like a free fall for at least one story, and then abruptly stopped again.

"Now you did it. You broke the elevator. The cops are probably on their way!" Marty was awake and on a roll now.

"I guess it's off limits. What do we do...," I didn't get to finish my sentence. The elevator once again was in motion and we were headed up to the top.

The doors opened on the fourth floor, revealing a stark white reception room containing only a desk and computer. "Where is everyone," I wondered out loud. I was half expecting to be greeted by security, and a little disappointed when we weren't.

"Georgie!" Martin called out from behind me as he exited the elevator, giving me a start. "He usually takes a minute to emerge from the back rooms."

"How many rooms are there, do you know?"

Some rustling sounds came from the hallway to the right, and then a person draped in a white protection gown appeared.

"Wow, it's kind of hard to see you, white on white," I tried to joke to break the ice. "Hi, I'm Dr. Wake, you can call me Alex. You must be Georgie." I started to offer my hand, but thought twice about it, as he was all suited up, so I wound up just offering a stupid grin.

A very pregnant moment passed before Georgie removed his mask and said anything. At that point, I was sweating a bit. Georgie and Martin went on to greet each other and make generalized small talk, making it evident that it was up to me to find anything out.

"So, Georgie, how long have you been working here?" I thought it was as good a starting point as any.

"About two and a half years, shortly after it started up, from what I understand," he said with a half grin and steady eye contact. I nodded and then paused before my next question. Something felt off, maybe rehearsed? Or, more likely, he was a nervous lab geek type who didn't meet too many people.

I grinned again and said, "Oh, so from the beginning, nice! Were you hand selected for the job by Dr. Ceta, then?"

"Oh, no. I responded to a job listing. I was just out of college, forensic science...well I guess that would be obvious....and I was in dire need of money to start paying off my student loans. And here I am," he concluded as if that was all there was to his story.

"Ah, yes, student loans....I know them well. I just finished paying off mine a couple of years ago, and I'm...well older than you." I felt a bit of color come to my cheeks. I don't know why my age would be an embarrassment, perhaps because the company in the room was so noticeably young. I changed the subject, "Martin said that you do somewhat regular trips to HQ, have you seen much of the place?"

"Oh no," he said again, "just to the reception area. I am required to return all evidence to headquarters."

Georgie was coming off as an insecure and apologetic type. Still, I wondered if it was an act.

"You don't have a storage facility here? Is it a space issue?" I think about the flashing lights on the elevator and the blocked floors.

"I guess we have room. I just figured the agency preferred everything to be secured at their main office. Maybe they don't trust us." Georgie was snorting a little in his attempt at a joke. Maybe he wasn't so bad after all.

33

"Who else works here?" I asked as I laughed along with him. He went on to tell me about Ani and Tadaaki, two other techs who worked on fingerprints and DNA, respectively. They both also work for another non-profit, AWO, where Dr. Ceta apparently had worked before starting STAFE, or at least that's what he was told. I guess there was not enough work here to warrant three full time forensic lab techs, and they had to keep their old jobs part time. All three of them were hired through the HR rep.

"Have you met Dr. Ceta?" I was going to see if it came up in more casual conversation, but I was growing more curious by the minute.

"Oh, no. Just the secretary. Well, her voice. I leave the packages on her desk in the reception area. She is usually in one of the offices, and just checks me in over the intercom. I hear Dr. Ceta is out of the country most of the time." Georgie paused for a minute just staring, and then continued, "They get all of our findings through the system." Georgie pointed over to the computer, and with that, he started with the thank yous, and good byes. I looked over to Martin to get a read on his take of things, and I saw the 'see-what-I-mean' look on his face. We were getting rushed out.

"But I was hoping for a tour of the facilities. I was working in a lab, well, part of the time, down in Florida in my last job....," and I was cut off.

"Oh, I'm sorry, Dr. Wake, only authorized personnel...which I'm sure you would qualify...it's just....there isn't much to see, really," Georgie was starting to sweat a little himself. "I suppose I could let you look see from the doorway....otherwise you'd have to suit up." I got the hint, no tour for us.

I did take him up on his offer to let me look through the door. What I could see was quite impressive. The usual benchtop workstations with ductless hoods, a new-ish looking fuming chamber, a couple of comparison microscopes, a ninhydrin development chamber, and towards the back I could make out a forensic genomic next-generation sequencing system. Beyond that, in the next room, I could see bits of digital surveillance equipment.

"Looks like you have quite a few high-end pieces of machinery." Now I could see where the money went- not that I was complaining about our office digs.

"Yes, well, all to get the job done, right?" Georgie feigned a weak smile.

I had enough at that point, and gladly headed back to the elevator.

We were headed back down when I got the distinct feeling we were being watched. I wouldn't be surprised if there were hidden cameras in there. In fact, at that point, I would have bet money on it.

"Dare me to push all the buttons again?"

We putzed around the office for the rest of the afternoon, writing reports on the evidence to the case we no longer had. We wrote up the details of the investigation, including tracking down the perp and his assumed demise. I kept going over the details in my head, as far as I knew them, but my mind would drift back to the organization. I didn't really know who or what I was working for. And, the more I looked into it, the less I felt I knew.

"What is AWO? I don't think I've heard of it," I asked Martin, who was bobbing his head with his iPod on. Never mind, I'll look it up myself, I thought, suddenly feeling alone. I did the usual search engine query for it. I didn't think it was in reference to waterways, auto workers, or weather. Arab Women Organization- maybe she was from Jordan? I doubted it, especially with two of the lab techs working there. I couldn't find anything on AWO, much like STAFE. How could there be so many animal welfare groups without adequate representation on the internet? Apparently, organizations that still use fax machines to communicate.

Martin and all three techs were hired by the human resources director, or rep. Georgie only heard the secretary's voice via the intercom. I only met a secretary who I assumed worked for Jaffey. Maybe they are all one in the same- the same woman. Ha, maybe it's Dr. Ceta, herself! Oh, now I was just getting cynical.

"I think it's time to call it a day," I tried to flag down Martin's gaze. He was glazed over, staring at his screen. I stood up and pretended I was screaming at him.

"WAIT, WHAT???" He jumped up pulling the buds from his ears.

"AHAHAHAHA! Oh, I needed that, sorry!"

"I'm starting to not like you so much...," Martin said as he sunk back down in his chair.

"I'm sorry," I said again, "I was just getting frustrated with everything. I'm calling it quits for the day."

"OK, I was going to offer you a ride, but now..."

"That's alright, I need the walk. All this sitting in front of a computer isn't good for me. The walk home will clear my head."

"Are you sure, this isn't the best neighborhood to walk in after dark," he offered.

"Yes, thank you, though. It's only seven blocks over. I'll be fine."

I shut down the computer wondering what we were going to do the next day. Maybe this organization is too small to have a forensic veterinarian full time here, and they didn't think it through. Maybe I was just worrying again. I have been doing a lot of that lately.

I headed down the street thinking about the eerie feeling I had in the elevator. I was sure we were being watched, but I wasn't sure why. The media group, ARM took up most of the building, I should look into them- maybe they were the ones watching. Or maybe I was just being paranoid. I rounded the corner, headed north towards my apartment. A half-moon and occasional light gusts of wind caused shadows to move in the partially lit night. "Strangers In The Night" was playing in my head, and I was too preoccupied with the day's events to notice the man creeping up on me from behind.

I heard a single 'pop', and felt a sudden burning on the side of my arm. I twisted around to see what was happening and saw a dark figure running into the shadows and out of sight. I think I blacked out.

Chapter 5

"Hey, hey....you OK?" It was Martin leaning over me. I was on the sidewalk only two blocks from the office.

"I think I hit my head when I fell...."

"Ya, and you did something to your arm- there's blood. What happened?" Martin was helping me up to my feet.

I looked around to get my bearings, and then to see if the shadowy figure was in sight. Feeling a little woozy, I reached for my arm to inspect it for any damage. The details were slowly coming back to me- the pop, the burning. A small rip through the side of the sleeve of my jacket was visible, as well as a small amount of blood. It appeared that I was shot at, but the bullet only grazed my arm.

I looked up at Martin, who was still talking about something, and said, "Someone shot at me."

"I told you this was a bad neighborhood to walk through after dark."

"I believe you said it was 'not so good' not that it was bad..."

"What? Same thing. Anyway, we should get you to a hospital and checked out."

"No, I'm fine. It's just a flesh wound, as they say." I was trying to joke it off to calm my nerves a bit, but I was quite rattled.

"Maybe we should start with the police station, then." Martin tried to walk me to his car, but I was preoccupied with my memory of the event. Was the dark figure shooting AT me, or was I just caught in the middle of something? It certainly wasn't a robbery, nothing was taken. By the time I looked up again, refocusing on the present, I was in the passenger seat and we were halfway to the police.

Martin took me home after I filed a report at the station. They wanted me to go to the hospital as well, but I insisted that it was fine, 'I'm a doctor', 'I can take care of it', yadda yadda yadda. I just needed to clean it and then get a good night's sleep.

I walked from room to room in my apartment- thinking of getting something, then forgetting what it was, and then repeating. It was over an hour before I settled into the couch to watch the news. Nothing on the dead guy in West Virginia, nothing on the dead body we found, and obviously nothing on my shooting. Maybe dead people were too common these days- that it wasn't news. I turned off the TV and stared at the ceiling for a little while, trying to calm my mind before I even attempted sleeping.

The traffic, although light, was audible, as well as an occasional bang or creak from an adjoining apartment. After a few minutes, I became aware of an intermittent clicking sound. Thinking that it was an over-sized cockroach (I loathe bugs in the place where I eat and sleep, and usually attribute any abnormal sounds or movement to these creatures), I went on a search to locate the source. I overturned every piece of paper, book, and article of clothing in the room with no luck, and although it was a little too dark to be sure, I was confident that it wasn't coming from under the sofa. Feeling paranoid, I looked into the lamp, the overhead light fixture and around any electrical devices for a 'bug'- not the cockroach kind, as I feared just previously, but a planted listening device. It could have been because I had seen all the surveillance equipment in the far room of the lab when we had our 'tour', or it could have been because I was shot at, and now I think everyone was out to get me. The infrequency of the clicking made it even harder to locate its source. I pulled the phone out of my pocket and stared at it until I was sure that it wasn't coming from there. I headed to the kitchen just in case it was the refrigerator or the stove, but then the clicking didn't repeat. It was nearing midnight by that point, so I resigned to the bed and did my best to get some rest.

The next day came way too fast, and my arm was hurting a bit. It was a difficult night of sleep, trying to avoid rolling onto my right side where the gunshot grazed me. I completely forgot about the sounds of the apartment the night before, and made my way to the office on the same streets where the night's activities had taken place. Things always look different in the light of the sun, and I couldn't believe how threatened I felt just hours before.

Martin was there first, and gave a bit of a startled reaction when I walked in. "I wasn't expecting you in so soon, if at all today. How's your arm doing?"

"It's been better. Thanks again for chauffeuring me around last night- I'm not sure I would've had my head on straight enough to find my way home." I offered a smile, but didn't make much eye contact. I felt embarrassed about the night's events. It was absurd, I know, but I wasn't used to feeling vulnerable. The smell of fresh coffee beckoned me, and I used that as an excuse to drop the subject.

Martin's iPod was turned on, and I could hear the faint sounds of Led Zeppelin wafting from the ear buds lying on the desk, 'Communication breakdown, it's always the same, having a nervous breakdown...'

"I didn't know you were into the classics," I said to him as I walked over to my desk with a steaming mug in my hand.

"Ya, I'm into lots of stuff...," he was cut off by the sound of the fax machine. "Well, it would appear that we may have something to do today, after all."

The fax finished printing, but we both stayed seated at our desks. Martin looked apprehensive to see what it said, but got up and grabbed it anyway. He glanced over it, handed it to me, and starting grabbing some supplies.

"Worcester County, Maryland, near Snow Hill. Well at least it's only about two and a half hours this time," I said to Martin trying to get him to smile, but he seemed impervious to humor today, at least this early. I was beginning to think he wasn't much of a morning person.

I decided to be the one to drive on our way out to the scene this time, to mix things up a bit. Who knows, maybe Marty would stay awake for the whole ride this time- at least for the ride home when he was driving, I hoped! Traffic was a pain all the way through Annapolis and over the bridge, but lightened up a little after that. I would usually be worrying about securing a search warrant, about the possible presence of the occupants of the property, and about the timing of meeting the law enforcement officer at the potential crime scene, but I was trying to adapt to the way that STAFE did things, and just rolled with it. Although, with the events of last night still fresh in my mind, I couldn't help but worry about confrontations and gunfire.

Glancing over at Martin, I caught him chugging his coffee again. "You really are going to burn the crap out of your mouth, you know." He just gave me a big grin and batted his eyelashes at me. After a few minutes he started playing with the radio, and I couldn't tell if he was bored or on a mission to find the 'right' song. He settled on Queen's "Another One Bites the Dust", and we looked at each other at the same time nervously.

"I hope that doesn't mean we are going to find another body....that was freaky...and kinda gross," Martin said with a laugh that quickly turned somber.

"I doubt it, how many dead bodies could there be...," I cut myself off and finished after a pause, "dealing with animal abuse is hard enough, I'd hope that there would be more police officers in Maryland resulting in a more thorough investigation, so that it wouldn't come down to us finding another person...." We both just stared straight ahead out the window, wishing it to be true, and thankful for the music filling in the space in between us.

The GPS successfully got us to our destination this time, with no need for my fumbling around on the phone. A couple of police vehicles were parked along the side of the street as we pulled up. It looked like a normal house, in a normal neighborhood, on a quiet street. I couldn't tell you how many 'normal' people were involved in dog fighting.

"Are we assuming this one is tied to the one in West Virginia?"

"We don't assume anything....but I'm thinking it is," I told Martin as we grabbed our gear and headed to the house. A police officer was flagging us over to the garage. It was a warm morning with a light breeze from the southwest, and a faint odor of decomp was evident.

After the usual introductions, we were shown to where a semi-permanent fighting ring had been set up. Screwed-together plywood made up the walls, with an old heavily stained carpet on the ground. There was a flirt pole in the corner with remnants of meat of unknown origin on the end, used to condition and develop hind leg strength in their dogs.

"We are going to need to get samples from the boards and carpet, as well as any other paraphernalia we find," Martin started explaining to the officer before he even finished showing us the findings.

"Did you find any animal remains?" I asked, as that was my specialty- or 'thang' as Marty says. I was not used to being on scene for any other reason, but I could tell already that that was not necessarily the case working for this organization.

"There's a lot more out back," the cop said looking annoyed that we interrupted him in the first place.

We followed him through to the surprisingly expansive back yard. There was a short slope down to the beginning of the woods, with a clearing about 100 yards further on. The smell of animal waste got stronger as we walked, and I could see the worn down areas where dogs had been chained and forced to stay for their short miserable lives. As we rounded the corner, we could see eight areas in total with heavy chains attached to car axles and heavy cinder blocks where the dogs had been tethered.

"We didn't find any living animals, so the perp must have moved them. I don't think they knew we were coming, but maybe they were tipped off," the police officer said to us as he continued on with the findings. We walked down a little further beyond the clearing to a thinly wooded area. "Over here is where they found the canine cadavers. I guess there was an area that looked like it had been recently disturbed, like maybe a freshly dug grave, but I think it's older than that. But, that's why you're here, right?"

"That's what they tell me. Do you know how many bodies they found?" I asked the officer.

"I think there's two or three. I'm not sure if they are all whole, though. There's at least one that's in pieces, I think."

I nodded to Martin, and we walked over to the graves. Martin took pictures of everything, documenting how we found the site as well as everything that we unearthed. The smell of decomposition was just as I remembered it, even one year out the loop didn't make a dent in my memories of that.

"We need to get samples of all of the bugs, which will give us the minimum elapsed time since death, at least. They don't appear to be wrapped or treated with anything, so it should be accurate," I said to Martin who was still taking pictures. "Hand me those vials. I need to put a few eggs into one with alcohol for court evidence and a few into a vial for hatching. Can you dampen a piece of paper towel with some water for me?" I went on gathering bug evidence before moving any cadaver parts from the burial site. "They're at least at the pupae stage. I need to collect those as well, but I don't need to preserve them. I don't think the bodies have been here that long. We will need to look up time tables of blow fly life cycles under these temperatures and weather conditions, to be sure."

I could tell Martin was used to seeing these kinds of things. He stayed diligent and methodical throughout the whole process. The smell didn't seem to affect him, either. It made me realize that I didn't know much about him, his past, or what brought him here to this job.

"There's still a good sized maggot mass around the head. It looks like it's localized around the left temporal region. My guess is blunt force to the head." At this point I didn't know if I was just talking to myself, as Martin was engrossed with his task of documentation, but I kept talking, anyway. "There has to be a wound there...eggs are only laid in orifices and fresh wounds. We should take the temperature of the mass as well as measure its size. Then we can bag up the body." I left Martin to finish those measurements, and I moved over to the second set of remains.

I took a breath and stretched before changing out my gloves to prevent cross contamination. Watching Martin document and bag the first cadaver brought on a sense of sadness. I usually don't allow emotions to crop up during an investigation, at least not on-site. My job was just to collect evidence to nail the useless excuse of a person for what they had done. It seemed I was a little rusty at putting up that wall.

I hunched down next to the second site, gleaning whatever I could from visual inspection while I waited for Martin to start with the photographic evidence. Procedure can be a long grueling experience, but it was needed to safeguard the viability of the evidence.

The second body had all the hallmarks of the first, including the head wound and estimated time of death. Nevertheless, we collected, documented, and secured all the evidence as we did the first. I asked Martin if he needed a break before we tackled the third site, but he wanted to press on and get it over with- I didn't blame him.

Martin walked over first, taking photos. I watched him eyeing the dirt and new growth around the excavation. He looked up at the overhang of the nearby tree, and then took a picture of the surrounding plants.

"What are you looking at?" I asked as I approached, trying to see what he saw.

"This site is older than the other two. Look at the amount of new growth around it and in the pile that they had dug to get to the cadaver. At least from last fall, I think- before the winter anyway."

"Well you would know better than I would, but we can see what the body parts say."

It was obvious that this site was different from the others right off the bat. The bones had a skin covering, but no residual flesh remained. Pupal casings were empty, and beetles scattered as I removed dirt layers from the remains. "Oh goodie, it's always fun trying to chase down beetles," I said out loud to myself as I reached for the forceps and a vial with alcohol. Beetles were fast and could be cannibalistic. If I captured them and kept them all alive in one vial they would mostly be eaten by the time I got them to the lab. They were much easier to deal with when dead, if I could even capture one.

I dug further around the remains and it became apparent that there were two bodies there, or a very strange creature with four femurs. I opted for the former conclusion, and dug gently around for the heads.

"The skulls are missing," I told Martin as I was still looking around. "Trophies, or hiding cause of death?" I asked to no one in particular.

We finished up with the burial site and bagging evidence. It took several trips back to the vehicle to carefully pack our new cargo. Martin walked the back field for a few minutes before joining me back at the house.

"I bet there are more burial sites out there...older ones. Who knows how long he's been doing this," he said to me without making eye contact. I knew it was part of his wall, his way of blocking emotions, so I didn't take it personally.

"In here, doc," I heard from behind me. It was the second police officer speaking from the back porch doorway. "There's some evidence in here you might want to see."

I was apprehensive to enter, thinking that the skulls from the last two bodies were sitting on the kitchen table- it wouldn't be a first. I entered and held the door open for Martin. We were in a small dated kitchen that was in desperate need of an update. The officer was walking through into the living room, but something caught my eye. I pointed to the counter and looked to Martin. He nodded and took a few pictures, turning the bottles sitting there to get shots of their labels. Performance supplements were a common find in these kinds of cases.

"I bet there's a butt-load of spinach in the freezer," Martin said, and went over to see if that was the case. "Well, either

Popeye lives here, or we have a dog fighter." People raising fighting dogs often supplemented the food with spinach for its vitamin K activity, which helped with clotting. It also had the amazing power of emptying the bowels, as retained fecal matter could cause overheating in an animal.

We rejoined the officer in the next room. He nodded toward the fireplace. Martin walked over and took pics of the trophies on the mantle. "'Gamest In Show', Oooh, impressive," he said and thumbed through a few books leaning against the cheap hunks of metal. "'Dogs Of Velvet And Steel', 'The Pitbull Bible'," he listed off a couple while looking through them for any loose pages.

I was glancing around the rest of the house for any computers or other documentation when I heard Martin call me. Finding him crouched next to the fireplace, I asked what was up while I watched him bag some severely burned pages.

"I think there's some pedigree information on these. Maybe we can track the lineage, connect them to the West Virginia case, even." I agreed and helped him label everything.

"I didn't see much in the way of conditioning equipment or even a crash kit," I said to both Martin and the officer. The officer said that's all they had found, and that the owner was missing. "Maybe he took it all with him as well as the rest of the dogs."

We wrapped things up, thanked the officers and climbed into our vehicle. I suddenly felt drained and was glad that I wasn't the one who had to drive home. I looked over to Martin and tried to assess his alertness.

"How you doin'?" I said in my best New York accent.

"I feel the need for coffee. An IV infusion is preferable."

"How about whatever they call large these days at the Dunkin's in the next town."

"I believe they call it large. You might be thinking of the 'other' place." Martin jokingly gave a shudder, but I knew he frequented any, if not all, coffee establishments he came across.

After a pit stop for a much needed bathroom break and essential caffeine supplies, as well as what constituted as food, we headed back to the office. It was getting on in the afternoon, and we were surely to hit traffic back through Annapolis. Just like Martin, I found myself fidgeting with the radio. I was going to settle on some calming classical to knock my tension back a notch, but thought better of it as I pictured a sleeping partner driving us off to our demise. I landed on the Doobie Brothers who were "Taking It To The Streets", and I felt an affinity for that sentiment.

It was going to be a long evening of necropsies when we got back to the office. There was a small exam room with stainless steel tables, an autoclave, and surgical instruments off the back of the office, and it looked like I would get to break it in today. I never asked why it was located here instead of at the main lab, but having met Georgie and seeing the set up there, I was OK with being ostracized.

I thought again about how little I knew about Martin and decided it was as good a time as any to do some good old interrogation.

"Marty, Mart, Martini..."

"Uh oh. This doesn't sound good," he broke in.

"Hahaha! I just want to get to know you a little more, you know, more than 'you're a James Bond fan'," I said with a big grin.

"What do you want to know....and don't say everything, the car ride isn't THAT long."

"I will settle for how you ended up here in this job."

"Welllllllllllll, my last boyfriend was a huge animal lover, and he rubbed off on me....I should probably rephrase that....we had a ton of animals at any given point. All, of course, were brought home from off the streets. Kind of like me, I always told him. Anyway, he helped me pay for school and here I am."

"Where is your boyfriend now, are you still together?"

"No, that was back in Philly." Martin got quiet for a minute, but I didn't jump in. I let him tell the story at his own pace.

"He was shot one day when he went out for a run...it was broad daylight. They police called looking for his next of kin, I couldn't believe it. It was just me...me and him....and a half dozen rescued animals. That was my third year of college. We, I should say he, had put away enough money so I could finish school. Of course, I had to get a night job to cover rent, but I managed....for him, for Tommy. He was the first person in my life to believe in me, and I wanted to make him proud."

"Tommy sounded like an amazing man." It was all I could think of to say. I worked in a discipline where consoling people was a daily activity, yet there were still times when I just couldn't find the right words.

"He was amazing. I had to do some unsavory things to make a living, having to get on my knees to make a buck, and I was smacked around more than once, but Tommy took me away from all that."

"I'm sorry, I had no idea." I reached over and touched his shoulder, half expecting him to flinch, but I was happy to find he accepted it.

"So that's why I work to help animals. It's all I can do to keep his memory alive. He really taught me a lot."

I wanted to ask about his parents, his home life, to dive in deeper, but I stopped myself. Instead, we sat for a moment taking it all in, and then he reached over and cranked up the radio. Boston's "More Than A Feeling" was playing, and it was as good as a closure that you could ask for- at least for that conversation.

Chapter 6

The next day was a cold and rainy one, not the kind of weather you want for your Saturday off. I found it hard to get out of bed, and the soothing patter of the raindrops didn't help. My arm started to throb as reality came back to me. I eventually dragged myself from under the warmth of the covers and made my way to the kitchen. The sound of the coffee dripping into the pot blended into the rain. Could it get any more drab? Yes, it probably could, and knowing me, I was going to get there.

A shower perked me up some, at least enough to go through e-mail and my social media accounts. It appeared that I had been neglectful, and let it pile up. I wasn't sure why I even had the accounts, really, I didn't think I could have recognized many of the people I was 'friends' with or following if I ran into them on the street. After scrolling through scores of work out routines, pictures of dinners, memes about the importance of wine (especially if one had children), and questionable political opinions, I concluded that I hadn't missed anything and closed the laptop.

Thinking that music might help the mood, I flipped on the radio and searched for something uplifting. Why was there so much talk radio in the morning? Play some good music for the poor people stuck in traffic, trapped in their cars, waiting for the time they could do the same thing in the other direction hours later. I searched the dial with poor results, ending up with The Carpenter's "Rainy Days and Mondays". So much for uplifting- at least it wasn't Monday.

I decided to unpack a few more boxes- I was never good at moving and always seemed to have a portion of my belongings boxed up. They were mostly filled with books, some of fiction, some of veterinary medicine, some of forensics, although most of the forensic books were already on the shelves for quick reference if needed in the new job. Books were always the quickest to unpack, if you had a place to put them, which at that time was my dilemma. This apartment was smaller than my last one in Florida, and even though I threw out and donated a lot of things, I was still left short on space. I opted for a smaller box of pictures to unpack, thinking there was always wall space to hang something, especially since my walls were stark naked.

The first pictures were of friends from college, the usual graduation poses, and a couple of degrees and certificates that I was surprised I found the time to put into frames. Then I pulled out a picture of my last dog, Moses, which I had to euthanize after struggling with kidney failure. My emotional stability, albeit not the steadiest at the time, went rapidly downhill from there.

Putting Moses to sleep was the beginning of the end of my life in Florida. My last job, my last boyfriend, my last dog all played a part in my need to escape. For a while I had thought that Florida might be my long term home, the place where I would say I was from if someone asked, the place where I would set down deep lifelong roots. I wasn't sure if my failed relationship with Eddie led to my discontent with my work, or the other way around, or perhaps they happened to occur at the same time, but it all ended up dissolving just the same. Moving was easier for me than putting down roots, and four years was a long time to be in one job, for me, anyway. So I used that as an excuse to move on.

Moses wasn't the first dog I ever had, but he was pretty special. I found him when I was young and spry, or at least young-er and spry-er. It was after I finished my master's in forensic medicine, and I was working at my first job in the field at a lab in upstate New York. Moses appeared at a time when I needed some reassurance for the decisions I made in my life up to that point. There's nothing like a furry four-legged creature when it came to reassurance.

The early years in the lab went by fast, and rather uneventful. Spending most of my time knee-deep in DNA samples, mostly human, mind you, as little was done in animal forensics at the time, at least as far as DNA went. Things were starting to progress in animal welfare legislation, making the need for animal forensics more crucial, with more cases of animal cruelty being brought to the courts.

In fact, just after high school, I had taken a different route entirely when it came to careers. I was enrolled in night school at Maine College of Law for animal welfare law while working as a veterinary technician at a local clinic. Although I found law to be a mundane topic, I thought it would be a more crucial role for me, as I had big plans to make a difference in the world. It's funny how plans changed over time.

I didn't know if it was my young age, my inability to get excited about torts and precedences, or my being involved in yet another bad relationship, but I soon decided that law was not for me. Laurel and I broke up my second year of law school, it was bound to happen, it was just a matter of when. We had met at an environmental demonstration in Boston, and got swept up in the excitement of the cause. Well, at least I had kept fond memories of the time, if nothing else from the relationship. That was when I decided that I needed to take a different route, and thought that veterinary medicine was a better fit for me.

By the time I wound my way through four years of Latin anatomical names, diseases that you wouldn't wish on your worst enemy, and names of breeds and species that I didn't even know existed, I was still sure-footed in the welfare camp, and I decided on anatomic pathology for my residency. It was my residency and subsequent conferences on welfare issues that led me to forensics.

Pulling out another picture from the box, another wave of sadness fell across me. It was of my parents and brother Darryl. A car crash in the early nineties took my parents from me, when I was just in college. Darryl was a few years older than me, and already had a life for himself in California. He barely spent a weekend back at home in Portland for the

51

funerals. Darryl and I had grown up under the same roof in Maine, but we were never close. I wasn't even sure when the last time we spoke.

It got me thinking about Martin, and what he told me about his life. Did he have any family to speak of? Maybe we were more alike than I had thought.

I put the picture down and took a walk into the kitchen for more coffee- not that I needed it at that point, but a warm beverage to cuddle with seemed essential for the wet morning. I took my time walking around the living room, as small as it was, picturing where the best location was for each picture, or if I should even hang them at all. After all, I wasn't feeling the happiest looking at them now- did I really want that as a daily experience? I stood in front of the window debating it after grabbing some java. Looking out at the rain falling on the street below became mesmerizing, and I soon lost half of my morning with nothing to show for it.

I went back to the radio, hoping something better was playing on one of the stations by now. I didn't know why I hadn't set up my iPod yet- chalking it up to being a victim of selective laziness. With The Police's "Every Breath You Take" playing in the background, I went back to the box of books and started stacking them against the wall. "At least they're not in a box anymore. No one can say that I didn't unpack," I said out loud. I realized that I was talking to myself again, and remembered the clicking sound from the other night, and my paranoia about being 'bugged'. I had to chuckle at myself- it all seemed a bit silly now in the light of day.

When "Living room" by Tegan and Sara came on next, I had to change the station again. It was a knee-jerk reaction that I blamed on my spying paranoia. But in doing so, I spilled most of my half-cold coffee on me, the table, and the floor. "Well that's awesome," I said and grabbed a dish towel from the kitchen. As I was mopping up the mess, "Living Room" came on again, this time on the station I just landed on. "OK, I guess we are listening to this," and I couldn't find the energy to fight the radio anymore.

The afternoon played out even less eventfully than the morning. I discovered that grocery shopping hadn't been a priority that week, and I was left with toast and peanut butter for menu options- not that I minded, peanut butter was one of the four food groups, after all.

A thunderstorm had developed, and I watched the dark clouds displace the lighter rain clouds over the city. A few flashes lit up the northern section of the city. I was reluctant to play with the radio again, so I flipped on the TV instead. Ah, the ever-so happy news to cheer a person up. Still no mention of the dead body, the dog fighting perp, or the smugglers in Africa, for that matter. I was starting to question if the work I was involved in made enough difference to make the news. Maybe it just wasn't big enough for the cable stations.

The thunder was reminding me of the elephant stampede, of Jaffey and Marcus, of our time on the savanna. I thought about Nkiru and her herdmates, and hoped they were still alive, knowing that poachers were all around reducing the population every hour of every day. And, why haven't I heard back from the organization regarding any follow-up to that case? Surely there were press releases, explanations to the government, and hordes of red tape to process. Wasn't my statement needed for any of this? I was growing more frustrated with the agency's communication skills and lack of transparency. We were all on the same side, right?

I remembered that I still had Jaffey's number somewhere, and I wondered what time it was wherever he was at that moment. I dug through the paperwork on my makeshift desk in the bedroom- copies of statements from previous cases at my last job, copies of forensic findings, pictures and diagrams of gruesome crime scenes, but no number. I tried to remember what clothes I brought with me to Africa, perhaps it was in one of my pockets. Lucky for me, I sucked at housecleaning and hadn't done the laundry since I got back. Finding the number on a piece of crumpled paper with dirt

53

smears and hairs from someone or something stuck to it (I didn't want to know or think about it, really), I sat down with the phone in my hand. I debated on calling at that hour, as it would have been after 11 pm if he was still in Kenya, but it would have been a perfectly acceptable hour if he was back here in DC. Since I had nothing else to do but unpack, I gave it a shot.

"Allo," he answered.

"Hello, Jaffey? It's Alexandra. I hope I didn't wake you..."

"Oh, no worries. What can I help you with Dr. Wake?"

"Please, call me Alex. I was just wondering how the case was coming along. Do you need my statement or anything?"

"Not at this time. The process is a slow one, Dr. Alex. Have you been contacted by someone at STAFE in regards to it?"

"No. That's why the confusion. I haven't heard a thing, and frankly, I was wondering if I was going to. The organization doesn't seem too keen on keeping me in the loop on much of anything." I heard a laugh at the other end of the line, then a pause.

"We do have some short comings to deal with, I agree with that. You will get used to it."

"That's what the people here are telling me, too. I guess I just have some questions surrounding the whole organization's identity. I can find very little information on them on the internet, and no one here seems to be able to fill in the gaps."

I heard a click and thought Jaffey had hung up on me. "Hello, hello..."

"Yes Dr. Alex, I am still here..."

"I thought I heard the line disconnect.... Do you know anything about STAFE that would help me here? Sometimes I worry that I jumped back into animal welfare again too soon. Maybe it was the wrong decision to work for this organization." I felt emotionally worn down at that moment, and suddenly felt like I was making myself appear vulnerable and weak, and I didn't like it.

I heard some static and another clicking sound, and I thought I had lost Jaffey, but then I heard, "STAFE is on the forefront of justice for animals everywhere. We are the leaders of the new future, where all animals have equal rights, regardless of how many legs, if any, they walk on. You are very much needed for this new world to happen." I heard some more static, and tried to re-establish contact with Jaffey, but it was to no avail.

I sat perplexed for some time. 'New world'? That was some rhetoric he used. I could see why that wasn't used as their mission statement- it would scare off too many people. A bit too strong of a marketing concept, I thought. Was STAFE an extreme animal rights group? I never saw the point of setting research buildings on fire and letting lab animals free only to get run over in the streets. Now I had even more questions than I did an hour ago, and my head was starting to throb. I laid back on the sofa doing some deep breathing exercises while I stared at the ceiling. So much for a relaxing weekend, I wondered what Sunday would have in store for me. Then it hit me, I was due in court on Monday in Florida.

"Crap! How could I have forgotten that?!" I was yelling at myself as I pulled my body from the sofa. I ran over to the stack of paperwork again, and sure enough, the summons for my testimony was among the documents I had just rummaged through. "Crap, crap, crap!" I spent the next hour online securing a flight, rental car, and hotel room for Monday- just in case the hearing ran late.

It was a case from my last job. Even though I tried to break all ties to Florida and my life there, I knew there were a few cases that were still on the books, and my presence would be required. It was part of my job, to show up in court and present my findings, to explain procedures, and to be a witness for the prosecution. I never got used to that part of things, to look at the perpetrator all dressed up trying to impersonate an upstanding citizen, to be cross examined by his skeevy lawyer who was trying to make me feel like I was the one who did something wrong, and to re-live the harshness of the animal abuse that I had witnessed.

It looked as though I would be spending my Sunday entrenched in the details of that case, preparing for court. My head felt like it was going to explode.

Chapter 7

Monday came around too fast as it always did, and I was left wanting an extra day to prepare, or sleep, or both. The Carpenters and The Boomtown Rats had it right: Mondays do suck.

After a restless night of sleep, if you could call it sleep, I was off to a grand start. I was down to the last few drops of shampoo and conditioner in the travel sized vials I had been using- chalk that up to my inability to grocery shop in a regular fashion like a normal person- and the last of the milk for coffee was long gone sometime yesterday. On top of that, I broke a nail, a heel, and had a small tear in my blouse. Well, I should be all set for court!

The heel didn't bother me, as I next to never wear them- aside from court appearances- and I had a plethora of flats to fall back on. The nail, on the other hand, bothered me to a point where I almost missed my flight out of Reagan International because I was obsessed with finding a nail file in my heap of belongings. At least it wasn't raining!

I thought things were getting better when I actually made my flight and even arrived on time. But, it went downhill again after that. My car rental reservation was lost, they had no vehicle to offer me, and I was forced to ride a bus from the Jacksonville International airport to the court house, which of course resulted in my being late, and the prosecutor was not happy, to say the least. After he managed to stall for almost twenty minutes, I showed up just in time to avoid a fine for holding up the court.

I knew the case was going to be an especially hard one because the defendant had managed to clean up most of the evidence before we could even get a warrant. I remember walking through the house: Medium-velocity blood spatter was running from the front door to a back bedroom. He had claimed that the dog had attacked him, and he had merely defended himself. The dog, even if he could talk for himself, couldn't argue his side of the story, as he had been brutally beaten to death with a hammer. I had the grisly job of documenting every blow, every contusion, every broken bone the defendant caused. Normally, I would get butterflies in my stomach at this point from being nervous on the stand. This case, in particular, made me want to vomit.

"Do you swear to tell the truth, the whole truth, so help you God?"

"I do," I said but thought about the lack of separation of church and state in this system. I would have used anything as a distraction at that point.

I went through my findings as the prosecutor went down the list of everything that was pertinent to the case. This was the easy side of things. He would let me explain the findings in full, expand on areas that had the most details, and give my interpretation based on my experience and knowledge. I made sure to make eye contact with the jury as much as possible and clearly detail the more complex concepts of forensics. Then it was the defense's turn.

"You said the injuries were consistent with a hammer," the perp's attorney said.

"Yes, sir. The blows to the...," and I was cut off. I was used to that.

"Did you find a hammer?"

"No, sir, we did not, but..."

"Then how do you know that it definitely was a hammer?"

"I said it was consis...."

"How did you conclude that my client hit his own dog with a hammer, when there was no hammer on site?"

"As I said, the injuries were...," and so it went on. He would grand stand, ask me questions that he didn't let me answer, and focus on the missing evidence, evidence that his client rushed around discarding and cleaning up before we could get into the crime scene. It went on for over an hour. The prosecutor was able to object a few times when the defense went on some side show without a direct question coming out of it, but honestly, the judge seemed awfully lenient on the defense and allowed quite a bit of the lawyer's statements in. Patience was never my thing, and when it was starting to look like the jury might be siding with the defense, I started to panic.

"Did you see the defendant at the scene when you were there?"

"No, I did not. He was already in route to the hospital..."

"So you didn't see the injuries that the poor man had suffered, the pain and anguish, the sheer shock of having been attacked by his own dog that he loved! Imagine, thinking you are safe in your own home with the animal that you cared for and fed and..."

"No sir I did not see him, as I said. That is not my area of expertise," I interrupted him this time. I may have surprised him for a moment, but only a moment. He was all up in arms about my unprompted statement, and asked it to be stricken from the record, and then went on to implore the judge for a reprimand and even went so far as to ask to treat me as a hostile witness. I looked over at the prosecutor to jump in and help me out, but he just looked down at the table and shuffled papers.

It was bad enough that I was on my own at that point, but now the judge allowed the defense attorney to be as argumentative as he wanted to be, which meant he was going to push his own testimony even more, and limit my answers to just yes or no, if that. As a forensic veterinarian, I was supposed to collect and document evidence as it related to the health and welfare of an animal. Although I get called to the stand by the prosecutor, I was supposed to be impartial. That meant that I couldn't play favorites, I couldn't keep my findings from the defense team, and I was not to offer an opinion as to the guilt or innocence of the accused. This was crucial to be able to do the job in an unbiased fashion. If I couldn't be a fair witness, I wouldn't be useful in court, and I wouldn't be useful in this career. Now I had been labeled a hostile witness, and I was afraid for my job.

If there wasn't anger mixed in with the fear and exhaustion I was feeling at that moment, I would have been in jeopardy of breaking down on the stand. Which, needless to say, was something to avoid at all costs. I was excused after several more minutes of beratement, and I couldn't leave the courtroom fast enough. The evil eye that I gave the prosecutor on my way through the gate was lost amid the stir of the jurors and onlookers to the controversy the defense lawyer created.

I sat in the hall outside the courtroom for a few minutes trying to decide if it was worth my time to tear into the prosecutor. What was done was done, and it couldn't be changed now, and I certainly didn't want to break down in front of him, either. Just as I did a year ago, I decided the best thing to do was to just leave town. I wasn't needed anymore for this case, and even if I was, it would just make things worse, and the prosecutor knew it. I turned on my phone as I hurried out of the building and booked my flight home.

The flight back to DC was a rough one through stormy weather. I normally don't drink on a plane, but I made an exception. Actually, I made three exceptions- there was a lot of turbulence.

"Stupid prosecutor, and sleazy lawyer," I said to the unknown and unlucky occupant of the seat next to me. He was graceful enough to smile back at me when he put his earphones on. I didn't blame him.

"Stupid prosecutor and sleazy lawyer," I said to my reflection as I spent the rest of the flight looking out the window at the storm clouds.

The flight back was delayed- some issue with landing in all the wind. It didn't matter all that much to me, I was going to head home and curl up in a ball. The other passengers, however, had a few things to say about it. By the time we landed and taxied in, my head was throbbing again. Too many whiny people or one too many exceptions in court, either way I really needed this day to end. The airport was crowded as usual, and I bumped into more than a handful of people as I attempted to turn my phone on and walk at the same time. Just as I turned it on it rang, and it was an unknown caller. I answered, thinking it had something to do with the horrendous case that I just sat through, or it had something to do with my new job. It was the latter.

"Dr. Wake....I understand you had some problems on the stand today." It was a woman's voice, slightly familiar.

"Whom, may I ask, am I talking with?" I tried to sound professional and put together, but I wasn't sure I could deal with this now.

"This is STAFE headquarters, your presence is requested."

"Now?" I said as I hoped against hope that she said no.

"Yes, please, if you would. We look forward to speaking with you. Thank you." Then she hung up.

My mind was reeling, maybe it was better to get it over with, if I was going to lose my job. I tried to put a face to the voice on the phone as I made my way to the metro. I finally decided that it was the secretary from HQ, the one who was present when I signed my contract. Maybe she wasn't a secretary, maybe she was head of human resources, like the techs in the lab had thought. Even Martin said that the head of HR was the only one that he met. I wondered if they were the same person. I continued wondering and worrying as I caught the yellow line to L'Enfant Plaza. What if they were the same person AND it was really Dr. Ceta? If it wasn't Dr. Ceta, would she be there at the meeting, would I finally be meeting the elusive doctor that no one else has ever met?

I continued on foot for the few blocks to headquarters, worrying about my fate. What about Jaffey? Would he be there for the meeting? When I spoke to him on Saturday, I didn't ask him where he was, and he didn't mention it either. I was assuming that he was still in Africa, but what if he was in DC this whole time? I wasn't sure if I wanted him to be there at the meeting. It would be nice to have someone that I was familiar with there as an ally, but at the same time, I didn't want him to be involved in the mess I seemed to be in. I'm sure he must have met Dr. Ceta, and maybe he was higher up in the ranks than I had previously thought. He could have been the one who called for the meeting, for all I knew. Or, maybe I was just being paranoid, taking it all too personally. I wouldn't know anything until the meeting. And there I was at the building.

Taking the elevator up to the top floor, I tried to think of anything but what I assumed to be my impending doom. At least it stopped raining! That was as far as I could go with positive thoughts. I supposed that if I had a mirror to look into, I could tell myself that I was important and good and that I mattered- like that character from the old Saturday Night Live shows- but even I wouldn't believe myself at that point. I just had to suck it up, or at least hold it together long enough to get through the meeting.

The doors opened to the lobby, and I was greeted by the secretary, or not the secretary, I didn't know anymore and I didn't know how to ask. She spoke first, with generic greetings and led me into big office at the end. Well, even if this is my last day on the job, I think I had made it further into the unknown than some of my colleagues back at the lab.

"Please have a seat, we will be with you in a moment," she said and closed the door. I was left alone in the massive space, and suddenly I felt small and insignificant. I sat on the sofa against the side wall, then moved to a small winged chair across from the huge desk. I was thinking of moving again when it dawned on me that she said 'we will be with you'. We? Maybe Jaffey was here, or maybe it was Dr. Ceta coming here to meet me. Why would Dr. Ceta be here just for my firing?

The door opened, startling me for a moment, and I stood up. The secretary- as I thought of her- and another woman walked in.

"This is Dr. Aquene, head of PR," the secretary said. I reached to shake her hand, and she held on, looking directly into my eyes. If I wasn't beside myself in nervousness, I would have been struck by her beauty. She was at least five foot eleven, with long dark hair, worn straight down, clearly Native American descent.

"Pleased to meet you, Dr. Wake, I have heard a lot about you. Please sit." When she released my hand I slowly sank into the chair. "Our head assistant here has been filling me in on your casework," she continued from the opposite side of the enormous oak desk. I glanced over and smiled at the woman whom I had previously thought of as the secretary, as she pulled up a chair to the end of the desk, treating it as more of a conference table.

"Yes, well, today wasn't...," I tried to say something in my defense before anything could be said about me, but I was interrupted.

"It appears that a defense lawyer has gotten the best of you, I'm sorry to say," Dr. Aquene said and paused to stare at me. I wasn't sure if it was my turn to speak yet, so I waited uncomfortably for what seemed like hours. She took a deep breath and sighed. "Please walk me through what was going through your mind when you were on the stand. I understand this was an especially brutal crime."

Her words brought back the images of the dog, with his head smashed in, all the blood, and the broken bones. I felt tears start to well up in my eyes, and I was once again in jeopardy of breaking down at a time when I desperately did not want to.

"The judge was letting the defense lawyer give testimony," I heard my voice cracking but kept pushing through, "and the prosecutor didn't object. I was trying to present the evidence, but the lawyer kept cutting me off. I didn't know how else to stop the man, the jury was starting to be swayed, I could see it on their faces."

"Did you consider that reputation was on the line? Are you aware that you are only valuable if you maintain your role and standing in your field?" Her tone wasn't harsh, but her eyes were. I could feel a lump forming in my throat, so I pinched the skin on my hand to distract me and keep it from progressing.

63

"At that moment, I admit, I was caught up in the emotion of the trial. I am aware that it is not my role to curb or edit the defense's words. I am there to present evidence, only....but I...," and despite all my efforts, the lump swelled like a goiter, and I couldn't finish my sentence. I couldn't even maintain eye contact with her, looking down at my feet instead.

"We are concerned. Do you think you are strong enough for this role, Dr. Wake? This needs to be addressed before we go any further with this working relationship."

"Yes, I do believe...I know I...," and I had to bite my lower lip for support. I looked off to the wall to pull it together, barely noticing the artwork hanging on the wall. "Yes, I am," I finally got out.

"Jaffey had so many good things about your qualifications and working rapport, I was rather hoping this would be a long term relationship. However, you would be of no use to us if your reputation became tarnished, you do understand?"

I couldn't respond, the tears were coming down, and the best I could do was nod.

"Carrie, could you get Dr. Wake some tissues?" I heard Dr. Aquene say, and soon felt the head assistant's hand on my shoulder. I didn't realize that she had moved her chair closer to me when she was offering me a tissue. I took it, nodding to her, and felt my despair turning to anger as I tried getting a grip on things.

"I just couldn't let the defendant get away with it. He was going to, I could tell. The jury was feeling sorry for him, and his lawyer went on vilifying the poor dog. I just couldn't let that happen. I know it's just my anger talking, but sometimes I really would like to see the perpetrators suffer the way they made innocent animals suffer...and their lawyers too, for that matter!"

I was still looking down through my outburst, and realized that the room had gone quiet except for a faint clicking sound. I was hesitant to look up, trying to avoid Dr. Aquene's eyes, but I needed to know if anyone else heard it. I lifted my head slowly, still hearing the clicks, and caught a glimpse of the side of the doctor's face. She had pivoted the chair to face the wall on my left. Was she smiling? She appeared to have a grin on her face, and pivoted her chair back around to face me. I dropped my gaze quickly, hoping she didn't see me watching her. When I looked up again, her face was back to the stoic version it was before.

"You don't have to worry about that defendant anymore. He won't be a problem ever again," Carrie said, and I looked at her, somewhat shocked. I don't believe she was supposed to reveal that information because Dr. Aquene shot her a look, and Carrie immediately left the room.

A different kind of fear crept through me, as I watched Dr. Aquene rise to her feet. She had a smile on her face again, but this time it was forced. I stood as well, not knowing what was happening next.

"Thank you for coming in and meeting with us, Dr. Wake. It was a pleasure to meet you. Please keep in mind what we discussed, your services would not be of use to us if your credibility was lost," she said as she ushered me to the door.

"Thank you Dr. Aquene, it was nice to meet you as well, and I'm sorry for, well for everything."

She stood in the doorway watching me leave. Carrie was nowhere to be found, and I couldn't get to the elevator fast enough. I'm not sure if Dr. Aquene had just threatened me or complimented me for my importance to the organization. Either way, I was pretty sure that I still had a job, for now, but I was starting to question if I would be terminated from the job or just terminated if I messed up again. I saw her go back into the office and start to close the door when the elevator doors were closing. I could still make out the clicking sound as her face disappeared behind the door.

Chapter 8

I woke with a splitting headache. It must have been all the crying the evening before. Dehydration, stress, and vocal outbursts could all lead to an emotional hangover. It was only Tuesday, and I had the whole rest of the week to look forward to. I got up and got ready as best I could without shampoo and conditioner, and knowing that I was out of milk for the coffee, I headed into the office early- at least there were supplies there.

Martin wasn't in yet, and I didn't expect him for a while. I figured he would take his time strolling in, as he didn't know I was back in town already. My first priority was caffeine, and probably my second and third as well. I sat down in front of my computer with the largest mug I could find in hand. I stared at the dark screen thinking about Carrie's words. Was the defendant dead? I managed to turn on the computer, and leaned back drinking my coffee while it booted up. I needed to search the news for any report of his death- if there was a report, and if there was a death. I got as far as Jacksonville in the search engine when the fax machine went off.

"Looks like we have another crime scene," I said to no one in particular. I started to walk over to it, but then slowed my pace as I thought about Dr. Aquene and her words of warning. One misstep and I would be next. They wouldn't kill me, right? I'm sure they didn't kill anyone- it was all in my head. I pulled the fax off the machine.

"Active crime scene, Kent County Maryland. One recently deceased canine needing immediate necropsy."

Martin wasn't around, and I wasn't sure when he would get in, so I left him a note and headed out alone. I didn't usually do solitary investigations, but this one was currently being investigated by the police and their CSI team. My job here was just to document the state and location of the body, and then bring it back with me to the office. At least this trip was only about an hour and a half, and I had plenty to think about on the way. I needed to focus clearly on my job- if I was going to keep it- and recent events were making that difficult. Jaffey kept popping back into my head, and I was left wondering what role he played in yesterday's meeting and what role he played in the organization. Was I working for an extreme animal rights group, and were they taking justice into their own hands? Surely there was a reasonable explanation for all this, and I was just jumping to ridiculous conclusions. I had to stay focused. Then Bob Marley's "I shot The Sheriff" came on the radio and I started laughing uncontrollably.

The crime scene was taped off, and just a single officer was standing guard. As I approached, I wondered why there was only one officer, and why we were letting the locals handle the rest of the forensics when we clearly took jurisdiction over the last scenes.

"Hi, I'm Dr. Wake," I extended my hand.

"Yes, hi, we've been waiting," he said.

"We?" I looked around.

"The rest of the team already left, I've been waiting with the cadaver for you to come and pick it up. Your director assured us your promptness and full cooperation."

"Yes, well, it is a long drive from the DC office. Can you please point me in the direction of the evidence to collect." I was starting to get tired of being caught off guard by the lack of information that the organization provided to me. Clearly, they were more than free with the information they shared with local officials. I followed him around the back of the property to an old trailer.

"Really? A trailer?" I probably shouldn't have said that out loud, but after that meet and greet, my ability to care about it was dwindling fast. The officer didn't have a verbal response, but his face contorted to something just shy of spitting acid. I thought silence would be a wise move on my part.

67

I stepped up into the trailer and was surprised by the lack of odor. Then I looked around and discovered why- there was little to no blood on the scene. There was, however, a deceased canine under a sheet on an old futon mattress in the corner. I didn't see any boards to form a fighting pit out of, but didn't know if the other officers had taken them, or anything else for evidence, and I was a little intimidated to ask.

"There's the body," the officer pointed to the corner, as if I didn't notice, but I'm sure it was more that he wanted me to take it and leave.

"Yes. Was there evidence of a pit set up in here or anywhere on the property?" Again, my question was returned with a death stare but at least he shook his head. "What led you to the crime scene, may I ask?" I almost cringed when I asked it, but it would be helpful to have as much information as I could get. I hated when there was more than one group working on a case at one time unless they were all really good at sharing and communicating.

"The neighbors called it in. Apparently there were several unfamiliar vehicles parked along the street, loud yelling, and the sound of an animal screaming in pain, according to them. We were sitting on them for drugs, so we pushed the warrant forward to raid the place. No one was here by the time we got back here, but we got some tire impressions. Then we came across this here," he indicated the body.

"There was nothing else? Any blood, break sticks, or training equipment found?"

"No, doc, like I said, this was it. We were busting our hump for nothing."

I didn't want to get into a discussion about the importance of animal welfare and ethics, so I let him mosey back to his patrol car and do whatever it was he seemed dying to do. Not being sure what had been done, if anything, I pulled out the camera and started the documentation process. As little evidence as there was, it was still going to take a while to process the scene. I hoped the officer was aware of that, and that he had enough to occupy himself for a while. I certainly didn't need him to be interfering with my work.

Finding a few drops of dry blood, I took some swabs just in case it belonged to the perp or even another dog. The samples were small, but we might be able to get mitochondrial DNA from them, and possibly establish a connection to the other cases. One of the other cases we didn't have anymore, I reminded myself. Why, exactly? Hmmm, because the perp in the first case died. I wondered if something similar was going to happen in the second case, the other one in Maryland. That case and this body were about a two hour ride apart. These two could very well be related, but the scene in West Virginia may or may not be. I wondered if the lab ran the evidence, or if they dropped everything when HQ said the case was closed. I was starting to wonder what the point was to collecting evidence, if the organization was just going to close the case, or take care of it on their own. All that kept going through my head was 'who was I working for?' and 'why was I working for them, again?'

I started bagging up the body when the phone rang and brought me out of a daze. It was Martin, I had forgotten all about him.

"Hey, you left me!" I heard while I was swiping the answer button.

"Sorry, but I had no idea when you'd be arriving, and it sounded like an urgent pick up. Good thing too that I didn't wait because the officer is a bit impatient...and a bit of a douche bag, if you ask me."

"Sounds like you're a bit on the grumpy side too," Martin deduced.

"It's been a sucky couple of days- that was for sure. Did I mention that I was called in to headquarters for a meeting? I'll tell you all about it when I get back."

"Ooooh, that doesn't sound good. Or does it? Tell me now! It's the least you can do for leaving me out of the loop on this one."

"There's really nothing here for you to do. I photographed what little evidence there is, and it's just one dog at this scene, thank god. Looks to be recently deceased- killed less than twelve hours ago. There's some fly activity, but no presence of

69

maggots yet. If it's related to the last scene, then we are getting closer. And I will fill you in on the details of everything later."

"Do you think they're related? We got the lab results on two of the specimens you submitted on Friday. You won't believe who the sire is to those dogs!"

"Who...," I started to ask, but the door to the trailer opened, startling me.

"Are you almost done in here? I've been waiting for you to finish up....they're expecting me back at the station," the officer said.

"Yes, just finishing up. Glad you're here, actually. You can help me carry the bag back to my vehicle, if you don't mind?" I asked with a smile and then told Martin I'd talk to him back at the office and tucked my phone back in my pocket. The officer agreed to help if it would hurry things along.

I was almost out of breath when I settled in behind the wheel. I was saying some choice words to the officer about his rudeness and demeanor, none of which made it outside of my head. No time for cynicism- must remain professional. My job was on the line, after all.

"Time for some driving music," I told myself as I was driving back and fiddled with the radio again. I almost didn't hear the GPS tell me to turn left- I was so distracted by the task- and nearly got T-boned by a large SUV. Maybe today was a little luckier than yesterday. Then "Secrets" by The Cure came on, and I spent much of the ride home going over yesterday's meeting in my head.

Pulling in in front of the office, I called Martin to come out and help me with the body. He was yawning the whole way over from the door, appearing as if he was napping.

"Help me carry him in," I said and opened the car door for him. He was definitely sleepy. "And I was thinking, do you think that the lab ran any of the evidence from the first scene, the one from West Virginia? I wondered if these were all connected. Do you think they kept the evidence, even? I know they were told to stop, that it was no longer our case, but do you think they might still have it? Or maybe it was sent to headquarters already?"

"Wow. You shouldn't be allowed to be alone and left to think for that long," Martin said with a sarcastic grin.

"Wise-ass. I'd hit you if you were closer," I said to him as I mimed a slap with my head. He then pretended to drop the body as we were walking into the office. "Why, I oughta...," and gave him an evil eye. I was glad that our office was on the first floor, no waiting around for elevator rides from hell. Yes, I liked being ostracized from the main lab.

"I don't know."

"You don't know to which part," I asked him as we set the body down on one of the steel tables in the back room.

"All of it. I don't know what they do or did over there."

"Well, I was thinking this could be a great opportunity for you, double-O-seven, to work on your subterfuging skills," I said with a grin.

"Is that even a word?" He paused to think about it. "Tell me more."

"I was thinking that you could question Georgie about it all, maybe tell him that the case was back on or something? You know, get him to run a sample for us, just to see if it's related to these from Maryland. They could use the blood samples from the pit boards, or even get DNA from the tooth pulps? The skulls may be too old or degraded, but it's worth a try," I tried to sell it to Martin. He was beginning to look intrigued. "And, yes, it's a word." I wasn't really sure about that last part- or any part of it, to be honest.

I was setting up for the necropsy- adjusting the light, getting the sample jars out and ready. I started in on the external exam, documenting scars, cuts, abrasions and the like when it occurred to me that I didn't hear the rest of Martin's news about the DNA results from our last case.

"Hey, what were you saying about the sire of two of the dogs we found in Maryland?" I shouted to the next room. I wasn't sure if he heard me or if he had his ear buds in again, so

I started to shout again, only to stop when he poked his head in the room before I get another word out.

"That's right, I didn't get to tell you. And you didn't get to tell me about the meeting!" He pulled up a stool next to the table to delve into the gossip. "The sire they found from the DNA turned out to be 'Darling Dan' out of Texas. He was owned by a guy named Martinez, who's serving a life sentence for double homicide. He was linked to the Twentieth Street Gang from Arizona. I guess they had ties to a drug cartel from Mexico."

"I heard about that dog- legendary, from what I've been told."

"Yeah, I guess he was a two-time grand champion. Those pups would have cost a pretty penny. I hear his line is in great demand. Why do you think they were killed?"

"Not sure yet. I do know that they were killed by blunt force to the head, as this one was. We are dealing with a sadistic and cruel group of people. Most fight dogs that I have seen were culled by gunshot or electrocution, once or twice by drowning. Beating is more graphic, more personal- a perp would have to have a lot of hate inside them to opt for this route of killing."

"Have you seen a plugging death, then? I heard they smell bad."

I looked at Martin to gauge his level of emotions- he was well versed at keeping his emotions in check. "I'm not sure that electrocution, "plugging" as it's known, is any smellier than the rest," I told him while reminding myself to keep my own feelings on a leash.

"Your turn. What's this about a meeting?"

I sighed and started in on my long day in court and the worthless prosecutor, the sleazy defense attorney, and his despicable client. Then I remembered Carrie's inference that the defendant was no longer alive.

"I made it all the way to the big office off the lobby at headquarters, and met a Dr. Aquene, head of public relations. Did you ever hear of her?"

"Nope, what was SHE like?"

"She had the most intense eyes- they could bore into you and stop you in your tracks. And intimidating- I think I was in a cold sweat the whole time." I started to relive the moment of meeting her, her striking beauty, and my fear.

"Was Dr. Ceta there?" Martin looked like he was about to fall off the stool, as he was sitting so close to the edge.

"No, I don't think we will ever meet her. Oh, and the woman that I thought was a secretary is Carrie, the head assistant. I wonder if she's the same woman that you and Georgie think is the head of human resources."

"What does she look like?"

"Average height, brown hair, I guess a little nondescript, I'm afraid. Does that much match up at least?"

"I suppose, but that could be anyone. What did Dr. Aquene say to you?"

"Not a whole lot. She stressed a couple of times that I would be no good to the organization if my reputation soured. I'm not sure if it was a threat or not. Looking back, I'm still not sure. But I do know that if I mess up again, it'll be the end of my role here, if not the end of me."

"Really? Don't you think that that's a little extreme?"

"Then, get this, when I had completely lost it, Carrie consoled me, handing me a tissue saying that the defendant would no longer be a problem- like he was dead!" I said that a bit too loud, and quieted myself, looking around the room. "Do you think that they bugged the place? You were hinting on that before."

"They do know what's going on without anyone telling them, that I know of. But, I've done multiple sweeps of the office, and found nothing even remotely suspicious. Besides, if the guy is dead, I'm sure he had many enemies waiting in line for that privilege."

I nodded and said, "Maybe you're right. Maybe I'm reading way too much into it." I thought about the clicking sounds at headquarters and at my house, but decided against bringing it up. Instead, I wanted to focus back on the case at hand and asked Martin, "Why don't you get the camera and document the head wounds. I haven't found any other external lesions.

73

Then, I can collect tissue and blood samples, while you start the paper work for me?"

He looked disappointed at the anti-climactic end to our gossip session. Feeling guilty about taking him on this roller coaster ride, I reminded him about our plan to get Georgie and the lab to run some tests for us.

"Maybe you can ask Georgie about running a comparison DNA test for us when you swing by the lab with these samples. Tell him the case was reactivated by HQ, and we really need to know if the dogs at all the scenes are related."

"I think I can pull that off. They don't call me Martini for nothing," he said with an evil grin.

"Who, exactly, calls you Martini?"

Chapter 9

Another miserable night of shoddy sleep. I had a dream that I was being chased by giant grasshoppers- those things were scary when they were mammoth sized. At least I made it to the store on the way home last night- I had a proper preparation before work.

It was a sunny humpday, and I was a little excited to get to work today. I had hoped the outcome of Martin's meeting with Georgie would prove beneficial, and I couldn't wait to find out how it all worked out. Getting in the office before him, I went about turning on the computers and checking the fax machine for messages. I was waiting for the system to boot up when I thought back to what Martin said yesterday. He had done several sweeps looking for bugs around here, maybe I should as well, for peace of mind. I didn't really know what I was looking for, but I had some confidence that I would know it if I saw it.

Sitting back down in front of the computer, I didn't know if I was happy that I didn't find something, or upset that I missed something that may have been there. I must have been making a face because Martin walked in and asked why I looked distressed. I brushed it off and smiled widely at him.

"There you are! So, how did it go at the lab yesterday? Give me the details."

"Oh, honey, I need some coffee first," he said putting his jacket on the back of his chair. I started to follow him into the back where the coffeemaker was, but he gave me a look that made me think better of that. I returned to my desk and waited, instead. I let him get settled and a healthy way into his first cup of joe before insisting on the particulars.

"Georgie looked worried, because he didn't hear it from the top, you know, but I went all double-O-seven and convinced him of his importance in the case and the urgency and all. I told him that the fax came in to us to see if there was a link, and that I figured he would have heard the same, but 'you know how it works around here', and gave him an eye roll. It seemed to work. We'll find out soon enough, though. The results should be done any minute now, I would think. They are super-fast over there."

"So we wait. Ugghhh! I wonder if all three scenes are related. They second two have the same MO. All we had were skulls from the one in West Virginia, but those didn't show a lot of trauma. One had a fractured orbit, but that could have occurred during a fight. They probably aren't related, and we are just grasping at straws."

"At the first Maryland scene we found two bodies buried together without skulls. Do you think the skulls from the West Virginia case are the missing heads?"

"It's plausible, but why the distance between the two sites? Was the perp carrying the skulls with him wherever he went? Seems like an odd practice, especially given the way he kills off his dogs. I wouldn't peg him for a sentimental guy."

"What if those two were somehow special to him? You said there weren't the same blows to the head as the others. What if he cared about the first two and then something happened?"

"Are you trying to make this monster into a person? I don't really care what happened to him, do you?" I was starting to let emotions creep in- and so early in the morning after such a great start! I reeled it in a bit and flashed a grin at Martin, trying to convince him that I wasn't taking it so seriously. It was just friendly discussion of what-ifs, after all.

"I just think that if they are related, those skulls belong to the bodies we found in Maryland. Couldn't you look for matching cut marks and things between the bodies and the skulls?"

"There are missing bones. C1 and C2 are missing from both bodies, and no cervical vertebrae were found with the skulls, so, no, I cannot go by similarities. We just have to wait for the DNA, if they found any that's viable," I explained to him.

A lull in the conversation had our gazes drifting over to our monitors and then over to the fax machine, but they all remained quiet. I could hear some birds chirping outside the window, and I pictured a happy couple building a nest together for their future family. Spring was filled with more than one type of anticipation.

My phone rang and I immediately looked at the fax machine again. It was on the third ring that I realized it was coming from my pocket. Pulling it out I saw it was a blocked number, and instantly thought of Dr. Aquene and her warning about messing up again. I managed to answer it before it went to voicemail, but my hands were visibly shaking.

"Hello?" I croaked out clearing my throat.

"Hello, Dr. Wake? It's Jaffey here." I let out a sigh of relief and collapsed backward in the chair.

"Jaffey, how are you? I meant to ask you the last time we spoke, are you still in Kenya?"

"Yes I am, in fact, that's why I'm calling. I wanted to give you an update." I think I went partly into shock. The organization was sharing information?

"An update would be splendid! How are things tidying up there? Has there been a press release yet?"

I'm afraid it's more serious than that, Doctor. The convergence of herds has split up, once again, and Nkiru's family is being shadowed, we believe."

"More poachers? Do you need me back there? I could fly out today and help with whatever I could..."

"No, no, we can handle it, at least for now. Besides, Dr. Ceta has told me that you are needed where you are." His words brought to mind the meeting with Dr. Aquene and Carrie, and I wanted to tell Jaffey about them, the conversation, and the related intimations. I scarcely got a word out when the connection started to break up.

"I'm sorry, Dr. Wake, but I must go now, we'll talk again soon," and the connection was lost.

I had so much more to say, to ask. I felt frustrated- having just felt elated for an update, then downcast by the lack of a report. I was no better or worse for disclosure than I was before the call.

"What's up in Kenya," Martin said, pulling me out of my preoccupation.

"Poachers. I think Nkiru is in trouble. I feel helpless from here, but there's nothing that I can do to help right now."

"That was a quick conversation," he tried to ascertain more details of the call.

"The connection wasn't good. He said that Dr. Ceta mentioned that I was needed here. That means that he must talk directly with her. How high up in ranks do you think he is? I never even thought to ask when we were together in Africa."

"I don't know. I don't know how any of this works. I just do my thang and get my paycheck." Martin looked a touch dismissive. An account of his place in this organization was emerging- he preferred not to be part of it.

I shook the mouse to keep the monitor from going into saver mode. The results should be coming in soon, at least from yesterday's case, if not from the West Virginia one. I looked back over to Martin, but he had put his ear buds in- not a bad idea. I could use some distraction myself. My thoughts drifted to Nkiru and her herd mates. I wondered why the group would break into smaller families and separate. What was their strategy? Would they even have one?

Elephant herd size was variable and were usually led by the dominant matriarch- that much I knew. Hundreds of individuals of all ages were not uncommon in one group. Sometimes the herds would congregate and socialize for a while, and then they would break up into smaller groups. The stable social portion that would remain together usually would be made up of closely related adult females and their offspring. Sometimes adult males would join those herds when there was a female in heat. Females can be highly protective of their young and some have killed those who were in close proximity to them in the African bush. Breaking into smaller groups might give them another advantage- forcing the poachers to split up or confuse them as to a direction.

I had read a lot about the intelligence of the elephant. They were brilliant animals who could display complex social behaviors. Several of these behaviors have been documented such as greeting ceremonies, group defense, vocal and scent communication, social play, courtship, and more. Elephant intelligence and their ability to cooperate have been thought to equal that of chimpanzees and dolphins. Some researchers documented that elephants could recognize signs of anxiety in another herd mate, and they would rush to the upset animal's side, making quieting sounds and stroking the head of another. When elephants came across the remains of a deceased elephant, they approached it slowly, and gently touched the bones with their trunks, but they didn't show the same interest in the body parts of other animal species. Elephants were also seen on many occasions kicking dirt over the skeletons of their deceased and covering them with palm fronds as if burying them.

I grew more worried about Nkiru the more I pictured her life on the savanna, and soon imagined a horrible demise- being followed, hunted, chased down. The fear that someone was going to jump out around every corner weighing heavily on their minds. The dream from last night resurfaced, and the image of giant grasshoppers chasing me started mixing with images of poachers chasing the elephants.

I was rattled back to reality by Martin yelling that results were back. He had his music booming and had no idea how loud he was. I refocused my eyes only to see the STAFE logo bouncing off the edges of the screen. Wiggling the mouse again I saw that results for the body from yesterday's case were back, at least part of the results.

"Only part of the results are back," Martin stated the obvious in a boisterous voice. I nodded and tapped on my ear giving him the hint. He smiled and unplugged himself.

"There was a familial match to the two whole bodies found at the other site. Looks like they had the same sire but different dam. The two more skeletonized bodies without

79

skulls from the other scene didn't match this body or the other two but had a familial match to each other. They haven't run those against the database of known dogs yet," I read out loud.

"So the dog from yesterday was related to the two whole bodies from the other Maryland site, but not to the other two bodies buried together. Do you think that the same perp buried all four from the first Maryland scene?"

"I don't know. The two older bodies could have been there from a related perp or someone from the same gang. Or it could be the same perp, and those were his first fighting dogs- I don't know."

"But the dog from yesterday's case could have been owned and killed by the same perp as the one from the four body site, don't you think?"

"Yes, it could be, but maybe not. I don't want to jump to conclusions. Although it would be a huge coincidence that dogs at two sites in the same state were killed in the same way and all had the same sire. I would think that the owners at least knew each other," I answered Martin. I did really think it was the same perp, but it was dangerous to assume it.

I wasn't sure what to do next. I wanted to wait and see if the skulls came from the two bodies from the Maryland site, at least I would have a better idea as to how many separate cases we were working, they could all wind up being parts of the same one. Since the perp from the West Virginia case had died, we may have been down to one perp who left the two fresher bodies in Maryland and the body from yesterday. If those two perpetrators were connected, then the dead person we uncovered from the West Virginia case indicated a larger crime ring.

"There was a case a few months ago that was intricately connected, like this one. Sean was putting the connections together, one from Arizona, one from New Mexico, and one from Texas. STAFE had multiple court cases going at the same time. I'm not sure how it sits right now, if they're in jail, awaiting trial, or what. Sean was all over that, but that was before he left," Martin said.

"I never even asked who worked here before me! Was Sean a forensic veterinarian?"

"No, Sean was a retired cop from Boston. He had a shady reputation- there were rumors that he was a dirty cop, but there wasn't proof. I think he probably just rubbed people the wrong way. I got along with him OK. We weren't buds or anything, but we hung out a few times."

"What happened to him?"

"He was here when I started, which was close to the beginning of the inception of our fine organization. I don't think he ever met Dr. Ceta. I'm pretty sure he was a low level like us. We were finishing with the forensics from a neglect case in Tennessee when I found a fax on the machine on a Monday. It said to stop work on the case, that it was closed, like our case in West Virginia. It also said that Sean resigned- he had a family emergency that he had to attend to. Thing is, he didn't have any family. It was the only thing we had in common."

"So what do you think happened to him? Did you keep in touch?"

"No, that's the other weird thing. I went by his place to see what's up because he wasn't answering his phone. The whole place was cleared out, no forwarding address. A couple of days later his phone was disconnected."

The warning from Dr. Aquene rang through my head, and I questioned the depth of the involvement of the organization. Once again the fear crept into my stomach and I began to feel queasy.

"I think his past may have caught up to him. Georgie said he heard that Sean was being stalked by some criminal he busted that just got out of prison. I don't know if it's true or not."

"Sounds credible, maybe that's all it was," I said but not believing a word of it. I was fidgeting with the mouse again and felt Martin's stare.

"Yeah, that's probably what it was," he said with an anxious look on his face. "What do you want to tell HQ about this?"

Alarmed, I said, "About Sean?"

81

"No, hahahaha! About the case. Do you want to fax your ideas over- about the dogs being related and that the cases may be as well?" Martin snickered.

"Oh, in a way I figured they would already know that somehow. Yes, I guess I should send over my findings thus far. I just don't want to include anything about the lab testing the skulls. We aren't working on that case anymore, wink wink, nudge nudge."

"Is that a reference to another old TV show?" Martin sounded disenchanted.

"Monty Python.....come on, you must have seen something by them? I give up!"

Martin rolled his eyes. "Whatevs, Doc. We don't have to say anything about THAT. Just tell them about the two cases in Maryland and the results so far. They may need to get the lawyers going on this or something, I don't know. That's just how we did things before. Sean would put a few things together and shoot headquarters a fax. We would then be told what direction they wanted us to go in."

"I wish there was some way to tie in the dead perp and the dead body from West Virginia, though. I think that they are key parts to the whole thing, if they indeed are connected."

"Well, we can bring that up when we get more results, right? That is, if they still want us working on these ones from Maryland. They can be quirky that way, dropping cases half way through."

"Does that happen a lot?"

"Here and there. Some cases go to trial, some cases get dropped. I don't ask. I guess I just assumed that it was a turf war with some other agency."

"Jurisdiction can be tricky. Maybe STAFE hands off their forensics to another nonprofit or government agency that is better equipped for certain crimes or locations," I offered.

I typed up the findings so far, being sure to point out the similarities of the two Maryland crime scene victims and their genetic connections. I noted that the two skeletal bodies that were missing heads were not linked by DNA to the others, and being from an older crime scene, might be related to other older crimes. I didn't specifically say an older crime that we had come across, nor did I reference the West Virginia case. I hoped the open-ended nature of the findings would lead them to same conclusions that I was drawing, but it was all I could do at the moment. I forwarded it to the same number that sends us our directives, and wondered how long it would take to hear back from them.

Martin was no help on the time estimate, so I was forced to entertain myself to his chagrin. I started with show tunes-finding the most outlandish ones on YouTube and inharmoniously singing along. Mortified, Martin put his ear buds back in, but after several songs, he gave up and joined in. I didn't even notice that headquarters had faxed us back.

Chapter 10

"An FBI agent? Seriously?" I said.

"No Way! Cool, never met one before. Have you?" Martin seemed almost excited about the prospect.

"I've worked with the FBI before, when they pulled jurisdiction on us, but it was just to hand over evidence and explain our findings. It was over a dog fighting ring that also dealt with human trafficking." Martin cringed when I mentioned human trafficking, one of the worst crimes I had been involved with tangentially. "Apparently the agent will be here later this afternoon. They want to question us about our finding of the dead body- the human- from West Virginia. It says 'bodies' though. Do you think they mean the dead perp as well?"

"We didn't even see the perp, though. By the time we got to the scene, they were removing the body. Did anyone even know we were there?" Martin was starting to panic.

"Someone seems to think we know something. It is kind of strange, I would have thought that the perp killed the person, then killed himself later....they must think otherwise." I tried to put it together before the agent came out. I was beginning to worry too.

"Looks like the DB is coming back to haunt us," Martin said and did his now-famous spooky music and wiggly fingers routine. I could tell he was still nervous, though.

I did wonder what the FBI knew. I wondered what headquarters knew. I couldn't imagine that STAFE would call in the FBI, so they're probably being forced into cooperating. Thinking it was the more prudent route, I started talking through the events of our first case in West Virginia with Martin, so our details matched.

"Do you think there's something more to the skulls than we know? I mean, it could be the hallmark of some mass killer or something, right?"

"I don't know...," it made me think about the skulls and the DNA test we were running behind the back of the organization. Surely, this would all come to the surface now if the FBI was involved. "How is the lab sending us the results of the DNA test from the skulls? Are they putting it in the system, I mean?"

"Oh, crap, I get what you're saying. Headquarters will see it and know we are still working a closed case. I'll call Georgie and have him fax the results and not enter it in the computer.....I'll tell him it has something to do with the FBI, but I can't talk about it," Martin looked very proud of himself.

"That's very Martini of you." I shot him a grin and proceeded to replay the day's events in my head. I didn't want to miss any details. It still seemed strange that an FBI agent was needed for this case. Maybe there were more bodies in the field behind the barn that we didn't find. Maybe there were other bodies elsewhere with similar characteristics. I wondered how far-reaching this case really was.

We filled our time waiting with paperwork- no matter where you go or who you work for, paperwork will drag you down. By the time the agent arrived, we were both drained and ready to go home. I didn't relish the idea of hanging around answering questions that I just spent hours answering over and over in my head in preparation. Still, I tried to rally for the team.

He was a tall man, younger than I had pictured. Wearing a dark suit and carrying a hat in his hand, the agent looked like he just stepped out of a film noir. I couldn't help but laugh when he walked through the door- I think he was taken aback by my response. Still, he offered his hand with an introduction- a mister Jon McDermitt, with the Federal Bureau of Investigation, hoping to have a few minutes for some questions.

"Yes, the organization said you would be arriving, please come in and have a seat. Can I get you some coffee," I tried to sound cordial.

"No, thank you. I should only be a few minutes, really." He took a seat at the long table against the main wall while looking around at our humble office. "I imagined a bigger place than this....not that it's small." He sounded nervous himself, and I wondered how many cases he had worked before this one.

"I really don't know what we can tell you about the case. I assume that the officer, Deputy Freeman or Sheriff Tinely would have filled you in about the body."

"Yes, we have spoken to both of them, but I wanted to get your perspective, from the dog fighting side. I understand you have worked several cases with criminals involved in dog fighting, and I need your take on things in this case. For instance, the manner of death of the dogs involved?"

"Well, we only found the two skulls at the location where we found the dead body, and manner of death was not able to be determined. There were peri-orbital fractures and several missing teeth, but that's all consistent with dog fighting."

"So you don't know if they were shot, drowned, or..."

"Usually when they are culled by gunshot, it would be through the head, but not always. We did not find any evidence of this with the heads discovered there, but it doesn't rule it out."

"I see. And, to your knowledge, are there any similar cases ongoing that might be related to this one? Many times there are several crime scenes related to one dog fighting ring...," he said, and I could tell he was fishing for something more specific, but for some reason he wasn't saying it outright.

"We are working a couple of scenes, but those are out in Maryland. We don't know if they are related at all." I didn't want to tell him about our pending DNA test on the skulls or my theory of the relationship between the cases. I had no real evidence that the West Virginia case was related at all.

"Could you tell me about the cases, anyway? They may indeed hold some insight into my investigation." He sounded colder, like he knew something more that he certainly wasn't going to share.

"OK, we have a case in the Snow Hill area of Maryland where we found three distinct burial sites. Two of them had one canine body each, bludgeoned to death by blunt force to the head. The third grave had two canine bodies that were almost skeletonized- clearly an older burial site than the first two. Those two bodies were missing their heads, and no cause of death could be determined. Also found at the site were several books and a trophy associated with dog fighting, and various other paraphernalia. The lab has it all, you'd have to talk to them as far as what forensics they could pull from all of it." I watched him watch me as I spoke, and I wasn't sure if he was more interested in my mannerisms or my words, but it made me nervous for some reason.

"And from what you have seen in other cases, did that seem typical...more brutal...," he was fishing again.

"I would say, more brutal, yes. It's a pretty aggressive act to physically and forcefully hit another living creature than it would be to electrocute or shoot." I said it matter-of-factually, and I found myself watching his mannerisms as much as he was watching mine. I felt, somehow, on the defensive.

"Any other cases pending?" Now I was sure he already knew our business, and he was teasing out details one by one.

"The second crime scene in Maryland, up near Chestertown, was a single body, no other evidence found. It was of a recently culled pit bull with a head wound consistent with the two from the other scene. DNA results indicate a familial link between all three dogs, but not the two from the older burial site."

"Familial link? Can you explain?" He looked sincere in his questioning.

"The three of them share the same sire. The two from the first burial site were siblings, and they were half siblings to the dog found at the last crime scene. A dog named 'Darling Dan' from Texas was the sire." I wasn't sure if I needed to go into who owned the dog, seeing as the FBI agent seemed to already know the answers to the questions he was asking.

"I have seen the file on 'Darling Dan''s owner. Glad he's locked away for life." He attempted a smile, but it didn't really go as planned. He looked more like a gargoyle or a really bad narc.

"So that's it. Just the two cases now. I hope that helped you some," I said, standing up, hoping he'd be finished. I looked over at Martin who was watching the whole conversation like a tennis match. He made a face at me.

"Just one more thing, did you see anything when you went to the perpetrators home address?"

I sat back down, somewhat alarmed. How did he know about that? Looking over at Martin, I saw him putting on his jacket.

"I need to run over to the lab, I hope you don't mind," he said when he was half way out the door.

"No, I think Dr. Wake's answers are all I need....for today," the profiler waved at Martin as he left.

"Today?" I gulped. "We," and I looked at the now-closed door, "We were on our way when headquarters told us we were off the case. We figured we'll just do a drive-by to see if there was anything to see. They were removing his body when we got there, so we just headed back...a long drive for nothing, really." I'm not sure what he thought of my answer, but I got up again and this time, so did he.

"Are you on your way home, then? Can I offer you a lift?" The agent looked more serious than I thought he should for the question, and it put me off a little.

"No thank you, I enjoy the walk," I said, lying somewhat. It was already dark, and I reached to touch my arm.

"Please, there's another item I wanted to ask you about, this way we can get it out of the way and you'd be home by the time we are finished." He attempted another smile, a better effort, but it wasn't his strong suit.

I agreed and we headed out the door. He did have manners, at least. He held the door open for me, both at the office and to his car. The ride couldn't be that bad. We were around the block when he set in with the questions again.

"I understand someone shot at you the other night," he said with no particular emotion.

"How did you...."

"You filed a police report, remember?"

"Yes, it was nothing, really. It was late and I was walking home. Martin warned me that the neighborhood wasn't the safest after dark. It was just an abrasion- my jacket got the worst of it." I made light of the event, not knowing what it had to do with anything.

"Did you get a look at the shooter?"

"No. I felt something, like someone was behind me, but it all happened so fast. Why are you asking about that? You don't think it's related, do you?"

"We have suspicions. It could very well be related to the dog fighting. We believe they are part of a bigger drug ring in this area. They may view you as a threat."

I didn't know what to say. I felt shaky. He asked if I wanted him to walk me to the door and check things out, but I declined. I was sure I wasn't being targeted, wasn't I? At most, I had pictured the shooting being related to the organization coming after me, now I had more to worry about. I said good night to him and walked up to my apartment fearing the shadows more than ever.

I popped some melatonin and tried to get some sleep that night. Dog fighting perps shooting at me? I didn't think so, but maybe. It took all my effort to believe the shooting was random, and not my employer coming after me for knowing something or doing something wrong. What happened to my predecessor, Sean, anyway? Now it might be the criminals coming after me? What have I gotten myself into with this job? My last place of employment had me in an emotionally wrecked state, but at least no one shot at me- that I knew of. Maybe I should have just stayed in Florida. But then, I wouldn't have gotten the opportunity to go to Africa, to see elephants up close and personal (a little too close!), and to help

89

stop the poachers- or watch them get killed, as the case may be.

Sitting up, I thought I would be better off doing something more productive than lying awake in bed all night. I could do the laundry, but that would entail going to the basement of the building at night by myself, and the FBI just told me that I might be a target. I thought better of it and looked around the room for something to do. It would be early morning in Kenya, maybe I could try to connect with Jaffey to see how they were getting on. I got up and went through the papers on my desk for his number. Realizing it would be in my phone from the previous attempt, I abandoned the search and reached for the phone. It went through to voicemail, and not knowing what to say really, I hung up. When he called before, it was from a restricted line, I wondered if he even had his phone with him this time or if something happened to it. He could have lost it, for all I knew.

I sat down behind the sad excuse for a desk in my room and glared at the scattered papers. I really needed to be more organized, I almost felt angry at the notes and documents for being in such chaos. It looked like a storm hit the corner of my bedroom, I almost expected to find some of them soaking wet. I read through some of the notes and began the arduous task of organizing the clutter into piles- constructive confusion at best. Maybe I could find a golden nugget in this mayhem that I could pass on to Jaffey. It was conceivable that there was some way I could still help Nkiru and her herd mates from here. I searched for the case reports that I received from him before I even started working for this agency, and certainly before I started regretting it.

I read through reports on ivory trafficking and the dwindling elephant population in Africa. The illegal trade was responsible for the killing of approximately 50,000 African elephants each year. A typical poacher could sell ivory for around three hundred dollars per kilogram. Since an average elephant would offer up around ten kilograms of ivory, an elephant would be worth about three thousand dollars to a poacher. The ivory goes on to be carved and polished after that, increasing the value to around six thousand dollars per kilogram. That meant that the ivory industry was worth at least three billion dollars. Most of the demand for ivory came from Asia, where it got carved into jewelry and other novelties, and the United States was the world's second-largest market for ivory, with San Francisco and Los Angeles being in the top three domestic ivory markets overall. Clearly the battle at the other end- the demand side- was just as important, if not more so, in stopping the mass killing of these animals.

I had helped Jaffey understand the recent studies that were done to locate the poaching hot spots and critical areas of this complex trade that crossed several international borders. The DNA studies, using stockpiled confiscated ivory, showed that a large portion of the ivory was taken from only two relatively small areas in Africa. They showed that most savanna elephant tusks harvested after 2007 came from Tanzania and Mozambique, and the most forest elephant tusks came from Gabon, the Republic of Congo, or the Central African Republic. Interpol was working with several groups and stressed the importance of stopping these poachers in these countries. There would be more poachers coming, and Jaffey had many more battles in his future, and much more ground to cover if he wanted to make a dent in the carnage. But what about me? What was my role?

Dr. Ceta had requested that I'd be on scene in Africa, but I never quite knew why. My expertise was in anatomic pathology, making me needed at crime scenes with animal casualties, not in the savanna fighting poachers. But, if she wanted me there before for whatever reason, why not now? I could certainly perform forensic tests on evidence that Jaffey brought back, I didn't have to be present for that part of the investigation. Were they trying to impress on me the graphic nature of the case, get me involved in all facets so I would be more invested in the outcome? I felt that there was more to the story than I was even guessing at.

I tried Jaffey's number again and left a message this time. Maybe he'd call back, maybe he wouldn't, but I had to reach out. It wasn't fair to give me the 'update', as he put it, that

Nkiru was in danger and then hang up. I felt helpless enough as it was. Getting up from the desk I stubbed my toe, and then hobbled my way into the living room. If I couldn't sleep, couldn't help the elephants, and couldn't get a hold of Jaffey, I was going to pout with some ice cream and Twilight Zone reruns.

Chapter 11

The next day was dragging before it even got started. I had had too much caffeine and too little at the same time, working at whatever was considered a functional level was not an option. Martin, on the other hand, appeared elated.

"What are you so happy about?" I asked while scrutinizing him through bleary eyes.

"Who, me?" He did his best impression of cheeky. "I had a good night. You, not so much?"

"Not so much. What was so good?"

"I had a date."

"Ooooh, details!" I wheeled my chair over to his desk.

"Cut it out, this isn't the beauty salon. I don't kiss and tell," Martin actually blushed.

"So there was kissing, then? Go on." I gave him a big grin.

"I'm not going to give you many details....he's cute, he's a drummer, and we have another date on Friday."

"A drummer? What kind of music? Where did you meet?" I could sense he wanted to tell me about it, but he was being modest.

"We actually met at a wedding....I know, corny. His band was playing, and we started chatting during one of their breaks."

"A wedding band? Hahahaha! Oh no, does he have to play the "Chicken Dance" and "Macarena"? That would drive me nuts!"

"Yes, unfortunately, it's part of their routine. But whatever. They make money, and this day and age, it's the only way."

Martin looked put off. Now I felt bad for laughing, but I wasn't making fun of the poor guy.

"Well I'm glad you got out and had some fun. When do I get to meet him?"

"Never," Martin said and stuck out his tongue for effect. I laughed and let it go. Rolling back to my desk, I hit my leg on the corner. "See, that's what you get. Karma," Martin sounded justified.

I checked the computer again for results from the lab, but nothing. Are they still going to process the evidence from the West Virginia case, or did headquarters find out and intervene? I didn't want to ask Martin about it, but I had to.

"So, when do you think Georgie will post the results of the DNA comparisons?"

"I don't know. Maybe he won't. I can't ask him, though, he might think we're up to something."

"We are up to something. But, as long as the organization doesn't tell him otherwise, he should just think we're working on a time-sensitive case." I was trying to reason it out to myself and to Martin at the same time. He wasn't buying the argument.

"Let's give him more time. I don't want to rock the boat or make any enemies here. What if headquarters stopped them?"

"I would think I would have heard from Carrie by now if that were the case. They would have come after us, wouldn't they?" I wasn't even sure at that point, but my best guess would have been that I would be no longer employed- or dead.

"Maybe that FBI guy shut it down, or took over. What happened after I left?" Martin leaned in across his desk as if some juicy scoop of gossip was about to be delivered. I didn't want to tell him about the shooter possibly being related to the dog fighting ring and the cases we were working on. I thought it might scare him or even make him overprotective. I certainly didn't want someone hovering over me, on my every move. But, at the same time, I was worried about his safety, too. What if the shooter came after him? That is, if the shooter was related to the case. I still wasn't convinced.

"He's concerned that the cases in Maryland are related to the one in West Virginia, but I didn't tell him we were running the test. I figured it would have definitely made it back to headquarters if I did that."

"So now what? Does he take over our cases? Does he have to come back here again? I don't think I liked him coming around- it kind of freaked me out."

"I don't know if he'll be back, I have a feeling that he will. He had....other concerns."

"Other concerns? Like what? Does he think that we had something to do with the murder?" Martin laughed nervously.

"No, nothing like that. He actually drove me home. He was concerned for my safety, citing the shooting from the other night."

"How did he know about that?" Now he looked scared.

"The police report, nothing nefarious. He thinks the shooter may be related to the dog fighting case. Can you believe it? I highly doubt it, but just in case it was, you should be careful, too. Not to sound overcautious, but keeping vigilant of your surroundings, especially when you are alone, isn't a bad idea." Seeing Martin's face drop made me wish that I hadn't said anything. I wanted to backtrack and take back the words, but maybe it was better that he knew. I didn't want to leave him exposed to possible harm.

"I never thought of that. I mean, connecting the shooting to any case we were working on. It makes sense though, don't you think? I don't know why I didn't think of it. Crap, should we ask headquarters for a bodyguard?"

"I don't think we need that. I'm not sure it's related at all. I'm actually sorry that I told you, I don't want you to panic."

"Too late for that." Now he truly looked scared, and there wasn't anything I could do.

"IF the shooting was related to the cases, and I don't think it was, then I think they would still be after me and not you. AND, they haven't made another attempt, so I think you're OK." That was the best I could offer up to appease his worries.

Checking the computer again, I hoped the results would be in. A distraction at this point would be most welcomed. Nothing. Maybe some lunch?

95

"Is there any good delivery around here, I'm famished. You?"

"Not so hungry now, thanks."

My phone rang, alarming us both. I fumbled for it, more to stop the noise than anything else. It was a restricted number again. I answered it quickly, thinking it had to be Jaffey, and it was.

"Allo? Dr. Wake?" The line was cutting in and out.

"Yes, Jaffey?" I was doing math in my head- never a good thing under any circumstances- calculating the time in Kenya. Seven pm-ish.

"Dr. Wake, your presence is needed here. Your statement....government here. STAFE has arranged transport for you...later today. The....will send you more details. I will....at base camp..." The line disconnected. I sat looking at my phone while Martin was saying something. I think I was trying to fill in the gaps where the line dropped out, but it didn't help me much. I looked over at Martin who was looking at the fax machine.

I had the whole flight to think about my guilt for leaving Martin to fend for himself back at the office, with the shooter at large, whether or not it was related to the case. Either way, he was panicked, and I couldn't help him with it. I also had the time to think about why I was needed in Africa. He said something about my statement and the government. Surely I could have done that remotely, why would I have to be there in person? I was getting more convinced that it was an emotional ploy, but for what reason, I didn't know.

I had heard that the government had problems with the wildlife services set up to preserve the wild animal populations and control poaching. Several officers had been convicted of aiding ivory poachers for a cut of the profits. There were accounts of corrupt wildlife service officers killing poachers to keep all of the profits or to keep them quiet after the fact. A government report had said some Kenya Wildlife Service staff members had even been implicated in the poaching of elephants and rhinos themselves. Maybe the government had a plan to flush out more of their corrupt officers, and we were part of the scheme. Or, perhaps, they thought we had information regarding the criminal activity.

The flight was about fifteen and a half hours long, and I needed to get some sleep if I was going to be helpful at all. Several hours into the flight, drowsiness took over. The giant grasshoppers were back, and were louder and more viscious than ever. I must have been tossing and turning because I awoke with bruising on my head. I must have whacked it during the turmoil- or we hit some incredible turbulence.

Marcus was waiting at the airport. It was a six hour ride from the airport to base camp, and he wasn't a chatty kind of guy. I made an effort to get information out of him, but he did the usual shrugging and smiling that I had remembered him doing before. I wondered why we were going to base camp if I was really in Kenya for my statement to the government. Obviously, there was another agenda, but I wouldn't be finding out about it anytime soon- or through Marcus for that matter.

Despite the amazing scenery, I dozed off again, awaking to the truck abruptly stopping in the familiar savanna setting. Marcus walked off toward the supply tent on the left, and I was left watching the hustle of a couple of unknown men packing another vehicle. I wondered where Jaffey was.

I almost fell getting out of the truck. Thinking back to Martin's comment about karma when I hit my leg on the desk, I chuckled and deduced that I was just a klutz. I grabbed the only bag that I brought. Packing light was my only option, really. I had no idea how long I would be here, or what I would be doing. It was that or bring everything I had, just in case. I opted for the former, as I knew I'd be the one carrying it.

I headed over to the main tent, hoping I would see or hear a familiar voice. I was seen first- Jaffey came up behind me and scared the crap out of me. At least he had a sense of humor, or he was a sadist. I was reminded that I really didn't know him. I extended my hand, but he went in for a hug.

97

"Dr. Wake, good to see you. I trust your travels were satisfactory?"

"Well, I'm here and alive, so I guess, yes."

He laughed and hit me on the back. Hard. "Good, good. Come sit. I will fill you in."

That was the first reasonable thing I had heard all week. We went around the backside of the main tent and sat around a small table covered in maps. There were small sticks and pebbles in various spots on the big map, and I wasn't sure if they were standing in for strategic positions or just random debris. Jaffey just ignored the whole thing for the moment.

"Nkiru and her herd mates were attacked. We managed to chase off the poachers this time, but I'm afraid they had some help locating the herd. There may be a wildlife officer or two involved. We are not positive yet, but if it's true, she is in more danger than I had anticipated."

"What can I do to help- I thought I was just out here to give my statement?"

"There are details that I cannot disclose, but you were sent here at the request of Dr. Ceta and Dr. Aquene. They thought that you needed to see what was going on."

"I don't understand, this isn't part of my expertise. This isn't what I was hired for. Why did they request it?"

"There's a lot going on. I needed the help for one, but they thought that you needed to be involved more, see what happens in other areas of an ongoing case. They want you to understand the importance of the work that we do."

"It'll be dark soon," Marcus said from behind us. Jumping a bit, I turned to see his somber face.

"Then we need to set out." Jaffey stood up and started to walk away before I could ask any more questions.

The Land Rover was fully packed with arsenal and camping gear and was ready to go. I watched the two unknown men get into the truck and head out. They looked like the men from the last time that I was here, but I couldn't tell for sure. Marcus was already behind the wheel and Jaffey was shouting for me to hurry up. I felt two steps behind and in slow motion. Shouldn't I know more before going on the battlefield? I squeezed into what little space there was in the back seat, and we headed out as well.

"Where are we going again?" I hollered in Jaffey's direction, but he just pointed ahead. Thanks, that helped a lot. About a half hour later, we pulled into a more heavily treed area and turned off the engine. I didn't see or hear the others in the second truck, in fact I didn't see anything but trees.

"So, where are we?" I asked again.

"We need to set up. We have reason to believe that they are planning an attack tonight. We have to move quickly."

Marcus and Jaffey went to task setting up a front, arranging firepower, and establishing sight lines for the impending battle. I tried to stay out of the way, having no idea what to do to help. I hesitated to walk off too far, but I wanted to get my bearings too. I wasn't much better than a sitting duck if I didn't, and I preferred to stay alive if I could. I still had no idea where our other guys were, and I wished I did. I'm sure I would have felt more at ease knowing the plan of attack.

Jaffey motioned me over. Stumbling in the dark, I made my way over to them. Marcus was preoccupied with something in the distance. He had night vision goggles and had already spotted motion not far off. I wanted to ask questions, but was silenced. It was apparent that the battle had commenced.

Grabbing a pair of goggles, I settled into a nook between the two men. Were those our guys, the poachers, or the elephants? All I saw was a small spot of heat in between the trees. After a few minutes, I could deduce that it was a person, no, a couple of people moving around through the trees.

"Are those..."

"Shhh," Marcus hissed.

A third body emerged from the cover. A shorter third body. Then I saw all three of them side by side in a partial clearing. One was clearly an adult, but the other two were dwarfed in comparison. Were they children? I gasped and immediately covered my mouth. I watched their movements- the more purposeful ones of the taller and larger person and the clumsier ones of the two smaller bodies. I was aghast.

I looked over to Jaffey to see his reaction, but he was unruffled by the development. Did he already know? He must have, if these were the same poachers that they just chased off. I couldn't believe it. I couldn't fight a child. Grabbing Jaffey's arm, I pulled him to me to explain.

"The children, usually the sons, sometimes take on the role of the father if the father has died. They have to assume the responsibilities of the lost parent and take care of the remaining family. It's not uncommon to find boys brought into this type of criminal activity," he whispered. He said it so matter-of-factually that I had no response. Certainly he wasn't going to shoot a child? I was horrified. I stumbled back a few steps toward the vehicle.

Then I heard a shot ring out. It wasn't from us, the poachers must have shot at...what, at us? I crouched back down and tried to get a visual. The bodies in the distance were running to the right. No one appeared to be chasing them, but I couldn't be certain. Maybe our other guys had set up on the far side, surrounding them. Another shot echoed. It was responded to by a trumpeting call further off to the right. I looked far down and caught a glimpse of motion. A small herd of elephants were gathered under the canopy in the distance. The poachers were on the attack.

My heart sank. Someone was going to lose, and I certainly didn't want it to be the elephants. But that meant stopping the poachers, the very young poachers, and it made me sick. Jaffey and Marcus were up and running, and I found myself running with them. I had no choice- I was in the fight alongside them.

There was little moonlight to help us negotiate through the trees, and the night goggles were no help with that either. Stumbling over branches, I barely kept up for the first hundred yards or so. I took a branch to the side of the face and was knocked over. I could see the bodies of Jaffey and Marcus moving farther away in the direction of the herd.

Hearing another gunshot, I pushed myself up and made my way after them, not knowing what I was running into. Jaffey had yelled to Marcus to cut to the left, and I caught up to them just as Marcus took a shot. Jaffey pulled me over to him and pointed off to the side. I could barely make out his arm, but I could see a heat signal further down from us.

"Our guys are over there. we need the poachers to think that we have them surrounded, or at least outnumbered." He whispered.

There was another trumpeting, and then there was sudden movement in our direction. The elephants were coming this way. Marcus took another shot, and a voice shouted out. There was a lot of movement between the trees, and I couldn't tell if one of the poachers was shot or not. I could hear more vocalizations by the elephants, and I felt strangely elated that the elephants were winning.

I couldn't be sure- it was very dark- but I could have sworn that Jaffey smiled at me just then, as if he knew exactly what I was thinking.

Chapter 12

I was crying and swearing at the same time. A calf had been shot, and it was left dying on the ground. The rest of the herd was in a panic, scattered about avoiding gunshot. I knew that elephants had a mourning process, and wanted and needed to stay with their sick and dying, especially the mother of this poor baby, but the poachers were keeping them apart. I was heartsick over the whole thing. I so desperately wanted to rush over to the downed elephant's side.

Jaffey touched my arm and pointed again. The poachers were still on the move, now trying to flee the gunfire from our side. I reached for his gun- I wanted to take a shot at them myself. I didn't know if I wanted to kill them, but I wanted revenge of some kind. Jaffey pushed my hand away and said, "No, I can't allow you to do that. You will regret your actions, and right now you are a loose cannon, someone will get hurt."

"No I'm not a loose cannon, I can handle it fine, really. That poor baby elephant....and the rest of them. This needs to stop!" I was yelling.

"I understand your empathy, but leave the shooting up to us. That's our job." He pulled away and set out after the poachers.

Still wearing the night vision goggles, it looked like there were only two of the poachers running away. One of the smaller bodies was missing, and I wasn't sure if he was dead or hiding. At that moment, I wanted him dead, regardless of his age, and that thought disturbed me greatly. My heart was growing harder in a matter of minutes. It was becoming evident why they wanted me there, to see all this, and become callous, ruthless even.

I made my way over to the Land Rover to arm myself. I didn't care what Jaffey said, I was going to take someone out if I had to. I stumbled over a few branches again, and it felt like forever before finding the vehicle. I honestly didn't know anything about most of the remaining weapons in the back of the truck, so I picked up a rather large handgun and hoped for the best. If I needed to use it, I would. I wasn't going to let anyone take out another of the herd.

Even though I wasn't equipped to do much as a doctor, it was my nature to try to aid the injured animal. I wish I had my medical bag at least. Since I was a good distance from the rest of our group, I decided to head over to the calf, while Jaffey and Marcus and the other men circled around and came up with a plan. The baby was down just beyond the fringe of the canopy, and the rest of the herd hadn't doubled back yet to tend to her. I certainly didn't want to get between the mother and her calf, or I wouldn't be making it out of Kenya alive.

Why did they shoot a calf, anyway? It didn't have tusks yet, there wasn't anything to harvest, no money to be made- just reckless actions by either desperate or greedy people, expediting the giant mammal's eradication. This was not acceptable.

There was a break in the short canopy that I had been traveling under, and I would need to cross an open space to get to the elephant. Crouching down, I tried to listen to movements around me. I thought the poachers would be too busy fleeing the area to take to their guns again, but I had no way to know that for a fact. Holding my breath, I made a run for it. I faltered a few times on the uneven ground, but made it to a tree on the far side of the calf. I slid down under the gum tree to catch my breath. So far, so good. But now I needed to sit with the elephant and at least get some vitals without being noticed. I feared the mother elephant more than the poachers, but I could be attacked from any direction.

I crawled over to the downed animal. It appeared to be a female, and she was barely alive. I was in agony over the needless suffering, and started gently caressing her head. She had been shot through the chest, and was laboriously

103

breathing. I'm sure she had a punctured and collapsed lung. I wished that I could imitate the cooing sound elephants make to sooth each other in times of anxiety or stress. I wished I could do anything to alleviate her pain. I thought of shooting her to put her out of her misery, but she took that decision out of my hands. The poor calf took her last distressed breath in front of me and died, and I never felt so helpless.

I sat crying next to her for a few minutes before hearing more trumpeting not too far off. I slipped the goggles over my eyes, getting a better look at the impending dangers and their positions. There wasn't much time to plan a safe getaway- the only choice was to run. The uneven ground got the better of me this time, and I landed face first. My initial thought was to stay down, but the idea of getting trampled played out in my head, and I got to my feet again. From what I could tell by the heat signatures in the distance, I was closer to the poachers than to my own people.

An overwhelming animosity swelled inside me. I wanted retribution. I darted for the edge of a clump of elephant grass. I started to make my way through the thicket, but it made too much noise. To avoid drawing attention to myself, I stayed to the edge of the grass, keeping low. There was no sign of my associates from where I ended up, and for a moment I was confused as to where our original set up was and where the Land Rover was parked.

There was some commotion off to the right, but I couldn't see through the tall grass. I was frozen, not knowing what direction to pursue. Without warning there was breathing at the back of my neck. I slowly reached my hand down and felt for the gun, but there was no time to grab it, let alone aim and shoot. A hand slipped over my mouth, and I heard an unfamiliar voice.

"I work for Jaffey. You are in danger here, come with me," he whispered. It was one of the unknown men from the other truck. He led me along the edge of a drying up stream and then cut through the deep grass to small partial clearing. Jaffey and Marcus were there discussing their next move. The man guiding me in, pointed to them, and pushed me off in that direction.

Careening into them, I reached out for Marcus's hand, but ended up with a handful of pectoral muscle with Jaffey catching me before I hit the ground. They both had a hand in getting me upright on my feet, and I held on to both of them a few seconds longer. I was more angry than sad, but the emotional roller coaster was taking its toll. I needed to take comfort in someone or something familiar, and these two were the best I could get out here.

"They shot a calf...a calf!" I yelled in a whisper.

"I'm not surprised. They will shoot at whatever moves and see what can be harvested later," Jaffey said.

"She died," I tried to hold back the tears. "It was a baby girl, and they shot her through the chest. She suffered and died." Anger was welling up inside, and I wasn't sure if I could hold it back any longer. "Do we have a plan to do something about this?"

I could make out their faces a little easier here, as there was no overhead coverage. The open sky above us allowed dim moonlight to reveal telling facial expressions. Jaffey looked intrigued, almost pleased, Marcus not so much. It didn't take long for Marcus to notice the gun tucked in my waist. He gave a sharp look to Jaffey who looked down at it too.

"I thought I told you that was a bad idea," Jaffey said tapping the gun at my side. He didn't remove it, though, to my surprise. "Do you even know how to shoot it?"

I didn't- not really. I mean, I had seen it done a million times on TV, but I had never even touched one before. I didn't want them to know, nonetheless. "Sure, but a few pointers wouldn't hurt."

With that, I got a raised eyebrow and a short lesson on how to hold and aim the giant weapon. Some doubt started to creep in, but I held it back the same way I held the tears back. I was determined to follow through on my silent promise to the elephants. No other majestic beasts were going down on my watch.

Marcus had drawn out a diagram in the sand, but the moonlight wasn't strong enough for me to make out the finer details. The two of them had already gone over the particulars, and I was playing catch up. I pointed to the drawing and looked at Jaffey for insight. He looked skeptical. I outstretched my hands, one holding the gun, pleading. Marcus interrupted, pointing to movement behind a distant tree. We all put our goggles on and followed the movement. There were still three of them, but only two were moving. There was more movement off to the right of them, but the grass was obscuring the view. Feeling the vibrations through the ground, I knew the herd was on the move, and it looked like they were headed right into the poachers.

I panicked, and attempted to run out and divert them, but Jaffey grabbed my arm and held me back. We were standing face to face, and I could see the intrepidity in his eyes. He turned and nodded to Marcus who then disappeared into the thick grass. He moved silently through the coarse vegetation. Jaffey moved off in the other direction, toward the elephants, leaving me in the thicket to watch their plan take shape.

I caught a glimpse of Marcus at the far edge of the grass, then heard a shot ring out. I couldn't tell who shot at what, but I could hear the elephant's trumpet and its change of direction. They were now headed toward me. Once again I felt panicked and was ready to run. Another shot resonated from an unknown direction, and now the poachers were running my way as well. This was it, I thought.

This time I saw one of the poachers raising a rifle as he was running. He was still going after ivory, after all this. The herd was closer, and he was bound to hit one of them. I raised my gun without hesitating and fired. I think I fired a few times, I wasn't sure. A voice yelled out, and a thunderous movement swept through the tall grass knocking me to the ground. I heard the pounding of feet and trumpeting echoing off past me. Dazed, I was reluctant to get up, but I needed to make sure the poachers weren't still in pursuit.

I heard a voice, but couldn't make out the words or the person. Rolling onto my stomach, I tried to get a visual, but my goggles had been knocked off, and I couldn't detect any motion. I felt around for the goggles and then got to my feet. The elephants were no longer in sight, and I couldn't see any large heat source on the ground. At least they didn't down another one...yet. They could have easily wounded an elephant, but for now they were all still among the living.

"Over here," it was Jaffey's voice, and surprisingly close.

I cautiously crept through the grass in the direction of his voice until I could make out his figure. He was standing over another body, motionless on the ground. I feared that it was Marcus, and strained to make out any facial features as I approached. Jaffey crouched down and pressed his fingers to the neck of the individual, checking for a pulse. He looked up at me shaking his head.

It was one of the poachers, shot through the heart. I was relieved, then concerned.

"Looks like you got one," he said in my direction. For some reason, I thought he was talking to Marcus, so I looked around, but we were the only ones there. It still didn't sink in.

"What?" I said and looked around again. I was reliving the details of the last few minutes and tried to put the picture together.

"You got one of the poachers." Jaffey walked around the body and put his hand on my shoulder. I still didn't understand. I had blocked out the whole part where I shot the massive weapon that was now on the ground somewhere in the grass. Then it hit me. I looked down at the person on the ground, at the person that I shot. Denial came back hard and I had to question who was responsible. How did Jaffey know it was me? It could have just as easily been him or Marcus or one of the other guys that came with us. For all I knew it could have been one of the other poachers shooting him by mistake.

"I don't think that was me. Was it? How do you know?" I was shaking my head in disbelief. My hands were still vibrating from the discharging. I remembered firing it now, but surely I didn't hit anything, much less a person!

"Marcus is off to the far left closing in from behind. He was set up to drive the poachers inward, here. I hadn't taken a shot when I heard your weapon go off. The two other poachers shot at the herd before they started in this direction. That leaves you." He was again so matter-of-fact with his statement.

"I killed him?" I looked closer at the man. I was relieved that it wasn't one of the children, but still, I killed a man.

There was some rustling off to the left. I heard Jaffey say something, but I didn't catch what it was. I couldn't stop staring down at the body. I heard a shot, and Jaffey said something again, louder this time. He disappeared into the elephant grass in the direction of the shot. I heard more rustling and assumed it was him, but I didn't know for sure. I was preoccupied with the murder I just committed. He could have been someone's dad, someone's husband, someone's son. I was responsible for taking him away from all of them.

An unknown person was running through the grass now. They were shouting someone's name? I couldn't make it out, another language I assumed. I still just stood there in shock. I heard Marcus yell this time. Was he chasing the other poachers? The footsteps were getting closer, but again, I didn't look up.

Jaffey's voice was louder than Marcus's, and I think it was directed at me. I looked up for a moment with the goggles on, but didn't see any immediate heat signatures. I'm not sure I would have responded accordingly even if I did. Everything was happening around me, but I felt so far away. I was lost in the minutes past, when I was in the middle of a charge of elephants running for their lives, lost in the flash of the vision of the poacher taking aim.

The footsteps were close by, and Jaffey's voice was coming from a different direction. I looked up in time to catch a glimpse of him running by, not ten feet away. A shot was fired and Jaffey yelled. Was he hit? I waited listening, frozen in place. Jaffey's voice again, "Get down!" But I stood, partly because I didn't know who he was talking to, partly because I didn't think I could have moved if I wanted to.

Jaffey stumbled into the partial clearing where I stood- he was bleeding from his arm. I started to reach for him when I heard another shot ring out. I fell backwards on the ground. I remember turning my head and seeing the face of the man that I had killed staring back at me before I blacked out.

Chapter 13

I awoke in a darkened room. There were no windows, only sparse medical equipment against the walls. My head hurt, and I had no idea where I was. Reaching up slowly, I felt the left side of my head. A small area had been shaved, and there were what felt like stitches. There was an IV attached to my arm, and I suddenly realized that I was extremely thirsty. I tried to lift my head, but it felt like a train wreck, and I fell back against the pillow, moaning.

The door swung open, and the lights were turned on, blinding me for a minute. Shielding my eyes, I heard a familiar voice.

"How are you feeling?" It was Jaffey, and I was remembering the shootout in the desert. I tried to answer, but nothing came out. I reached for my throat, still squinting from the harsh room light. Jaffey saw my motions and went to a side table to pour a cup of water.

"You had me scared there for a while. I wasn't sure you were going to make it." He walked over and handed me the cup. "You were flat lined at one point. Glad to have you back."

I gulped at the water, spilling some of it on my gown. The room was getting blurry, and I was fading in and out. I tried to speak again, but still nothing. Jaffey was talking, but I couldn't make out the words anymore. I passed out again.

At some point later, I had awoken once more. The lights were on, but dimmer this time. I was still parched. Attempting to lift my head resulted in the same pain as before, thus I was relinquished to lying there until someone came along. I wondered where I was, and tried to remember the details of the shooting, of my last memory. It was all hazy.

Jaffey entered again after a while, heading over to the table first, anticipating my need for more water. He looked more concerned this time, but I didn't know why. The memory of him bleeding came to me, and I motioned to his arm.

"The gunshot? It was just a grazing, all stitched up now, see?" He lifted his sleeve revealing the handy sewing job. "What do you remember?"

I could hoarsely speak now, telling him of what little memories I had from that night.

"Do you remember the elephant calf, the one that died?" He asked me.

I nodded and asked, "Did they kill any others?"

"No, the rest of the herd got away, thanks to you."

"Me?" I pointed to myself, not remembering what else had occurred.

"Don't you remember what else happened?" He asked with a pained face, but I didn't know what he was referring to, my mind was blank.

"The poacher, the older one," Jaffey said trying to coax the memory out of me.

I nodded, "There were three. An adult, and two smaller ones, right?"

He nodded and tried to pull more information out. "The elephants were charging toward you, and the poacher was shooting at them."

Then it came back, almost causing me to blackout. The memory, the picture in my head, looking down at a body. The poacher was dead, and I had shot him. Suddenly, I heard bells going off, and someone rushed into the room. It all went dark again.

I was remembering more the next time I awoke, and I was in need of answers. Jaffey was already sitting beside me, but I had no idea how much time had passed since I was last conscious.

111

"Where am I? Is this a hospital in Kenya?" I was confused by the room, not looking like any hospital that I had seen in America.

"Let me get you some water, and we can talk some more. I don't want you to crash again, so we have to go slowly."

He handed me another cup, and I sipped at it this time. Jaffey pulled the chair to my bedside.

"Do you remember what we were discussing before?"

"Yes," I said, "I had shot the poacher. He's dead, isn't he? And what about the other two, the children? What happened to them?"

"The man died, that is correct. The two boys were taken away. The government will deal with them. Nkiru and what's left of her herd will continue on to fight another day, again thanks to you."

"I didn't mean to kill him- at least I don't think I did." However, I doubted my intentions already. The memory of my anger and pain was seeping back in, and I was feeling shame and remorse for my thoughts and actions.

"It was because of your actions that the rest of the herd made it. If you didn't take that shot, another elephant or two or more would have been killed. Your actions were vindicated. Besides, you almost lost your life as well. The youngest of the boys shot both you and me. He will face stiff penalties before the government."

"What will happen to me? I murdered someone in that country..." My mind started to drift again, in and out, but I tried to hang on to reality.

"No worries, no worries. It's taken care of."

"What do you mean? Won't I face charges before the government, too?" I think I said that, but I wasn't so sure it made it out of my mouth. "And where am I again?"

"We had to fly you in to DC. You needed specialists. We weren't sure you were going to live."

I thought Jaffey was talking and saying these things, but it didn't sound right. Why would I be flown all the way to the states? That sounded much too risky to be real.

"DC? Why? Which hospital?" My mind was fading fast, pictures of my parents and brother were cycling through my head, memories of friends from somewhere along the way, my old dog Moses.

"Yes, DC. We had to bring you to headquarters."

There were grasshoppers and elephants and gunshot. There were pit bulls, eye-level thick grass, and killer mosquitoes. All of it was jumbled together, and someone kept saying my name. Opening my eyes, I saw three people through the haze. It was still dim in the room, yet too bright for my eyes. Voices were seriously discussing something. Was it about me?

"We can pull her...this would be a good time if we're going to do it."

The voice was familiar, but I couldn't place it. Were they going to pull the plug on me? Wait, I was alive, right? Jaffey said I had pulled through, that I made it. They couldn't be talking about life support, could they?

"I don't think we should. She is too valuable where she is now." That was Jaffey's voice- that much I could tell.

"They're already gunning for her- this is the second time she was shot." It was a woman's voice, but I still couldn't tell who it was.

"Exactly, and she's still alive. Let's keep her where she is. For now, anyway." Jaffey was on my side. See, he said I was still alive. Keep me, whatever that meant.

"But if we pull her, we could use her as an underground operative. It would be very easy to fake her death. No one knows she made it, she was coding when we left Africa. As far as anyone knows, she's already dead."

"Doesn't she have family? I thought you said she had a brother?" Jaffey seemed to be trying anything to get them on our side.

"Yes, a brother. We didn't know that at first, it was uncovered after her hire."

113

I tried to speak at that point, to interject my opinion on things- after all, it was MY life. However, my voice failed me again, and my mind was quickly following suit. Blinking heavily, the shadowy people approached bedside.

"You have a brother, yes? Just nod your head if you do." I swear I knew that voice.

I nodded, and reached my hand toward her face. She stepped in closer.

"Is that your only relative?" I nodded again, but wasn't sure why they were asking. Do they need next of kin?

"Does he know where you live, how to get in contact with you?" I had to process that question. I hadn't thought of it before. My brother and I weren't close, and he would have no way of knowing if I died. She asked again, holding my face toward hers. I shook my head, and she let go. Why such interest in my brother?

"Well, we could go either way with this decision," the woman said.

"Are you sure she won't remember this if we decide to keep her on?" It was a new voice, a woman's as well. It was Carrie's voice. What was she doing here? What did Jaffey say last time- I was at headquarters? That couldn't be. I would be at a hospital if I was in such bad shape as they said.

"Yes, we have her on a large dose of Dilaudid- it's a morphine derivative. Everything she sees and hears will blend into her dreams, if she remembers anything." Was that Dr. Aquene's voice? I didn't understand. Why would I be at headquarters? It didn't make sense.

"Was the surgery a success?" Jaffey asked the Doctor. I couldn't tell if she responded, I didn't hear her say anything.

"Well my vote is for underground. We need more scientists, especially if it was successful," Carrie said.

"My vote is for staying in the same position. We can use her talent AND name and credentials more here," Jaffey voiced.

"That's if she doesn't ruin her reputation. She can be so volatile at times," Dr. Aquene said, and I could tell without doubt that it was her. Her reprimand echoed in my head for several days after our meeting.

I thought I heard them agree, but when I finally opened my eyes again, no one was there. The room was dark, and just the persistent beep on the monitor could be heard. I was sweaty, and my head hurt. Closing my eyes, I drifted in and out, unaware of how much time was passing by.

Jaffey came to visit again, after what seemed like forever. He looked happier this time around.

"How are you feeling?" He had brought flowers and was putting them in a vase next to the bed.

"Better." The words came out of my mouth easier now. I tried sitting up in the bed and still swooned a bit. He helped me adjust the pillows.

"That's good, good. A few more days and you should be good to go!" He was smiling and reached for my hand. He squeezed a little too hard, and I pulled my hand back.

"Sorry, don't know my own strength. I am glad you are feeling better, though. I will need to get back to Kenya again. I leave tomorrow."

"Is there a problem? More poachers?" It alarmed me, I didn't even think about going back there or what the next steps were.

"There are always poachers, always. Our fight is never done, not yet." There was a look on his face that I couldn't interpret. He looked sad, happy, hopeful maybe? No, it was more like he knew something, that he had a surprise waiting.

"I wish I could help you out again," I said but really didn't mean. I wasn't in a rush to commit murder again, but the impact of having done so was dulling with time- or maybe with the drugs?

"No, you must heal. STAFE needs your help here for a bit in the meantime." Jaffey was back to squeezing my hand.

"Speaking of which, was Dr. Aquene here? I vaguely remember her and Carrie and you engrossed in a conversation. something about the ground and my brother? Does that make any sense?"

A momentary panicked look shot across his face, but it quickly faded. "No, no one has been here. I've been your only visitor, well, me and your nurses, of course." Was the whole conversation all in my head, a dream? It felt so real- I could've sworn it was real.

"Why am I at headquarters, then, instead of a hospital? I am at headquarters, yes?" I looked at Jaffey with skeptical eyes, watching his reaction.

"We brought you here for legal reasons." His eyes were darting around the room, as if he was looking for an answer in the back regions of his mind.

"Legal reasons?" I tried to establish eye contact with him, but it wasn't happening.

"Yes, when you shot and killed the poacher, then got shot yourself. And I got shot trying to get to you before the poacher did," he surmised. "It was tricky getting you out- politically, I mean. If we brought you to a hospital stateside, we would have to explain to officials what happened. All gunshots get reported, you know. And, we couldn't leave you in Kenya, it wasn't safe."

"So headquarters? That was the only option?"

"Yes, we have run into this before, as you can probably tell." He motioned around the room. It was clearly an established medical facility, not just a storage room done up for my sake. I wondered how many more people had been in this bed, and how many of them lived on to tell about it. Well, lived on anyway- I got the feeling not too many actually told anyone about anything that happened around here.

"It's all part of a cover up, for the shooting? Because I murdered someone? Should I not be telling anyone about what happened in Kenya?"

"It's best we don't speak of this to outsiders. Who would you tell, anyway?"

Flashes of the conversation about my brother came back. Is that why they were asking? Or was that all a dream, like Jaffey said? Things were still too jumbled in my mind. "I don't know, Martin, my partner, maybe?"

"It's best we don't include him. You can tell him about the poacher shooting you. He was recently informed of your accident, requiring a lengthy recovery. He thinks that you've been in Africa this whole time. You can tell him that you were here in DC at another hospital, however."

"Did anyone contact my brother?" I knew no one had, but I wanted to see his response.

"I wasn't aware you had one. As far as I know, he has not been informed."

What did he say in the dream? Did he ask about my brother, or was that Carrie? I couldn't remember how the conversation went. Either way, he knew about my brother, in the dream at least.

"I need to be off now. So glad you pulled through. It was really shaky ground for a while. I will be in touch soon."

"Give my regards to Marcus. Oh, and Nkiru and her family as well. If you see them."

With that, Jaffey left, and I was alone for the rest of my recovery. I didn't recall ever seeing a doctor check in on me, just a few nurses taking turns in shifts.

The hair hadn't grown in yet where it had been shaved, leading me to believe that I hadn't been there that long. By the time I was discharged, again without meeting a single doctor regarding my care, it had only been a week since the shooting.

I was surprised and worried about the seemingly early discharge. After a head wound, I was picturing several weeks of recovery. Don't get me wrong, I was elated to be leaving the dreary room. Even the flowers that Jaffey had brought were wilted and depressing. My little apartment was looking like a mansion by the time I left.

They sent me home on a decreasing dosage of Dilaudid for the pain, put me in a cab, and sent me off. There were no discharge instructions, no follow up appointment, not even to get the sutures out. I was on my own, a familiar scenario, yet still unnerving in a way. I could die from complications and no one would know.

Arriving at my apartment, I barely made it up the stairs before succumbing to exhaustion. I hoped and assumed it was

117

from the meds, and decided to curl up on the sofa. Well, it was as far as I could go, so it was an easy decision. Dreams plagued me, none of which were good. Giant grasshoppers turning brown, jaws wide open, making some sort of noise, were following me through thick grass. An elephant was walking next to me, telling me something really important, but I couldn't understand what it was saying. A woodpecker was pecking at the side of my head. I awoke with a splitting headache.

The clock said it was four in the morning, but it was as good a time for breakfast as any. I wasn't sure when my last meal was. I was given Jell-O and broth several times when I was recovering in that room, but I couldn't recall a real meal. Not that I had food in the house that would pass for a real meal. I at least had oatmeal and herbal tea. It was enough to satisfy the pangs in my stomach.

I went over the conversation from my dream again, the one with Jaffey, Dr. Aquene, and Carrie. Even on heavy doses of pain medications, I think I'd still be able to tell a dream from reality. Then again, the grasshoppers seemed real, too. So did my headache for that matter, and I decided I should go back to bed. I wasn't going to make any sense out of any of it tonight- the Dilaudid was still coursing through my system. I was thinking that I'd go into work the next day, if my head was feeling up to it. I wanted to get the skinny on the investigation, anyway. The rest of that night I dreamed about dog skulls morphing into human skulls morphing into the dead poachers face staring at me as I lay next to it on that desert ground.

Chapter 14

It was Friday morning, or so my smart phone told me. I crawled out of bed and made some coffee. To work or not to work, that was the question of the morning. No one would fault me for taking another day off, but what would I do? I was tired of being laid up in a bed, and besides, I wanted to find out what was happening on the dog fighting cases.

Walking was out of the question, my head was still too painful for the echoing of my footfall. I opted for a cab- as short as the ride was. Maybe half a day, I negotiated with myself on the ride over. The weather was just a little too sunny- for my current state, anyway. Being stuck inside in the office wasn't a bad thing today.

Martin was already there, as I was at least an hour behind my usual schedule. He jumped out of his chair when I walked through the door- I guess he wasn't expecting me back so soon. The negotiations started again in my head- maybe just a few hours then, it's not as if anyone expected me back yet, apparently. Martin's eyes were popping out of their sockets when he saw the shave job on my head.

"Welcome back," he went in for a hug, "How are you feeling, and what happened!?"

I gave him a weak smile, it was all the energy I could muster- healing sucked a lot of your energy up. I carefully walked over to my chair and fell into it. I didn't think I'd be moving from that spot for a while.

"I'm doing OK...been better. How are things here? Did you manage without me for the week?"

"I'll tell you about the week AFTER you tell me what went down! What happened to your head, to your hair!? All they

119

told me was that there was an accident, no details. I was dying!" Martin was beside himself with anticipation. He pulled his chair over for the particulars.

"When did they tell you?" I wanted to know if it was before or after my so-called dream of the conversation. Were they planning on letting me die or something- if it was real?

"Wednesday I think. Yes, day before yesterday. Why, when did it all happen? And WHAT happened?"

From what I could calculate, I was shot on a Friday night, and must have been in DC since Saturday night or Sunday. The conversation, or dream if it was, would have been Monday? I wasn't even sure about that.

"I got shot. In the head." I pointed to the incision, "And almost died, so they told me. I guess I had coded at least once. Jaffey said he wasn't sure I was going to make it. I've no idea how they got me to DC."

"You weren't conscious by the time you flew back?" Martin looked about as baffled as I felt regarding the whole incident.

"They flew me back sometime right after the shooting, for medical attention. I actually had the surgery and recovered here in the city."

"Why didn't they tell me! I would've come to visit or something. I was worried when I didn't hear from you for a week!"

"I guess they didn't know what was going to happen, so they didn't want to get you worked up for nothing. I made it, though. Here I am." I grinned trying to mitigate his worries.

"Well, I wish I knew. Chalk it up to another crappy communication by the agency." Martin sounded hurt, like he wanted to help or at least be a part of what was going on. I couldn't offer him much more in the way of details, though. Jaffey was clear about leaving him out of the loop on the rest. Still, I had the urge to spill it all, to let him in, to share the intricacies and oddities of the last few days.

"Tell me about the shenanigans here. Skulls?" I did my best to divert his interests.

"Ooh, that's right. We didn't have the results yet. Tadaaki was able to extract DNA from the tooth root like you suggested. They matched the skeletal remains we found in Maryland." He was excited relating this tidbit.

"Who's Tadaaki again?" My mind was floating around, but I wasn't sure if I ever met her.

"She's the DNA tech that works with Georgie and Ani, remember?"

"Did I meet her?"

Martin looked at me weird. "No, she wasn't there when we visited the lab. How bad was the gunshot wound, anyway?"

I reached up and touched the wound on my scalp. "I'm just a little fuzzy from the meds. They still have me on Dilaudid, though it's a small amount."

"Oh, the good stuff! I was on that once. Enjoy it while you can, coming off it can be tough sometimes. I had a buddy who...," he noticed I was squinting a little and stopped mid-sentence. I tried to look more interested, but I couldn't pull it off.

"Sorry, your head must be killing. Why don't you go home. I can fill you in when you're feeling better."

"No, it's fine. I'm just dizzy. Things are a bit muddy upstairs right now, go on." I still wanted him distracted enough to drop the subject of the shooting, but I didn't think I was up to following a drawn out story.

"It wasn't that interesting. Just that he got addicted to the pain meds and had to go to rehab. So moral of the story: better ween off them sooner rather than later. But, better wait until you feel up to it. Are you sure you should be out of the hospital so soon?" He reached over and patted my hand.

"I wondered the same myself. But honestly, I was dying to get out of there. And I concur on the weaning. I'll just take it slowly for a while. What else went down? Any new crime scenes?"

"No new crime scenes, but Jon came back looking for you." Martin cocked his head and smiled.

"Who's Jon?" I was starting to worry that there were gaps in my memory now.

"Jon the FBI man. Did you not even remember his name? After all, he did drive you home." He grinned again.

"No, I didn't remember his name. What did he want?" I was relieved that it wasn't a huge blank spot in my memory, but I was disturbed that he came around again. I had put all that business of being shot at by a possible gang member away in the back of my brain- it didn't need to resurface this soon.

"I'm not sure. He left his card there for you." He pointed to the right hand side of my desk. Sure enough, Jon McDermitt, Agent, in black and white along with his phone number on an otherwise plain looking card.

"Do you think it was important, or can I get away with blowing him off?" I tried to smile again, but I think it came off more pained than anything.

"I think it was important. He had this scowl on his face and everything. Very FBI. It might be a lead to the perp, why not call?"

"Are we even on those cases anymore, or is it strictly FBI territory now?" I wasn't sure how things were left, nor was I sure if things had changed since I'd been gone.

"We haven't been called off the Maryland ones, if that's what you mean. Actually, I haven't heard squat from headquarters since you've been gone except about the accident.

"What about Georgie? Did anyone say anything to him or his lab mates about ID'ing the skulls?"

"Nope. He faxed me the details when the results were in, but didn't post them to the system. FBI man- Jon- came sniffing around that day, come to think of it. Haven't heard anything else from the lab people. What do you think they do all day?"

"Well, the two women work at the other place and probably don't get over to our lab too often. I have no idea what Georgie does all day. Sometimes I wonder what we do all day." I laughed, and it hurt my head. "I'm glad no one got busted for the work, though. I didn't tell FBI- Jon- about it, but maybe I should."

"How about you go home and rest some more. You can call Jon tomorrow and figure it out from there. Take that with you," Martin said and nodded in the direction of the FBI man's card. "Why don't you start your weekend early? I'm worried that they let you out too soon. You know how they do things these days, the insurance companies don't want to pay for your stay, so they boot you out as soon as they can. What hospital were you at?"

I panicked and said the first thing that came to my mind, "Oh, my head, you're right, I should go home. Can you do me a favor and call a cab?" It did the trick, and I evaded the question, this time.

Sleep was rough. I wasn't sure what parts were dreams and what parts I was awake for. The sounds around me seemed a whole lot louder than they usually were, and my eyes were still sensitive to the light. I wondered what areas of my brain were affected by the bullet- I never actually saw a doctor. No one gave me updates or summaries of what was done. I never heard of hydromorphone having oversensitivity as a side effect. It could just be that I was in a confined space for a week with limited stimuli. Time would tell.

I slipped out of bed ever so slowly, and made my way to the kitchen. I could tell it was going to be a long day, but what it would entail, I didn't know- nor did I care at that point. All I was focusing on was getting coffee and settling on the sofa as quietly as possible. I left the curtains drawn and lights off and waited to acclimate. It didn't happen.

A couple hours later, I got up and searched through the pockets of yesterday's clothes for FBI man's card. Jon- I need to remember that- Jon was waiting for my call. I figured I should get it over with, then maybe a nap. Going over what I could remember about our last conversation, I thought about telling him the results from the skulls. He needed to know, after all, to catch the perp- that was everyone's goal. I just needed to figure out how to tell him and not get in trouble with the organization. What if the results were pending when we were called off the case? They don't know when it was run, technically. Sounded like a plan.

123

I called figuring I'd get a message service. Why would he be in an office to answer? Turns out, it was his cell phone number, and he answered. I awkwardly told him who I was, and immediately he asked for a meeting. Couldn't it be done over the phone? No, in person. I informed him of my injury and somewhat compromised condition, but it was urgent. Not being in any mood to venture out today, I agreed to a meeting at my apartment. I wasn't thrilled with the idea, but I didn't have options.

Showering and dressing were the only things I was up to doing to prepare for the meeting, he'd have to deal with looking at a mess. I had just moved, anyway- I had that as an excuse for the clutter. I debated taking my next dose of meds, I didn't want to be groggy during the discussion, but I was hurting. I compromised at half a dose, swallowing it down with a healthy gulp of coffee. Nothing like downers and uppers at the same time.

He arrived about an hour later. We said our pleasantries, and he sat down on a lounge chair near the TV. I let him start the conversation- it was his idea for the meeting.

"We have a lead on the killer in regards to the body that you found," Jon said.

"OK, so it wasn't the dog fighter perp that killed himself in West Virginia?"

"No, and we aren't positive that he killed himself. The killer, we think, is linked to a drug ring out of the DC area. We think he's the same guy who owned the dogs in Maryland. There was another body, we haven't told the public about yet, found in a warehouse here in the city. He had ties to the Maryland area where you found the last dog. Kent County?" He was looking at his notes now.

"Yes, the single pit bull was found there, but no other paraphernalia. I assumed no fighting had taken place at that location, but I could be wrong. I have seen fighting pits put up in all kinds of places."

"The body we found was the owner of the property. We think he leased it out, or was killed and his property used after the fact. Your lab had discovered that the dogs were all offspring of 'Darling Dan' out of Texas?"

"Yes, the first site in Maryland near Snow Hill yielded two dog bodies that were sired by 'Darling Dan'. The body found in Kent County was as well, but had a different dam. There were two other bodies, the skeletonized ones, also found at the first scene. We haven't found a match to any other dogs on the database- that I know of anyway. I was away for a while, but Martin didn't mention it." I didn't add in the information about the skulls yet, I wanted to see where he was headed.

"Well, we know Martinez, who owned 'Darling Dan' was part of the Twentieth Street Gang from Arizona. They had a connection to a Mexican drug cartel with operatives here in DC. We think they may all be connected."

"I had heard that about the dog's owner. In the dog fighting world, amateurs would cultivate their bloodline while working their way through the industry. Many act as 'yard boys', doing errands and miscellaneous tasks for professionals while learning the trade. Maybe the perp we are looking for worked under Martinez?"

"That could be. We don't yet have anything linking the West Virginia case- where you found the body- to the Maryland dogs though." Was he fishing for the information, did he already know it? Somehow I got the feeling like I was being played with.

"Well, we did get some results in, or so they informed me yesterday. The lab was able to extract enough DNA from a tooth root in the skulls we had found at the West Virginia site, and it matched the two skeletal remains found near Snow Hill." I watched him closely for a reaction.

"So the skulls came from the bodies in Maryland? Then we do have a link." He didn't even blink.

"Apparently. Does that help your investigation?" I could ask questions that I already knew the answers to as well.

He smiled slightly, "Yes, yes it does. And it brings us to why I am here."

That didn't sound good, and it sent hundreds of images racing through my mind. Was he really from the FBI, or was

125

he from STAFE, undercover? Didn't Dr. Aquene and Carrie say something about undercover or underground in my dream- if it was a dream? Did they already know I went ahead and had evidence processed on a closed case?

"Oh? Why is that?" I was recoiling as I said the words, fearing the worst was about to come.

"We need to ask you to do a favor for us- when you're feeling better, of course. But it is rather urgent." Jon had a worried look on his face, and the suspicions that he may be working for the organization were melting away.

"What can I do for the FBI? You have all the information that I was able to get out of the evidence."

"I, we, were hoping that you could go undercover for us. We don't usually ask this of a civilian, but you are uniquely qualified for this. We would be watching and monitoring your every move, so your safety would never be jeopardized."

"Why me, and what would you have me do? I'm not exactly in any state to be playing spy games," I said and pointed to my gunshot wound.

"We can prep over the next few days, after you rest a bit. Maybe start tomorrow or Monday? Then we can assess how ready you are for this. We think they might be smuggling in the drugs through a pet shop. Importing birds and exotics for the store is how they traffic the merchandise across the borders. The imported animals may be illegal captures. You could give us a better idea of their set up from the inside. We can put you in as a contract veterinarian there to evaluate and treat the new arrivals or whatever." He sounded shaky on the idea- like he wasn't sure it would work. Not a convincing sell.

"How do you know that whoever took a shot at me won't recognize me in the store? If that's who really shot at me in the first place."

"The hit men don't usually spend time in store front, it shouldn't be a problem."

"Shouldn't be? Gee, that sounds so safe and all, but I think I'll pass."

"It'll be safe, trust me." Jon tried to look reassuring.

"I don't even know you enough to remember your last name. How am I supposed to trust you?"

"It's McDermitt. Jon McDermitt, and I need your help. This may be the only way we can get into the ring and shut it down. We already know they murdered two people and killed who knows how many dogs, but they're also moving drugs through the territory and quite possibly endangered animals."

I'm not sure that last part was true yet- he may have just thrown that in to get my cooperation.

Chapter 15

I was a sucker for an animal-in-need story- don't even bring up the Sarah McLachlan commercials. Agent McDermitt knew enough to use it against me, and so I was sucked into his plan.

"How's this going to work? I don't know all that much about avian husbandry, if that's supposed to be my specialty there." I was concerned that I wasn't the shoe-in that he thought I was. Just because I was a vet, didn't mean that I knew everything about all living things. I needed him to know where we were starting from.

"You don't have to know everything, just enough to fake it through for a day or two..."

"Or two? Maybe we should start off with the overall picture of your plan. How long do you see this going for, it's not like I don't have a job. I will be missed, you know." At least I hoped I'd be missed, Martin was doing OK without me for the past week.

"Well, I'm not sure how long it'll take. They have a storefront on Florida Ave, and we've been monitoring the traffic in and out of there. We know they've been getting parrots in from South America. Most of them are brought in during the hatching season, from the beginning of January through mid-May, so they are still actively bringing them in now. How much do you know about bird smugglers or CITES?"

"I do know that most if not all parrot species are protected under the Convention on International Trade in Endangered Species of Wild Fauna and Flora, or CITES. They try to regulate international trade on various species listed on its three levels of protection." I was trying to recall the legal overview we had in school regarding wildlife trade.

"Yes, in fact over forty parrot species are listed on CITES Appendix I, the highest level of protection. Trade is completely prohibited with these species because these birds are currently threatened with extinction. I believe most other parrots are listed on the second appendix of the CITES agreement, which means that they cannot enter trade without export permits from their country of origin." Jon was well versed in the legal aspects of the case.

"I also know a little about the regulations that APHIS set up due to the outbreaks of exotic Newcastle disease in the U.S. from imported birds. A thirty day quarantine at one of their facilities is required for travelers entering the country with birds. They also have to get a health certificate for the bird from the country of its origin as well as arrange for the shipping of the bird to its final destination after it gets released from quarantine. But that's about all I know about bird smuggling. You're going to have to tell me a whole lot more before I feel comfortable enough to go in on this." I was starting to feel woozy, mostly from the drugs, but also from the anxiety that was building inside me.

"You're looking a bit peaked, are you alright?"

"Maybe we should call it a day. Can we take this up tomorrow? And bring visual aids- I do better when I can see things."

"Of course. Then you're in? I can talk to your employer for you. As I said, I don't know how long this will take, and we need you to be clear headed, obviously."

I nodded yes, and walked Jon to the door. It was a long day for me- in this state anyway- and tomorrow was going to be worse, I could tell. I immediately popped the other half of my Dilaudid dosage, and put the kettle on for some tea. I needed some serious down time.

Curling up on the sofa, things still seemed overly bright and loud. I was hesitant to put on the radio or TV- I didn't think that my head could tolerate more stimuli. I closed my eyes and slowly sipped the herbal tea while listening to the sounds of the

129

apartment building. Some creaking, muted voices, and traffic discord blended together and I slipped into a troubled sleep.

I was running in the dream- running from the grasshoppers that turned into crickets chirping away, running from the poachers chasing the elephants, and running from the elephants as well. They were all trying to talk to me, but I couldn't understand them. I had fallen in the deep elephant grass, surrounded by crickets and elephants. The poachers, at least, were gone. Their sounds slowly worked into words- almost words. I could almost make out the words....so close. One of the elephants started to poke me with her trunk. More words, sounds, buzzing, but not understanding. I felt wet, like it was raining. Then I woke up, in a sweat, with half a cup of tea soaking my shirt.

Sunday morning didn't start out any better than the night before. I was groggy and couldn't shake the feeling that I needed to remember something, but I had no idea what. Things weren't as bright and loud as they had been. Maybe I was adjusting to the meds, or maybe I was healing from the surgery that I had. What exactly did they do to me? A big pot of coffee was needed for what I anticipated was in store for me that day, and I was actually glad that agent Jon was coming here instead of meeting him elsewhere. I had no patience for the outside world today.

I turned on some classical music and hopped into the shower. The hair was growing back in over the sutures, and the incision was healing nicely, but the resultant hairdo left much to be desired. I supposed I could dye that area another color and do the punk/rebel thing for a while, but it probably wouldn't go over too well in professional settings. Perhaps hat shopping was in my future instead.

Grieg's "Peer Gynt Suite" was playing when I passed through the living room on my way to get dressed in the bedroom. It always reminded me of Bugs Bunny cartoons. Bugs would wake up and rise out of the rabbit hole to

"Morning" from that Suite. Later, the "Ren and Stimpy" cartoon utilized all the movements from it at one point or another. Even though "In The Hall Of The Mountain King" was used over and over in commercials, I never grew tired of it.

Dressing was slow for a couple of reasons. One was lack of clean clothes. A long distance trip followed by almost dying and then a long hospital stay somehow got in the way of the more mundane tasks such as laundry. The other reason was an overwhelming inability to decide what to wear. Sunday was for sweats, casual wear, socks and big sweaters- not the kind of thing one wears when entertaining a guest. I went with something in between: khaki's, socks, and a big sweater. It would do.

I sat down at my little desk and worked my way through a backlog of emails and social media notifications. Almost an hour went by before I got through most of them, and I realized that none of it was important. Why did I spend time on these things again? The doorbell rang, saving me from the last of it. I guess the rest will have to wait, oh no.

Agent Jon McDermitt was on time, and I got the feeling he was always on time. He came equipped with a small dry erase board and stand, taking the request for visual aids seriously. Good, I liked that. I helped him set it up in front of the sofa. After pouring some more coffee for both of us, we settled down on the sofa and stared at the white screen.

"So I think we should start off with a little more about smuggling to give you more of a footing in the legal aspects of things," Jon started.

"OK, we had some legal courses both in veterinary school and in grad school for forensics, but it's all rusty by now. Hit me with some more." I tried to make light of the process, as I was beginning to dread having agreed to the whole thing.

"Well, for starters, every year there are around 25,000 birds that are smuggled into the United States."

"That many? I had no idea. Where are they all, I mean where do they go?"

"Many of the smuggled birds die from illness or stress, and many of the rest are often disease carriers- as you are already aware of, I'm sure. In fact, most of the birds don't make it alive. An official had once estimated that only one in six parrots survives the trip across the border from Mexico."

"Why do they bother doing it then?" I was greatly disturbed about the sheer volume of birds needlessly being killed for this black market.

"Smugglers plan for the deaths of parrots and capture four times as many as they need to supply the market. The demand driving the market in parrots is by collectors and breeders and surprisingly, largely by regular people who want them as pets."

"So, many species of parrots, and other birds, are being killed off because we want pets. Nice." My stomach was turning. And we weren't really even getting started yet. "What happens to the birds when the smugglers are caught? Do they go back to their natural habitat?"

"No, unfortunately, most wild parrots smuggled into the U.S. will never fly free again. Usually they are auctioned off by the U.S. Fish & Wildlife Service or occasionally adopted by zoos. Some get sent to shelters or sanctuaries if there's room available." Jon sounded unemotional reciting these facts to me. I wondered how thick his skin must be to do his job.

"And what happens to the perps? A slap on the wrist or something? Our laws are slowly catching up to the heinous crimes that people are committing against animals, but not fast enough."

"Right now, bird smugglers can be sentenced up to five years in prison and fined up to $20,000 per violation, if they are convicted. It's covered under a law administered by the U.S. Fish and Wildlife Service. I know, I agree, not much for devastating populations of species to the point of extinction."

"Great, so that about covers it, I risk my life and they get five years. Sounds like a plan." I was getting less into this the more I thought about it.

"Don't be that way, Alex. I know it's a fraction of what they deserve, but remember that most of these people are involved in other criminal activity. These perps in particular are involved in drugs and dog fighting, not to mention murder. For all I know, there could be human trafficking as well. Getting them off the streets is our primary goal, and with the other charges, they'll go away for a lot longer than five years."

He did have a point. It was too easy to get caught up in the smaller aspects of their crimes- I had to look at the big picture. "Tell me about the plan."

Jon smiled, stood up, and cracked his knuckles- something I hated- but whatever. He went to the board and started drawing. If he were playing Pictionary, we'd lose. But other than that, his drawing was understandable- if there was a whole lot of dialog that accompanied it, that is.

"This is the storefront of Feathers And Fur..."

"Sorry, Feather And Fur? Are you kidding me?"

"No, why have you heard of it?" Jon was either great at straight-face or he had no idea how absurd the name actually was.

"No. It's just....it's a stupid name." I giggled a little saying it, and a smile finally dawned over Jon's face.

"Yes, I suppose it is a stupid name. Anyway, the storefront is on Florida street on the east side. Here is the back room where most of the birds come in and are stored, or housed I guess you'd say, but in a room below is where they keep most of the newly smuggled parrots." Jon began to draw again, this time depicting the lower level, or so he said it was, it could have been Piccadilly Square for all his drawing was worth.

"Where's the cellar door, and is there a second way in or out?" I wasn't claustrophobic, but the idea of getting stuck in a basement with drug pushing mobsters was making me sweat.

"Good questions....the door is here," he indicated by underlining a seemingly random spot on his drawing, "And there's a walk down from a bulkhead in the rear." He again made with his random underlining. "We will have an agent stationed back here in the building behind the store, as well as out in front."

"Oh like in one of those nondescript vans with no windows?" I chuckled thinking of all the parodies involving flower deliveries and plumber trucks with FBI agents secretly tucked away inside.

"No, they'll be in a car." He looked at me weird, again missing the humor in the whole set up.

"OK, Jon. What will I be doing? I assume I'll be wired?"

"Yes, wired, so we can keep close tabs on you. I don't think they'd suspect you, as we have a complete profile set up for your character. You're the sister of a frequent customer, who we just so happened to bust the other day, but they don't know that yet. Anyway, the sister- you- is veterinarian from Oregon with a history of recent family problems. You came here to get away from your abusive husband for a while and could use the money."

"So am I licensed to practice here?" The details were starting to accumulate, and I needed to get a notebook and start writing this stuff down. Not to mention, more caffeine would be very helpful at this point. I got up and stretched, then rummaged around in the kitchen for something to write on.

"No, you are working under the table," Jon answered while watching me mull around the apartment. "We figured if your character was a little shady too, that they'd be less suspicious."

"Nice," I replied after returning to the living room. "Did you need any more coffee?"

"No, thank you. I'm good. Do you think you'll have trouble remembering the details?" He looked at the paper and pen as I sat back down.

"I just want to get it all straight in my head. There are a lot of details, and I've learned over the years when I was a witness on the stand that details go out the window when you're the slightest bit nervous." I began writing down my back story of an abusive husband, family issues, from Oregon, under the table, how hard could it be?

"They know you didn't specialize in exotics, but you know enough to nurse some of the sick and dying back to life. The more that live, the more they can sell."

"Sounds reasonable....I guess. Where did I go to school? And what about this customer of theirs, my brother?" I had more questions the more we discussed it.

"I'll have to get back to you on the school, although I really don't think it matters. The customer, Brad Polasky, wasn't quite that chummy with these criminals. Brad, by the way, is your older brother, always getting into trouble. He has an impressive rap sheet, from theft to racketeering. Nothing violent, though." He said it like I should be relieved, as if Brad was my real brother, and the fact he didn't murder anyone would make me feel better.

"Impressive, indeed. Big brother has been busy. What was he busted for this time, anyway?"

"Grand theft auto. Part of a ring we busted that stretched from Detroit to Daytona. He was a cog in the wheels, but useful in the information we got out of him. The take down was just last week, so there shouldn't be any way that our friends at Feathers And Fur would know." We both had to giggle again.

"OK, so I go in there and, what, document? Will I have a camera as well?"

"We are really looking for the shipment coming in. There will be a bigger sweep if we wait for all parties to be present. We are hoping that someone will say something or you will come across shipping information that we can use. I don't want you there when it all goes down, if we can help it."

"IF we can help it? Do you foresee things going awry? I need a little more confidence from you, I believe." Nope, things were not headed in a convincing direction.

"I'm sorry. We can only go on the information that we are given, and as far as I can tell, the next shipment of smuggled birds is due several days from now. The sooner we can get you in, the sooner we can get you out, and avoid any run-ins or jeopardize you more than you already will be."

"Seriously, the confidence is overwhelming me. Stop, stop." I gave him the 'what-are-you-going-to-do-about-it" look.

135

"Again, I'm sorry. But I don't want to make you think it'll be a walk in the park. This is a dangerous mission, I just want you to be as safe as we can make it. We can send you in, maybe just for a day, if you can get a hold of the information."

I was starting to feel like this was all on me- my responsibility to find the information, my fault if I get stuck in crossfire, my ability to slip in and slip out without raising an eyebrow. My head was throbbing, and the only thing I was certain of was that I had to stop the pain meds cold turkey to get clear headed enough to pull this off.

"I can't afford to get shot again. Tell me you'll have this under control." I was feeling pissy, and it was coming across in my voice.

"We'll have your back. If anything, we'll pull you out too soon and scrap the plan. I mean, if things look dicey or take a turn for the worse." Jon tried the honest sullen face, but my confidence was as shaky as my hands after all that coffee.

Chapter 16

The next day felt like Mondays always did, and then some. I had to use the day as a washout, making sure there were no drugs in my system clouding up my thinking. I also had to deal with the pain in my head. It was lessening enough, but it was something that needed getting used to. Going to work sounded like a good idea, in theory. At least it would keep my mind occupied, and I wouldn't have as much time to worry about this undercover stint.

I walked to work, thinking it might be good to get some fresh air after spending the weekend holed up in my tiny apartment listening to an FBI agent go on about bird smuggling. I'm not so sure it was the wisest move, as my head started to pulse with the movement and noise of the traffic. I had to close my eyes and cover my ears once I got to the office and threw myself into a chair. Just for a few minutes, I told Myself. It'll be better in a few minutes. When I finally opened my eyes again, Martin was sitting at his desk staring at me.

"When did you get here?" I asked.

"I was here when you came in. Are you OK?" He looked concerned, but somewhat humored at the same time.

"Yes, just trying to adapt to the pain. Traffic is loud around here!"

"I'm glad you noticed, but it's always been like that. I'm going to guess you've weaned yourself off the meds already?"

I nodded with a grimace and watched him get up and head into the other room. Martin came back with two aspirin and a cup of coffee for me. I accepted them with a hint of a smile- it was all that I could muster up.

"Tell me why you came in today. If you're not feeling that great yet, why don't you go home and take another day? I mean, it's not like you were shot in the head or anything." He tried to smile back at me, but it came across more sympathetic than aloof.

"But you'd miss me terribly, I can tell. I'm really here for your benefit," I joked with him getting him to laugh about it.

"Ha! I'm pretty sure I could find things to take my mind off of you....like this cup of coffee...or this shiny penny."

"Ah, I'm no match for shiny objects! I will head home early, if no new cases come in, though. I just need a distraction right now. I've got a big role coming up, and I'm a bit nervous."

"Do tell, does this have to do with FBI man?"

"Yes, apparently, he wants me to go undercover and ferret out information about this dog fighting-slash-bird smuggling-slash-drug cartel that we've all been working on, in different parts."

"Our dog fighters are bird smugglers and drug cartel members? Awesome. Will you be shot again, then?" He sounded a little pissed this time.

"Maybe, are you jealous? I will gladly switch with you. You can be a veterinarian from Oregon with an abusive husband, I'm sure it'll go over just as well. Actually, it would be right up your alley, pulling a double-O-seven routine."

"You're kidding, right? Are you trying to get killed, or do the circumstances just come to you often?"

"Not kidding. Jon the FBI man said so. I told him I was still on pain meds and it probably wouldn't be the best idea, but he sounded a little desperate. And he told me they were decimating the parrot populations in Mexico. I'm always a sucker for things like that."

"And when does this all go down?"

"Sometime this week. They want info on the next shipment which is coming in soon. Hopefully I will be in and out of there before it all goes down." I wasn't sure courage and determination came through in my voice, they certainly weren't in my heart at the time.

"Shouldn't you wait until you've healed from your last gunshot, which, may I remind you, wasn't even the first gunshot since you've been working here." Martin was getting visibly upset, which was nice in that he cared, but yet upsetting to me that I was causing him grief.

"I would prefer to get it over with. The sooner the better. Actually, maybe even tomorrow. I should call Jon and see if we can set that up this soon."

Martin watched in dismay as I dialed Jon's number. I reached his voicemail and left my thoughts about the timing of things. I knew he wouldn't be thrilled to go for it this soon, either, but the fear of getting caught in the middle of another shootout was building up, and I needed to remedy that.

"So did we find a match in the database for the skeleton dogs? Are they related to any previous cases of dog fighting that's been documented?" I thought Martin could use a diversion of his own, and why not throw some actual work into the work day?

"Oh, no, no matches. I was thinking it might be related to some cases that never had DNA run. Not many of the cases had funding to get fully worked up like that. What do you think?"

"Sounds reasonable. A lot of old dog fighting cases were processed on the evidence found at the location and weren't linked to other rings. I don't know how we would even begin to find that out, though."

"Well maybe you'll get a little more insight into the perps when you go out for target practice again." Yup, Martin was a wee bit uncomfortable with the plan, maybe even more so than me.

I took a deep breath and was saved by the ringing of my phone. It was Jon, uncertain if it was wise to go in this quick. Did I have my character down? Did I remember the layout of the storefront? Was my head well enough to pull this off? I reminded him that the sooner we get this done, the less likely I was to get shot again, if the shipment was truly due in the next few days. He reluctantly agreed, and we once again agreed to meet up at my place for one last run through the details.

Well, as it was set up, I merely strolled into Feathers And Fur (trying not to smirk) and introduced myself.

"Hi there, I'm Renee, Doctor Renee Polasky, from Oregon? I was told you guys needed a veterinarian to look over a few birds. I love parrots- I didn't get to see all that many in practice in Oregon, but the ones I saw were sweet. Ya know?" I figured if I kept talking they couldn't get many questions in. Trouble was, I had to come up with enough crap to keep the dialogue going, and somehow I felt like I should be chewing gum. I also felt like I should have an accent, but I wasn't sure if people from Oregon actually had one. Oh well.

"Yes I heard you were coming in..."

"Great, I know it may have been short notice and all, but I wanted to get working. I hope it didn't throw your plans off or anything?"

"No, it's fine. We were just..."

"Great, great. Where are the little cuties anyway? Do you get a lot of them through here- I mean it being DC and all? Seems like the hub of everything here. Oh what a nice looking Boa. Do you feel like you have to feed some pets to others, I mean I figured you sell mice as pets too?"

"Uh sure. Let me show you where the new arrivals are." She sounded annoyed- excellent. My acting skills weren't too shabby after all.

We walked through the main part of the show room into the back work space. A small kitchen area was set up where the food was prepared for all the animals. A bathroom was to the right, down the hall. She brought me to the door on the left, the one to the basement.

"We keep them down here, away from the rest. You know, like quarantine?" The woman had a heavy South American accent, or possibly Mexican, I wasn't good at faking an accent or telling ones apart.

She led the way down the stairs and pointed out where they all were and how old they were supposed to be. I walked over to a table and put my bag down.

"So, how long have you all been here...." I turned around to look at her, but she had retreated up the stairs in a hurry. I guessed that I had a knack at being annoying. I should keep that in mind in case the need comes up again later in life.

I looked around at the collection. Most were Amazons and Macaws with a few conures thrown in for good measure. I wondered how many were brought in originally to get this many still alive. There had to be about twenty five or so of them ranging from fledglings to juveniles, from what I could tell. If they were any younger, they didn't make it, as would be expected. It would be hard enough to try to feed the fledglings and weanlings, but at least they could attempt to eat some food on their own, albeit not enough to survive.

I pulled out my pediatric stethoscope and a notepad and started with rudimentary exams. This was going to take a while to get through them all, then I remembered that I was just there as the vet as a cover story. Whoa, got to keep the concentration up a little better than that, Alex! I felt bad for all the bird-napped babies, but hoped the bust would go down soon enough to rescue most of those that lived.

Hurrying over to the stairs, I looked up to make sure the coast was clear- as they always said on spy shows. Then I made my way around the mostly open, spread out room looking for any details that looked incriminating. One of the young conures was following me in its cage, from one end to the next, chatting. I stopped and took him out, checking him over. They really are personable birds, but I had to focus on the task at hand. I started to put him back when he latched on to my hand. OK, maybe there was no harm in having a sidekick for this charade.

Snooping around, I came across a piece of paper wedged under the corner of a cage. Of course it was written in Spanish or Portuguese, I couldn't tell. It was times like that that I really wished I knew more than one language. I leaned over so the camera in my fake glasses could get a better view. If it was important, it was in evidence now. I suddenly became paranoid that I was being watched, too. Checking the walls and ceiling, I did my best to 'sweep' the area for hidden cameras, but found none. "Didn't mean there wasn't one around," I kept saying to myself. The conure started looking sleepy, so I slipped him into my over-sized doctor coat pocket for a nap.

I continued my investigation of all the nooks and crannies for leads or incriminating evidence. I could hear creaking in the floorboards above, sounding like another person had entered the store. A male voice, speaking Spanish- maybe? - was talking in a somewhat stern fashion. A full dialogue was then ongoing between this man and the woman I had met upstairs. The voices were loud enough for me to hear the words, if I had only known the language. The name 'Espinoza' was mentioned a few times. Perhaps that's one of the contacts smuggling in the birds? Or maybe it was another member of the drug cartel?

In a matter of minutes, the voices escalated into shouts. I could distinctly hear the stomping of someone's foot and then the sound of something smashing against the floor. I nervously eyed the door to the bulkhead at the back of the room. Maybe I should make a break for it while I was still alive. I didn't see this turning into anything resembling a pleasant situation.

I grabbed my bag and was turning toward the back door when it busted open. Two large men came through the bulkhead and immediately began shouting at me in another language.

"I'm just the vet, you know, animal doctor?" I showed them my bag and indicated my coat and stethoscope, but they persisted with the interrogation.

"I don't speak....Spanish?" I tried to look for any clue on their faces as to the accuracy of my assumption. A slight nod and an irritated look, I was getting somewhere.

"My brother, Brad set this job up. Do you own this place?" They looked at each other then at me and started in on the berating in their language. I didn't have to understand to know that this was not going to end well for me, and I was starting to wonder where the Calvary was. Surely, the FBI could hear all this??

I was sweating and afraid that I was going to pass out, so I leaned back against the table. One of the men walked over to the stairs and yelled something up to the two above. The man came running down with a look like he had no idea I was even there. Some heated words flew among the three of them, ending with a death stare at me by all involved.

One of the guys came at me and I thought that was it, but he grabbed me and shoved me to the stairway. Pushing the whole way up, he barked out to someone some more commands. As I stumbled through the doorway to the upper level, I saw the woman bringing a roll of tape. She immediately backed away, out of harm's way and out of view, and I envied her ability to do so. More words were growled at me, but all I could do was hold up my hands to show that I had no understanding of the language.

I felt a stinging across my face and realized I had just been slapped. One man was pulling a stretch of tape off the roll, and I knew what was coming. The other guy intensely continued with the interrogation in Spanish, occasionally shoving my shoulder while the tape was sealed across my mouth. Clearly whatever he was saying, he wasn't expecting a reply back. There was a lull in the yelling and I looked up into the face of my attacker. I saw the resolution cross his face as he slowly reached into his jacket, and I could make out the glint of metal from the gun being pulled out.

The next few minutes happened in genuine slow motion. Footsteps from the stairs behind the men produced a fourth man, this one dressed in a uniform and a bulletproof vest. The one in front of me spun around, raising the gun before the intruder got to the top step. A shot rang out, bodies flew in all directions at once, mine included. After pulling off the duct tape, I watched from under the counter as the rest played out. The uniformed man fell to the floor. Shouts, now in English, were heard from the front of the store, and the door was kicked in. Two more uniforms ran in, and the three men

143

scattered down the stairs and out the back before the agents could reach them.

One of the FBI agents that entered from the front was Jon, but I was still too paralyzed with fear to move. He approached slowly, talking me out from the nook I took shelter in. All I could focus on was the man on the floor and the other agent tending to him. Jon reached down for my hand and reluctantly I reached up.

"Is he going to be OK?" I found my voice, but couldn't stop staring.

"I hope so," Jon answered and tried to walk me out of the shop to the street. I protested at first, wanting to help in any way I could, but then let him lead me out. I was in no shape to help someone else, I wasn't even sure I was in any shape to help myself.

I sat in the back seat of his car, with the door open. I felt like I couldn't breathe. My head was spinning, and there was a good chance that I was still going to pass out. The buzzing in my ears turned to low humming and then to quiet. I looked up and around at the scenery. Such a benign and passive front for such a corrupt and destructive organization. Then I heard a soft chirping, and it took me a moment to realize that the baby conure was still in my pocket. I was about to pull him out when I saw Jon on his way back to the car. I couldn't let him see the bird, knowing that he would make me put him back as evidence, to be collected, impounded, and then be sent off to a zoo or auction. No, this one was staying with me. It's the least I could do to save these guys, as it looked like the criminals got away again, and it was all for naught.

"How is he?" I was still concerned for the agent that saved my life. Well, saved it first, before the other two came in and saved it again.

"It looks like bruising- the bullet hit at close range, but the vest protected him. Got the wind knocked out of him, too, but he should be fine."

"That's the best news I've heard all day. What about the perps, they got away?" I had little hope for a positive response, but there was always a chance.

"For now. We got some credible information on the wire. Espinoza is a major drug lord from Mexico that we've been watching for a long time. You did an excellent job." I couldn't tell if he meant it or was just placating me, but I didn't care. The only thing I could think of now was to go home, take a hot shower, and take a nap.

I pulled the door closed and watched the ambulance transport the agent away to the hospital. Jon got into the front seat and was about to start the car when his phone went off.

"Agent McDermitt.....yes.....she's fine, she's.....OK......I understand. Do you.....OK, thank you." He clicked off and tossed the phone to the seat next to him.

"Boss? Upset at the outcome?" I asked him.

"Yes and no."

"Yes, boss? And no, he's OK with outcome?"

"Yes, a boss and upset, and no, it's your boss, not mine. That was Dr. Aquene from STAFE. Somehow she found out about what happened already. You are not allowed to participate in any more FBI sting operations. She said you are much too valuable now."

Chapter 17

Jon dropped me off at my apartment, declining to come in. I wasn't sure if he was intimidated by Dr. Aquene's order to not include me on another criminal bust, or if he was too tired from the day's events. Either way, we left it as 'talk to you later' and went our separate ways. We would still have to talk, as the case wasn't settled, the perps were still on the loose, and other dog fighting rings that they are connected to may still come up. Not to mention that my life would still be in jeopardy, probably more so now that I had been involved in that sting that went so wrong.

It was a long exhausting day, one that could only end with a large pizza with extra garlic being delivered, and then an early bedtime. My muscles ached for no apparent reason, and my head ached for several good reasons. Then the chirping started. Oh yeah, that baby bird. Pulling him out of my pocket once again, I got a good look at him in the light. Cute- of the Green-Cheeked variety- but now I doubted what I was thinking. How was I supposed to take care of a young bird with my schedule? And taking evidence from a crime scene? Now I was on dangerous ground. After all, the last time I spoke with Dr. Aquene- the only time actually that I knew of for sure anyway- she was threatening my job (and possibly my life?). Now she tells Jon that I was 'too valuable now' to risk on another FBI mission? I pondered this while I waited for the pizza to arrive. I added to the order a salad and a fruit cup- it would have to make do for the little conure for now. It looked like I would be doing some shopping at a pet store tomorrow- just not at Feathers and Fur!

I popped a couple of Advil PM's hoping to get a good night of sleep, it was oh-so needed. If I couldn't take the Dilaudid anymore, I knew I still needed something for the pain. I set up the conure in an empty moving box, complete with a blanket for snuggling and a small paper cup cut about a half inch deep filled with water. More make-shift arrangements for now. I was just hoping the bird would sleep through the night. I didn't even know if it was male or female yet- I could do a pelvic exam in the morning, but DNA testing was really the most reliable method for identifying the gender. It had gray feet, though, and rumor had it that- in green cheek conures at least- males had gray feet and females had pink. We will go with a boy for now, whether or not that figures into a name for him, I didn't know yet, but it might help.

After engorging on way too much pizza, sleep starting setting in fast, so I made my way to the bed, barely getting ready before I had to crash. As I hoped, I fell fast and hard to dreamland, not hearing if the conure had anything to say about it at all. I'm not sure when the recurring dream started, but it soon took over my peaceful state and worked my mind up into frenzy once again.

Chirping crickets, trumpeting elephants and now chirping parrots. I was surrounded, each with its own agenda it seemed. They needed to talk to me, tell me something they so desperately wanted me to know. Running through elephant grass in the desert, ducking under tree limbs through a jungle- there was no escape. I found myself backed up against a wall, with all of them closing in, getting louder and louder. A line of parrots cut through the masses speaking in Spanish. "Socorro! Socorro!" was repeated over and over, and soon they all joined in the chant.

"Socorro!" I woke up saying.

I walked into work with a headache and a weird sleep hangover. I must have looked off, as Martin made a face like he accidentally bit into a lemon.

147

"You're here....I think? Eat any brains on the way over?"

"What?" I gave him a look letting him know I wasn't in the mood for a lot of ribbing today.

"Sorry, you just look like the walking dead. I take it things didn't go well with the FBI take down, spy thing?"

"Not so much." I filled him in on the details, including the grand finale gunfight at the OK Corral. I found myself unconsciously playing with the fuzzy new hair growth around my scar, and I remembered that I should be pulling those stitches soon, before I couldn't find them anymore.

"Bullets seem to like you. I'm getting afraid to be around you now. So do you see Jon again? I mean, professionally, of course." Martin was being cheeky, his usual state.

"Oh, and Dr. Aquene told him that I was 'too valuable now' to go on another sting. Can you believe that?"

"She likes you too. You're surrounded!"

"I have no idea what that means...what Dr. Aquene said. What you said, I get, and stop it. Help me name my new pet."

"What now? A day of working at a pet store, and you bring home the merchandise? Clepto..."

"Haha. I sort of pocketed a young conure. I couldn't bear to put it back with the others after carrying him around with me."

"Like I said, clepto. Male or female? Orange, blue, green? I'll need some info to help you out with that one. And does Jon Jon know?"

"His name is just Jon, and no, he doesn't. And, it's going to stay that way, right?" I shot him a hairy eyeball, and he nodded with a scowl.

The better part of the next hour was spent coming up with and then shooting down scores of potential names. The fax machine went off as we were losing steam on the name game. I guessed Uri would have to suffice for now, as Conrad was just too obvious for the little conure bird. Maybe something more clever will strike me as I got to know him.

Martin grabbed the message off the machine and began reading it. A landscaper had called into authorities about a private zoo collection he had seen while working the grounds at a very expensive property on the west side of Virginia. It appeared to be a case of neglect, and we were to meet the police at the scene.

"Any note on what the collection entails?" I hated the sparseness of our communications with headquarters. How were we supposed to prepare for that? Do we bring tranquilizers and dart guns, large quantities of euthanasia solution, or everything and anything in between?

"Nope. As usual, short and sweet. I'll grab a couple more rabies poles, I guess more pentobarbital?"

We gathered up what we could, knowing the vehicle was fully loaded with more things than I know what to do with, and I figured we would just wing it from there. If any of the animals were healthy enough to move, and if we had the need and authority to move them, we would have to send for transportation at that time.

"Do you know if there's a facility that STAFE uses to move these animals to, if needed?"

"There's a large warehouse and lot that we have used not far from here. I think it's empty most of the time, but can be geared up quickly for larger seizures of animals."

I called shotgun, loaded up the forensic mobile, and we headed out. Traffic wasn't too bad for a late morning on a Wednesday. Clear skies and warm weather, it almost felt like road trip weather. Too bad the trip was only about half an hour this time. It was long enough for road trip music, however, and I nominated myself for the position of keeper of the music. I came across Morrissey's "The More You Ignore Me The Closer I get"- sounded good to me. A mellow start, no need to get hyped up on the way to a probable heart-sickening situation.

A policeman was stationed at the end of the long, gated driveway. We showed credentials, asked about the scene, and headed up to the main house with little more information than when we started out. I hoped it would get better than that.

149

"Wounded" by Good Charlotte was just starting when we pulled up next to a cruiser and got out.

Two officers were mulling around the front of the house, looking concerned. We made with the introductions, and they informed us that the owners were not home.

"No one was here when we arrived with the search warrant- at least no one we could find. One of us will have to accompany you around the grounds, in case someone shows up. We don't need this to escalate into anything serious, but your safety is at a higher risk here now because we couldn't secure all parties involved."

"Great. I feel a theme coming on."

"What, ma'am?" The officer, maybe mid-twenties- maybe- said to me.

"Nothing. Can you direct us to the collection? We'll need to pull the vehicle as close as we can to access our equipment."

The young officer took us on a tour of the grounds, pointing out the inadequate, cramped cages along the way. Two ostriches, three llamas, seven Capuchin monkeys, an orangutan, five black and white ruffed lemurs, one giraffe, a brown bear, and a Bengal tiger.

"Are there any in the house?" Martin asked before I could.

"Yes, there are a few snakes and a couple of birds. No dogs or cats, though. Weird. What's wrong with the old fashioned pet dog? Rich people are weird."

I nodded in agreement. What people choose to spend their money on was beyond me. What was the point of having an endangered animal pent up in a confined space for the rest of its life? Who was even around to see it, anyway?

Martin went around to the front of the house to bring the vehicle closer. I made my way around the enclosures to get a better look at injuries and body conditions. They all looked emaciated, the Capuchins and the tiger being the worst. I could see open wounds on the legs of the giraffe, but I would have to get a better view before knowing the severity of them. The Bengal tiger also had a prominent swelling along the left mandible- a possible tooth root abscess. I figured that would be a good place to start. He looked to be in quite a lot of pain.

The officer was mumbling something about a dog he used to have, and I was inserting my "uh-huh"'s here and there, as needed, but I was mostly trying to figure out an approximate weight for the giant cat. I needed to dart the boy, in order to get a better look at abscess and to check for other wounds. He would definitely need to be removed from this property, and cared for elsewhere until a proper home could be found for him. I had high hopes we could pull him through.

"Then he bit my grandma's leg. But she was alright. Ya know?" The officer was still recounting his dog story. I think I came out of my concentration too soon. Saved by Martin, he was just pulling around with the equipment.

"Hola!" I went for the back door to pull out the lock box. I wasn't that familiar with the meds that we carried, and I would need to figure out what I was going to use on Tigger.

"When did you start speaking Spanish?" Martin hopped out and was helping me with the medications.

"Ha. I don't know the language, but have been hearing a lot of it lately. First it was at the pet store yesterday, then in my dream last night. It was the weirdest thing..."

Loud shouting echoed across the back lawn. A scuffle of some sort had broken out at the main house. Perhaps an owner had arrived? Our young officer immediately headed over the grassy hill toward the voices with his hand on his gun. I wasn't sure if I should proceed with the tranquilizer or wait to see what went down. I certainly didn't need a third party in the middle of a tricky enough situation. The tranq in anyone else's butt could result in death. I thought I should load up the dart gun, just in case.

I was looking down when I saw a couple of people run by out of the corner of my eye. I didn't see who they were, and they were gone by the time I looked up. There was more shouting coming from the direction the people went in, so I assumed it was an owner with a police officer in pursuit. Martin, being the brave, double-O-seven-loving guy that he was, was hiding in the front seat of the car.

151

"Can you get out here? I need you to cut the lock so I can get into the cage." I knocked on the driver's side window, and gave him a pleading look when he raised his head.

"Not 'til they got the perp in custody. I'm not getting shot today, thank you."

I was on my own. Not the first time, surely wouldn't be the last. I grabbed the giant twenty-four inch bolt cutters, and had my way with the lock. It wasn't as hard as I thought it would be- not exactly high tech security for these animals.

I remembered pulling the remnants of the lock through the hole in the door and putting down the bolt cutters. After that it was a blur. Shouting came out of nowhere, spinning me around to catch a glimpse of the source. I felt, more than saw, a hand grab the collar of my shirt. I heard the clanging of the bars, of the door, and then of my body against the bars- as I was then inside the cage lying on the ground- and the door had been closed behind me.

I managed to lift my head to get a sense of what just occurred, and found myself eye to eye with the tiger. He had stood up and walked toward me as I was lying there against the bars, and all I could do was to stay as still as possible. I knew I shouldn't be looking the massive animal in the eye, locking gazes with him, but I couldn't look away.

I felt off-balanced and bewildered. Things started whirling around in my head. Inexplicably, pieces of my dream were coming back to me. All I could see were giant crickets, and hearing their overwhelmingly loud chirping sounds. I felt drugged. I felt out of my body. Was I going crazy? What exactly did they do to me when I was in surgery back at headquarters? The chirping then turned to voices, parrot voices, and the chanting, "Socorro! Socorro!" My head was swimming with images of elephants, of dogs, of birds, all chanting while I was staring into the huge eyes of a predator. I really wished that I took the time to look up the meaning of that word from my dream this morning!

Voices mulled and faded in the background, a shot rang out. I didn't move. I had no idea what was real and what was a dream. There were images of elephants talking to me, first in trumpeting, then in Spanish, then it morphed into some other language. I thought I heard Martin's voice somewhere in the middle of it, but it turned into some other dialect as well.

I managed to pull myself up to a sitting position, still maintaining eye contact with the tiger. Why hasn't he eaten me yet? Clearly he was starving. "Socorro!" I heard, over and over, in so many voices, in the tiger's voice now too. The cat now dropped to his belly, sitting in a sternal position. The voices kept coming, the visions kept coming. I wondered if this is what prey animals went through- a paralyzing connection with the predator, a complete helplessness that brought on- what, delusions?

Another gunshot rang out, this time close and loud. It brought me back to reality, back to my immediate situation. I managed to pull my gaze away in that split second, and I held it still, this time on his body, waiting for a reaction. I had no idea how much time elapsed during the whole ordeal, much less at this particular point, but when I looked back to the tiger's face, he had put his head down, and was looking just past my head as well.

I closed my eyes and took a breath. When I opened them, the tiger was doing the same thing. I nodded to him and lowered my gaze to his paws outstretched in front of him. He mimicked the action. There was a cool sense of calm between us, and my monumental fears were slipping away. I looked over his body, nodding to his emaciated condition, he dropped his gaze. I looked at the swelling along his jaw, and reached up to feel mine, he looked at me and blinked slowly.

Our eyes locked again, and I nodded to him as I slowly stood up. I kept his stare as I backed- ever so slowly- to the door. Feeling for the handle through the bars, I managed to get the door open, and step through.

I didn't know how long I was standing there looking at the magnificent beast. When I broke my gaze at last, I turned to see Martin standing there. He was the shade of Martha Stewart linen, and all I could do was look at him now. He tried to speak, but nothing came out. I knew exactly how he felt- I was truly at a loss for words too.

153

Chapter 18

Apparently the owner did come home, and didn't like the fact that his property was overrun with police officers and animal welfare workers. I was told that he had punched one of the cops in the face and took off running through the yard, dodging behind the animal cages. I didn't really know why he pushed me into the tiger enclosure, perhaps showing his disdain for the situation, but soon thereafter he was shot by one of the officers. I hoped he was shot by the one who got hit in the face, just for some payback, but I didn't know for sure. An ambulance was taking him away in serious condition, so he may live to pay for his crimes against these poor animals. I was surprised that part of me wanted him to die, but more surprised that part of me wanted him to live just to suffer for what he had done.

STAFE went ahead and hooked us up with transport vehicles and animal wranglers from the National Zoo. I was hopeful we could get them loaded and unloaded with minimal tranquilizing. I wasn't sure some of them could handle even mild sedation with their weakened body conditions. The tiger was the one I was most worried about. We needed to get him started on antibiotics right away, as well as re-hydrating him. If we could get the infection under control, and get him strong enough, then we could get a veterinary dentist in here to deal with the tooth root. It would probably have to be pulled, but I'll leave that up to the specialist.

It took most of the day, as you would have guessed, to corral and load the animals. I was beyond happy that we had professional help for this part of the process. Martin and I helped with most of the animals in the outdoor enclosures, as well as the birds inside, but I let them take care of the snakes. Not that I had an aversion to snakes, it was just a trust issue thing I had with a creature that could move so fast while having no legs. I was OK with relinquishing duties for those ones, thank you.

Martin's color started to come back the more we got into the tasks at hand. I could tell he had put the whole incident away somewhere in the back of his mind. I had as well, but I could still feel strange adrenaline bursts course through me from time to time. The daylight was pretty much ending, but we had a lot of work left to do.

The trip back started out without a word. I'm not sure either one of us had enough energy to speak, and if we did, we didn't want to talk about what happened. We were headed to the holding area set up by STAFE and the zoo, just to the north of our office, and the city. I remembered as we were cutting through the west side that the new edition to my family, Uri, was at home, probably starving himself. I took a turn off the highway, and headed for a pet store for supplies. Martin looked at me quizzically.

"Sorry, but I'm going to have to make a couple of pit stops...for Uri." Martin nodded in reply, and then went back to zoning out again.

We both went in, probably hoping to see some cute healthy animals to cheer us up. As luck would have it, it was adoption day, a collaboration with one of the local shelters. Rescued dogs were brought in for the day in hopes of finding adopters for their forever homes. They certainly put smiles on our faces, and made shopping a lot easier. We took our time finding the right food, the right cage, and of course, the right toys. That's where I left Martin for a little while- he was enamored with all the swings, knots, and even piñatas they made for a bird's entertainment, and apparently, Martin's. I left the store with a whole lot more than I intended to!

The next stop was my apartment. Martin helped me carry the goods inside, and he took right to Uri. They made fast friends, and I think the food helped a lot, too. I put the cage in the corner of the living room, near the kitchen. I figured

155

he'd be in the middle of the action there and far enough away from the bedroom so that I could get some sleep at night. The little conure was exploring his new digs with a full belly by the time we left.

We headed out to the holding area to assist in the unloading of the zoo animals and get a few rudimentary exams in, if possible.

"Why don't you wait until tomorrow, when there are a few more people around to help, to do the exams?" I think Martin was too tired to work anymore, and this was his way to try to get out of it.

"I just want to get a good look at everyone indoors, in the lights. The giraffe needs its wounds cleaned up and bandaged as soon as possible, and I want to get the tiger started on a course of antibiotics. I need to get his schedule set up as soon as possible- I can't imagine the pain he must be in."

Just the mention of the tiger brought on a hush in the car. It was several minutes before anyone spoke again, and then it was just to point out directions.

The holding area was really just a giant warehouse. There were a few 30×30 pens, and a 50×50 pen in the back. All the animals today, though, would go directly into the warehouse. Cages and containment areas of many shapes and configurations filled the space inside the building. They were all on the small side, but they had to be for treatment and observation purposes. The National Zoo personnel were about to unload the Capuchins when we arrived.

"Do we have enough side by side cages for them? It would be easier if they were in separate cages for now, but I want them to be able to see each other." I told one of the workers on loan from the zoo. He agreed and we found an area set up that would work fine for that.

They already had the tiger and ostrich unloaded- and far apart from each other- and the rest of the workers were handling the snakes and birds. I figured that I would get the meds ready for the tiger and giraffe, while Martin helped getting the food prepared for everyone. Feeding a zoo was no easy task, especially when they were in such a sorry state.

"Not that I want raw meat for dinner, but some food for us would be nice," Martin muttered. He could get cranky when he was hungry. I had witnessed that enough times in the short while that I'd known him. I needed to start carrying crackers or something with me for these occasions.

Most of the workers had gone by the time we got the bigger animals fed, and it was down to Martin and me by the time we got around to feeding the monkeys. I felt bad for keeping him at such an hour, but I wanted to at least address the open sores on the giraffe before calling it a night. I filled a small bucket with supplies and started to head over the giraffe pen when I noticed Martin asleep on a pile of paperwork. I let him nap- he'd be no help to me if he was that drowsy.

I had to take a few pictures first, to document the wounds for potential legal action. Then, after flushing the open wounds with sterile water and cleaning them up with a Betadine solution, I dressed them with a light gauze wrap to keep them clean. The giraffe seemed alright with the ordeal, perhaps even grateful for getting the food and care it needed. I was grateful that I was stared down by a tiger and lived to tell about it. That is, if I ever spoke about it, I still had no words to describe the incident.

I took a detour on the way back to check on the Capuchins. Suddenly, I felt alone among the zoo animals, the only human in the building- well that was awake anyway. My head started to swim again. That feeling of disassociation with my body and the blurring of faces was setting in. The room tilted and the faces floated slowly, steadily right toward me.

"Socorro!"

"Madad!"

"Ajuda!"

"Nisaidie!"

"Ungisize!"

"Socorro, socorro, socorro!"

The elephants, the ostrich, the parrots, and the tiger were all speaking at once. I was going mad. Swooning and teetering, I grabbed my head.

"Socorro!"

"Madad!"

"Help!"

It was one of the Capuchins. It said 'help'. Were they all saying help?

"Help!, Help!"

"Are you OK? What happened?" This time it was Martin, and I was wondering why he was so tall.

"You were slumped against the wall yelling for help. What happened?" Martin was standing over me in the walkway between the monkeys.

I must have looked bewildered. I certainly felt lost. Another dream? I was still holding my head. Looking around, I tried to get my bearings, tried to form a sentence, but 'help' was the only word I could say. My partner helped me to my feet, and I leaned on him heavily. Slowly, we made it over to the office area where he was just sleeping.

"I could hear you from over here. Are you OK? It couldn't have been the giraffe attacking you- you were clear away from the enclosure. What were you doing over there?"

"My head. I think they did something to my head."

Martin looked at me strange, and not knowing what I was talking about, he replied, "I think you may have come back to work too soon. Maybe even let out of the hospital a little early? I think we should get you back there for a checkup."

He didn't know the circumstances surrounding my surgery nor of the details of my recovery, and I certainly couldn't tell him about it. The best thing to do, I decided, was to have him take me home. Then I was going to confront Dr. Aquene, Carrie, and whoever else I could find. I needed answers. They did something to my head, and I needed to know what it was, or if I was just simply going insane.

I didn't sleep that night. I was too hyped up to get rest, and part of me really wanted to storm into headquarters that night, but I didn't think anyone would be there. Certainly not Dr. Aquene. I wasn't sure she was even there on a day to day basis. Carrie might have been there, but that wouldn't get me anywhere. It wouldn't get me the answers that I needed. So, I occupied myself with little Uri. Poor guy probably wanted to get some sleep himself, but we had things to discuss. Well, I had things to discuss, and I really hoped he didn't have answers. I didn't think that I could take any more critters talking to me in tongues.

A big pot of coffee and a bottle of ibuprofen were going to help me get through the hours until dawn. I started to pace, but soon felt fatigued, and opted for sitting on the sofa instead. Lost Girl was on cable- a marathon of episodes- and they helped me feel not so out of place. Surely things weren't as bad as all that? I tried to think through the facts, put the pieces together.

Brain surgery plus fatigue- emotional as well as physical- plus having the life scared out of me in the tiger den, all added up to confusion. That's all it was, right? I turned on the computer thinking I could throw a few symptoms into the internet and diagnose myself- a huge pet peeve for doctors of all kinds. Unfortunately, my specific symptoms weren't found, at least not all together, and the results were always 'cancer'. Not a hundred percent sure, but I really didn't think it was that. Crazy, yes. Cancer, not so much.

What was that word the parrots kept saying? The tiger said it too, but it also said something else. 'Soco'...something. 'Socor', 'soccor', I tried different spellings. Hmm, towns in New Mexico, Texas, and an energy company. 'Socoro', a Manchurian clan surname- pretty sure they weren't telling me that. Maybe they weren't saying anything to me- maybe it was all just jumble in my head, my poor, muddled up head.

"Socor...or?" I said it to Uri to see if he could make sense out it. No luck there. He was too young to talk, in any language.

159

For the life of me, I couldn't remember any of the other words that were said, if they were words at all. I was just crazy, that had to be it. Or, they really mucked with my head. Would they do it intentionally? I didn't see why. How was I so valuable now, as Dr. Aquene put it to Jon, when clearly I wasn't last week? I mean, I kind of feared for my life for a little while there after that meeting. What was it that they said in that dream I had in their homemade hospital? I was worth more in my current role? More than what? I believed I truly was going mad.

It was around six thirty when the sun started to rise. Another beautiful day ahead, weather-wise- not so much in other aspects. Uri had napped out at some point. Even my madness couldn't keep him interested in our one-sided conversation. I showered and made myself eat something. Toast was better than nothing, and nothing but a whole pot of coffee in the stomach can make for crazy behavior. I definitely didn't need any more of that on my plate. I waited until almost leaving before waking the little bird to feed him. Poor little bugger didn't know what he was in for when he met me in that basement the other day.

It was just past seven when I headed out the door. I had no idea what time anyone got in to headquarters, but I would wait if I had to. I was determined to get some answers, even if the answer was that I was mad. What if I was crazy, and they saw that and fired me? Or worse? I wasn't sure there was anything much worse than the state that I felt I was in.

I took the metro, taking the red line to the silver line to L'Enfant Plaza. The cars were crowded, everyone heading into work. There was a sea of business suits, smattered with a few uniforms, and the occasional casual wear of probable tourists. Usually the tourists weren't up that early, most of the touristy buildings weren't open yet, but the early bird go-getters didn't mind waiting in line.

Some hallucinations were still haunting me. The animal faces would come back, appearing out of nowhere, and disappearing as fast. I was glad that I was sitting, at least for the first leg of the trip. The silver line was a little more crowded, leaving me with part of a pole and a wave of bodies to prop me up. I fought the visions, but the voices had started as well. It was hard to tell what was in my head and what came from all the people around me. I was thankful for the ibuprofen alleviating the throbbing between my temples, but I had no remedy for the swimming sensation.

I had to walk the last few blocks from L'Enfant Plaza. The cool breeze helped me along, but as I got closer to headquarters, I started to slow down. I doubted my ability to find the answers I was looking for. I doubted the level of transparency my employer would have. I doubted the openness of a conversation, if one would even occur, that was needed to find out what was happening to me. Maybe I should have called Jaffey. Maybe he could have found out things for me, things that I wouldn't be able to find out on my own. Or maybe he was in on the whole thing, I had no real reason to trust him any more than I trusted anyone else involved with STAFE, even though I had known him slightly longer.

What was I going to say? 'Hi, you messed with my head, didn't you?' 'Oh, by the way, I hear voices in my head, and animals are talking to me. What's new with you?' I tried out several lines in my head, but none of them worked- none of them seemed to convey my fears, or direct someone to an answer. Then I found myself there, at the door of the building, and the time for thinking it through was over.

"I guess I'll just have to wing it," I said out loud to the questioning look of those people around me. The elevator ride was shorter than I remembered, and I wasn't even sure that it would go all the way up to the top floor without special clearance, but surprisingly it did.

The door opened to an empty reception area. My heart skipped a beat. Maybe no one was in yet. Or maybe they were in the office just beyond those doors at the end of the waiting area. Taking a few steps in closer to the head office, I carefully listened for any sounds, any telltale signs of life beyond those doors. I took a deep breath to ready myself, one last attempt to muster up the courage. Then I stormed in. It took me a

161

moment to assess the situation. I found myself face to face with three people, two of whom I knew, and one that I didn't.

"We've been waiting for you."

Chapter 19

It was Dr. Aquene that had spoken. She was standing in front and to the right of the large wooden desk. Carrie was seated in the wing chair pulled slightly to the side of the desk, with half of her face visible as she turned toward me. The third person was seated behind the massive piece of furniture, looking straight at me. She had exquisite features, dark hair, and piercing eyes. Could this be the elusive Dr. Ceta?

I had been staring, almost mesmerized by her eyes, and I had forgot why I was there in the first place. I knew I was angry about something, but I had no idea about what.

"Dr. Wake," Dr. Aquene started in. "May I introduce you to Dr. Dubashi, head of communications?" She laid out her hand in the direction of the new person in the room, as if she was an item on display in a store. I barely stumbled through my greeting, ending up in the previous staring state again. I'm sure I looked like a buffoon, as if drool might make an appearance out of the corner of my mouth at any moment. Was everyone here at STAFE beautiful? Suddenly I felt inadequate and self-conscious.

I managed to reach up and run my fingers through my hair, probably out of nervous intents, and remembered what brought me here, as I felt the incision line on my scalp.

"What did you do....wait, what.....why did you say you were expecting me?" My faculties were coming back up to speed- made a little easier by keeping my gaze on Dr. Aquene instead of the distraction behind the desk. "Dr. Wake, Alex, why don't you have a seat. We have a lot to discuss." She offered a smile that turned sinister at the edges, and I was overwhelmed by a bad feeling- one of many, I assumed- that were on the

163

way. I found myself wishing that I could turn back time, go back to the start of the day and that none of this happened.

Dr. Aquene stepped toward me with her arm outstretched, and I recoiled by instinct. I heard a faint laugh from someone in the room, but couldn't tell from whom, and wound up letting Dr. Aquene guide me to the sofa. She sat down next to me with her hand on my knee.

"You are here because you have questions, questions about the surgery, the voices,......the things that you are experiencing that perhaps you hadn't before." She was talking slowly, as if I was mentally incapacitated. It scared me more than soothed, making me fear that something worse was going to come of it.

"What did you do to my head?" I didn't want to look at her so close, but looking around the room wasn't an option. I didn't want to get stuck in the mental molasses that occurred when looking at Dr. Dubashi.

"I should start at the beginning..."

"That's usually a good place." My anger was starting to creep back in.

"We noticed that you have....certain abilities that are unique to you and to a few others. Your ability to empathize, not just with people, but with animals, creatures of all species. You have a certain rapport, a connection, if you will. That's one of the reasons we chose you for this position."

"I thought I applied for this job?"

"Yes, well that was after you had communications with Jaffey. We had him contact you, get you interested in our work, get you on board. It's really much more involved than you'd realized."

I was confused and could feel the dumbfounded look on my face, but I couldn't do anything about it. "So you researched me or something?"

"Or something." She grinned, and my heart almost stopped. "STAFE has been in the works for- well let's just say many years. It's only been recently that certain opportunities arose allowing us to move forward."

"I don't understand." Her cryptic talk was annoying me, and I was losing my patience.

"You don't have to, not yet anyway. But what you do have to understand is...the wonderful gift that we have given you." She was smiling again, and I knew it wasn't going to be pretty.

"What...gift?" I was biting the inside of my cheek.

"There was the most opportune time to try out- to first implement- a new device that Dr. Dubashi has spent years creating." She looked over at the woman behind the desk and then back at me as if I should feel special for being chosen as the guinea pig du jour. "When you were shot- most horrendously- we really didn't know if you were going to survive, we were able to turn a bad event into a life changing moment. It really was the perfect opportunity."

"Opportunity for what? You keep dancing around the topic. WHAT DID YOU DO?!"

Dr. Aquene's smile dropped to almost a snarl, then recovered. "Dr. Dubashi's research is in communications with other species, primarily with dolphins. She has invented a device that can help translate animal sounds and vocalizations into words that humans can understand. It's amazing, really." She paused, possibly for dramatic effect, possibly because she overwhelmed herself, "We implanted this device in your brain. I mean, the doctors had the access, and we weren't sure what was going to come of you, so we thought it an auspicious moment, a fortuitous one, if you will." She looked at me as if I would be grateful, happy to be toyed with, to have my brain mucked with. I was livid.

"And you just felt that you could take advantage of me, when I was in the most vulnerable state a person could be in, you exploited me?!" I stood up, uncertain if I should storm out the door or throw something. Dr. Aquene stood up as well.

"Dr. Wake, I assure you, our intentions were not malicious. We did save your life, after all. I know it's a shock, but the quicker you come to terms with it, the quicker we can move forward with the training."

"The training?! There's more? You put some foreign piece of equipment into my BRAIN, and then want my compliance

165

to study the effects?! You are all insane!" I started for the door, but Dr. Aquene grabbed my arm, spinning me around.

"You don't really have a choice..."

"Let me help explain." It was Dr. Dubashi who rose up from her seat behind the desk and approached. "Please sit, Alex. We would all like to make this as pleasant an experience as possible."

I sat back down, reluctantly, and continued to bite on the inside of my cheek. I didn't want to risk getting overly emotional, but the lack of sleep on top of these revelations had me tweaking. She sat down next to me.

"It's simple, really. I will work with you personally, and together we can hone your skills of interspecies communication." She spoke with an enchanting Indian accent, making everything sound exciting. I had to keep shaking my head to break the spell.

"What if I refuse? I mean, it is my body, my brain after all." I didn't know where I was going with this, but I felt like I needed to know if I had any control over the situation.

"We don't need to go down that path, do we?" It was Dr. Aquene who answered, adding her twisted smile for good measure.

"Let's not start out on the wrong foot." Dr. Dubashi once again took over. She reached over and put her hand on my back, putting me off guard. "Why don't we go to my research lab and start some basic training. You can get a feel for things. I'm sure you will love your new found ability. Think of all the animals that we- you- can help with this power." She was stroking my back as she spoke in her soft voice. I was lulled into submission, yielding to her suggestions.

"Please, get comfortable. It will take me a few minutes to prepare." Dr. Dubashi had led me down to the basement level of the building, through several limited access entry points, and into her subterranean laboratory. It was just the two of us- that I knew of- here in this hidden space. I was intimidated, yet thankful that Dr. Aquene hadn't accompanied us. She was really starting to scare me for a minute there.

"What exactly are we going to be doing here, Dr. Dubashi? And, is it going to hurt?" I was trying humor in the face of fear, but then I worried that maybe it did require pain.

"Call me Anoushka, please." She didn't answer my questions. Instead, she was preoccupied with a piece of machinery against the wall. She rolled across the tiny floor in the chair she was seated in, headed in my direction. She didn't look up, staying focused on her work.

"So you work with dolphins?" I was restlessly trying to start a conversation- anything, really- to get a grasp on a situation that was clearly out of my control. Why did I agree to this again?

She abruptly stopped, and turned to me as if she knew what I was thinking. "You don't have to be nervous. It will be brilliant, trust me." She smiled and went right back to work.

It's not that I didn't trust her, well, I didn't, but I'd do better with more information. I'd do better with more information when it comes to my brain, and to risking my life for unknown end results. I was working up the nerve to stand up and declare my desire to abort the mission when lights started to turn on in the adjoining room. There was a large Plexiglas separation between the rooms, and the lights revealed a huge aquarium of sorts on the other side. It was a wondrous sight- deep shades of blue and green swirled and sparkled in the light. For some reason, I was holding my breath.

Anoushka was looking into the darkened sea in front of us- looking for something. She then turned to me, laughing. "You can breathe, we are not the ones under water."

Complying, I took in a breath while staring at her, and once again I was at a loss for words. I could, however, pull off an inquisitive look, as eccentric as it may have appeared. It was successful in eliciting some more chuckling, but no explanation.

Several minutes of typing on a computer, echoes of underwater machinery moving, and flipping switches led to the moment. It was the first trial, officially, of a ground breaking communication device- one that could change the world. And I was the guinea pig they were trying it out on.

"Get ready, there's going to be several series of sounds coming at you at the same time. Just try to focus on one for now."

I had no idea what she was talking about, then I looked up, through the giant window and saw them all. At least half a dozen, I'd say. Gorgeous bottlenose dolphins, all with something to say. Their vocalizations were overpowering, paralyzing me. I had to cover my ears, gripping my head.

"Make it stop!" I fell to my knees.

Anoushka pressed a few buttons and turned off the intercom. Peace. She helped me back up to my chair. The throbbing was intense- I needed a few minutes to recover.

"I'll have them start slower," she said in her quiet tone, still holding my arm.

"How about just one of them?"

"Ha, It doesn't work that way, I'm afraid. They all have equally important things to say- or so they think- so you will need to learn how to handle that. We will start softer, slower. You will learn."

"You know, I never could learn another language, I sucked at Spanish, and my French is beyond resurrection. Perhaps someone with better language skills would have been more useful." I smiled, once again trying to make light of the situation.

"You will be more than useful, Alex. I am quite satisfied with our choice." She smiled back, this time with a hint of gratification.

I headed back to the holding facility to complete the physical exams and document any other injuries. I was hopeful that the tiger was feeling better, although twelve hours wasn't long enough to really see the effects of the antibiotics. I just felt so bad for the regal animal. I was also hopeful to try out the skill, even if I was a long way off from mastering it.

Dr. Dubashi's smile haunted me on my ride over. I wasn't being told the whole story, and I knew it. I knew it well. They were probably playing good cop/bad cop, and Anoushka got the good role. Not a bad role for her, though- she worked it well. I had to stop being so vulnerable. Next time, I will stand my ground better.

I found Martin filling out the mounds of paperwork that was already accumulating. He looked exhausted, but not as exhausted as I felt. I was going to crash and burn fast, so I needed to speed through as much of the work that I could. I was hoping he already did the rounds with the camera and got the documentation needed for the future court case or cases, depending on how things turned out.

"Hey partner, tell me things are moving along nicely."

"It's about time, Doc. I've been trying to call you all morning. You missed the feeding frenzy. The zoo workers really are a big help. So, were you sleeping in, or just playing with the new addition to your family?"

I wanted to tell him everything that happened, really I did, but I was sworn to secrecy. I couldn't tell him about the whole hospital stay at headquarters to begin with, and I certainly couldn't tell him about the implant. "I had the hardest time sleeping- I guess I didn't nod off until early this morning. Then, well, it all got away from me, sorry."

"Until after noon? Sure sure. Well, I got the photos done, and put a dent in the deskwork. You'll have to do the exams, though, and I have half a mind to make you do them by yourself!" He sounded like he was joking, but I could see a glint of animosity on his face.

"That's fine. Again, I'm sorry. How about you help me with the big critters, and then you can head out? I can do the birds, snakes, lemurs and Capuchins by myself. We have the squeeze cages, if needed." I was not only hoping to get back on his good side, but to have some time alone with the animals to practice. I knew my head couldn't handle a whole lot more of the communication exercises today, but I figured a few trial runs with the cross section of species here would be a good test.

169

We started with the giraffe. I pondered what one would say, as they weren't known to have any voicings at all. We made it through the exam and redressing the leg wounds, but nothing came to me- no voices in my head. Part of me was happy, relieved almost, yet part of me was worried that I wouldn't be able to make this work. The tiger was an easier exam, as we couldn't get too close. He was still too weak to knock down for a physical, so external observations were all we were left with. I didn't try to hear his voice, it was still too soon since the encounter in his cage, and I was worried about flashbacks. The bear and orangutan were similar in that we did observational exams. These animals needed some time to heal, gain weight, and re-hydrate before anything intrusive could or should be done.

I let Martin give me the run down on the rest of the day's events, and was surprised when he said that the owner was still in serious but stable condition. I was surprised because I hadn't even thought about him or his condition, and then I was surprised because now would be the time when our perps would mysteriously 'commit suicide'. I wondered if that would be this fellow's fate as well, and I found myself not caring either way. Wow, when did I get so hard?

I sent Martin home to get some rest. He didn't protest, I think he may have had another date lined up with that musician. I was envious of his life, now that I was tagged for the more complicated pathway of research patient-slash-communicator extraordinaire. I shook off the jealously and set out to finish the exams. I did the Capuchins last, as they were the ones I wanted to test my new-found craft on. After all, they were the ones that spoke some English. It was my best chance at understanding their message- if there was one.

It took almost two hours, but I finally made my way to the monkey cages. I realized there was an eerie quiet in the massive building, even with all of its living contents. I sat myself in front of the line of cages, worried that I would get dizzy and fall over or slump down again. I focused on one Capuchin in particular, hoping that I could isolate one voice alone. Then it hit. All twenty plus animals decided it was a good time to talk, all at once. If I hadn't been sitting already, I certainly would have been bowled over by the sheer volume. I once again was reduced to a lump, ears covered, head clenched, rocking back and forth. The pain was unbearable.

This wasn't going to work, this wasn't going to work at all.

Chapter 20

Maybe I was just exhausted or overwhelmed, but I had no faith in this 'gift' that I was given. A glass of wine and a dark apartment weren't helping my mood any, either. At least it was quiet here. Uri wasn't saying much at the moment. Why was I the one who got to be the guinea pig? What got me here, to this messed up position?

I felt the tears start to build up. I had to tell myself, "not this time". Crying wasn't going to solve anything. But it couldn't be helped. It was the kind of crying where you couldn't stop long enough to take a breath, where your nose ran as much as your eyes, and sometimes there was no sound at all. People have said that it was good to let it out once in a while, to not keep it all bottled up inside. Well, it didn't make me feel better. In fact, I felt pretty stupid for letting it happen. Ten minutes of crying and half an hour of trying to un-puffy my eyes and empty out my sinuses. Not a pretty sight.

Maybe Uri would have some insight, even for a youngin', he might have something to say. I felt bad about waking him up, but I was going to need to feed him soon anyway. He always looked so cute when he first woke up- not that he wasn't adorable the rest of the time as well! I gave him some mashed fruit, and he proceeded to make a mess of it all. And I set out on my feeble attempt at communicating with him.

"What do you think, Uri? Is this a gift or a curse?"

"Food," he said back, at least I think that's what he said.

"What was that?"

"Food." He looked at me, waiting for my response, waiting for me to offer up some more treats for his consumption.

"Food? Is that all you have to say? You're no help at all, are you?"

"Food."

Great, my only one on one with an animal to get a grasp on this new-found talent, and all I got was 'food'. What was the point of this again? I put Uri back in his cage with more of his food, and settled back onto the sofa. Well, I would have imagined that most animals would be consumed with their basic needs- food, water, and mating. Just glad he was concentrating on the former, I guess.

Maybe that wasn't such a bad thing after all. If I could find a way to filter out all the common, mundane vocalizations, I might be able to hone in on just the important ones. Maybe that was something that I could work on with Anoushka. For now, all this talk of food had made me hungry. A little road trip in search of some food and quiet time would be appropriate, I thought.

I got the car out of the garage, something I didn't do often- not since moving to this city with the public transportation, and use of the company vehicle. I had no idea where I was going, but I instinctively went east, toward the sea. A little ocean air never hurt anyone- well aside from people in a few horror movies. I headed out on Route 665 and picked up a pizza in Bowie. I headed east again, but took a southern turn down Route 2 to find some little nook and cranny road along the water.

I found a little turn off where I parked the car, then made my way down an embankment to the water- pizza in hand, of course, that was the point of the road trip. I had no idea who owned the land I was on, or what town I was even in, but I figured if I was quiet enough, I wasn't doing any harm.

There was a good sized rock by the water's edge where I sat and put the rest of the pizza down. I was in a small cove, surrounded by trees, with no people or houses in sight. The moon was waning, about three quarters that night- enough light to see rough details of the area. I could hear the occasional splash in the water, probably just a fish catching bugs, although I didn't know they did that at night.

173

Thinking that I was somewhat alone, I tried my communication skills again. I figured the worst case scenario would be a bunch of birds telling me to be quiet, and at best, perhaps a fish telling me he was hungry. I gave it a whirl.

"Anyone here have anything important to tell me?" I felt foolish at first, what if a person was out there listening? But I was getting used to weird things happening, and quite frankly, I wasn't caring that much anymore.

"Food!" A voice came from behind me, and I whipped around, startled.

"Food!" Another voice came from just to my left. Great, it was a thing. Now I got to hear all about the hunger woes of the woodland creatures, and most likely, the dogs in the neighborhood, the birds along my walk to work, and while we were at it, the squirrels in the park. I sighed heavily, feeling disappointed. What was I expecting, though? This was exactly what I figured I would have to deal with. Maybe there was a way to filter out this aspect of it; maybe there was some tweaking they could do to the device. At least I hoped they could, before I went mad.

Two raccoons showed up- the owners of the demanding voices. "Food! Food!" in unison they cried. If they weren't so cute, I'd be beyond frustrated with them. But instead I tossed them some pizza. No 'thank yous' were heard, of course. Manners- if only we all had better manners- I chuckled to myself, feeling amazed that I could find some humor in my situation. I was starting to feel determined to make this work- I mean, what else could I do? I had thought of demanding that they take out the device that they so cavalierly put into my brain, but that would open up the opportunity for them to do more harm. I couldn't risk it.

I downed that last piece of pizza and let the coons inspect the empty box, just in case there was something left behind. They lumbered off without another word, probably to knock over some garbage cans in the neighborhood. "Night Swimming" by REM came to mind as I was taking off my shoes to dip my feet in. Pondering a full-on skinny dip in the cove- why not, who was there to see? - I figured it might be a good time to try communicating underwater. What if the fish had something more to say than 'food'?

I undressed and stepped in. There was a steep drop from the edge- maybe five or six feet- so it alarmed me at first. But after a few splashes and minor panic, I relaxed and actually enjoyed it. The water was still cold, but warming up faster than I expected for April. After a few moments of acclimating myself, I took a deep breath and went under.

I opened my eyes and looked around. I didn't hear anything. Peace and quiet. I was feeling grateful for the stillness, for the silence of the underwater world. I was hesitant to attempt communicating again. I could just stay here, be at one with the water. Gills would've been a better gift, I thought. Still, I felt it necessary to try. Try to focus on one voice, just one at a time.

"Hello?"

No response. Maybe fish didn't talk? Maybe it doesn't work underwater. Maybe everyone was asleep, and that was where I should have been right then. I was about to try again when something swam by me. I stayed very still while I watched and waited for it to come by again. Surely it wasn't a shark this far inland? They have been known to come alarmingly close to shore. I needed to surface for more air, but I didn't want to draw attention to myself in case it was there to feed. After holding out as long as I could, I slipped upward and broke surface for a breath. No fin circling me- that was a good sign.

Another deep breath and I went back down. I was immediately met by the face of a harbor seal. As cute as they were, they still had teeth and could be dangerous, so one so close to my face was a bit disconcerting. I took a moment to gather my wits.

"I suppose you want food, too?" I said as it swam a lap around me.

"Help!"

"What? Are you OK?" I looked it over for any wounds or impairments, but superficially it looked fine.

"Help!" The seal repeated and started to swim off. It circled back as if it were waiting for me to follow, so I did.

We were headed out of the cove into open waters, and it worried me- a lot. I was an OK swimmer, but put anyone in the current and anything could happen. I had to go up for air a couple of times as I followed, but the seal waited and circled back for me each time. I tried to ask if it was much further, but all I heard was 'help'.

A little bit further out, just before I was about to give up and head back, I heard a second voice. It was saying 'help' very quickly and repeatedly. I knew something was in distress. The seal swam back and forth more frantically, eager for me to aide its friend or relative. A web-like substance hit my face and arm, causing me to recoil. At first I reacted by fighting with whatever it was, then I calmed myself and worked through the situation. The harbor seal's offspring (?) was entangled in old fishing gear, netting and wire. It could barely break the surface with its snout to breathe. I managed to lift up the weighted section, to alleviate the weight pulling on the line, and then unwrapped that section from the seal's flipper. There was a gouge around the base of the flipper- something that would probably always be there from now on for the life of the little animal- but now it was free.

The older seal swam around several times. At that point I was up at the surface catching my breath. I thought maybe they were chasing each other, but when I went back under, it appeared that the two of them were overjoyed and were frolicking around in their merriment. I started laughing under water and almost choked. after catching some air again, I went back down to see them off. I asked if they were going to be alright first, and I was surprised to hear 'thank you' in both of their voices. I smiled and told them they were welcome, and watched the two swim off.

I was giddy with joy. Maybe this gift really was a gift. Maybe I could put it to good use- if I got the hang of it, of course. Swimming around thinking about all of the potential, I clear forgot that I was out in open water, and now all by myself. Not that the seal could have or would have protected me, but somehow I felt safer when it was there. Now I was all alone.

I started swimming back as fast as I could- not knowing what else was out there. If everything seemed as focused on food as I was beginning to think, I was setting myself up for someone's next big meal. I made it about two-thirds of the way back when I ran out of steam. I was feeling more confident being closer to the shore again, but not enough to not worry. I just took a little more time getting through the last leg of it.

Back at the cove, I decided to try talking to the sea once more. Why not? I felt safe enough that if it came back as 'food', that it wouldn't be me they were going to find as a solution.

"Hello?" Once again I said underwater.

"Hello? Hello?" I heard faintly. Was it far off, or from something small or weak? I couldn't tell.

"Hello? Where are you?"

A somewhat small fish- compared to the size of the seal- appeared slowly out of the murky darkness. It looked like a catfish- not that I was any kind of fish expert. Some people think that just because someone is a veterinarian, that they know every species of every animal alive. Nope. We only got four years to learn everything we could about as many things as we could- that wasn't a lot of time. So my best guess was a catfish- it had those barbel things that looked like whiskers. If there were other fish with similar characteristics, I supposed it could have been one of those instead. It looked hesitant, unsure what my motive was.

"Help?" It turned sideways to look at me, and its problem was rather apparent. There was a plastic six-pack ring around its body, caught over the fin.

"Oh hey, I can help with that," and I tried to reach for it to help, but the fish kept swimming around. "You have to hold...still," again I tried, but failed to capture the fish. "You have to hold still!"

That time I think I frightened it away. It swam off, and I had to plead with it to come back. This dodgy behavior was

177

repeated for several minutes, interrupted by my needing to go up for air, and its need to swim off out of fear. I finally grabbed part of the plastic rings as it swam by and pulled. Off it came, done and done. The fish did another pass in disbelief.

"Wait, what happened?" It looked like it was trying to see itself, swimming in a circular fashion. Then I thought that maybe I wounded it with the pulling of the plastic, but it swam by with a 'thank you' and off it went. Another satisfied customer. I was beginning to like this gift- as much of a pain in the ass as it was, not to mention the invasion of my body.

I swam back to shore and rested on the rock before getting dressed again. What a night! Feeling cocky, I went about designing the superhero costume in my head. Of course I'd need one, right? I had a super power and helped those in need. But the hours will have to be worked on- these night visits couldn't be the norm if I was going to keep up my day job as well. Speaking of my day job, I had to get back home and get some sleep. Not only did I have the recently acquired zoo animals to tend to, I also had my next training session with Dr. Dubashi. I was eager to find out if we could somehow screen the messages coming through, to weed out the demands for food and focus on things that were more important.

The noise and clamor set in as I was climbing back up the embankment. Raccoons, skunks, mice, owls, etc., all wanting food, or a mate, or the occasional fear for their lives as they were part of the food chain. At what point do I interfere? It was getting awfully loud in these woods, and I needed to get out of there before the blinding headaches started in again.

The hope that I could get inside the car and close the door and all the voices would cease disappeared when it all kept droning through my head. I turned on the car and flipped on the radio to drown them out. "A Wolf At The Door" by Radiohead was playing. Turning it up, I headed back up the road to Route 2. The drive back wasn't that bad. I had a lot to think about, and my thoughts took precedence over the outside world. I found that if I could keep going on a stream of thoughts, my mind couldn't find nor focus on outside voices. It was a reverse kind of meditation, I guess.

"Birdhouse In Your Soul" by They Might Be Giants was rounding out the songlist when I pulled up to the garage. I toyed with keeping the car out for a few days, maybe making a nightly drive part of my routine, then I thought better of it. I wouldn't have the energy to keep up with that kind of schedule. I was getting older, and besides, I had a feeling my time was being managed by someone else. I'm sure soon I would find myself wrapped up in some other plan- whatever that would turn out to be.

One thing about the city- the wildlife was a lot quieter here. My walk from the garage to the apartment had few voices calling out, and it gave me time to practice shutting them out. It also gave me time to decide that if I did ever have a superhero costume, it should be green. I didn't know why, but I figured it was earthy, and I looked good in green- something all superheroes should factor in when picking out an outfit. Not that I would ever wear a costume, but if I did. Just not spandex, anything but spandex.

Chapter 21

"Food, food," Uri said from the living room. I wasn't sure I was going to like waking up like this. It was a cloudy morning with a threatening feel to it- probably just the weather, but maybe I was developing 'Spidey-sense'. For all I knew, I could start growing hair or feathers all over. Speaking of Feathers and Fur, I wanted to check in on those confiscated birds at some point, maybe they had something to say.

Getting out of bed was always hard, but it was a Friday, so the future fun potential was looking good. I decided to have a little chat with Uri once I got ready for work. He was a youngin' and a perfect age to teach some basic behaviors and words. I thought I would start with the more important ones, since he clearly had 'food' down pat.

"Love," I said and petted his little head. "Love."

"Warm," he replied. Well, it was a start. I petted him some more and repeated the word, hoping it would catch on at some point, but for now, 'warm' was all he was giving me.

I wasn't sure where the day would take me, so I put ample food in with Uri and left a light on in the kitchen, in case he was afraid of the dark. Actually, it was more for me, as I wasn't a fan of stumbling into things when coming through the door. And after getting shot at a few times, well it made me feel a little safer.

My first stop was a training session at headquarters. Dr. Dubashi was expecting me, and I had a few questions for her regarding the implant. She was the one who created it, I figured she would be the one who could tweak it, perhaps even add that filter aspect to it. I headed out to the metro.

It was weird walking into headquarters without feeling like I was in trouble. Let's face it, the first time I was threatened, the second time I was almost dead in their 'hospital', and the third time I wanted someone to pay for the pain in my head. Yesterday's training session went alright, after all the yelling in the upstairs offices. I was hopeful that the training would go smoother than all that, especially since it was with Anoushka. She still made me speechless just thinking about her. There was just something about her.

She had given me a special pass card to get through security for these sessions. I made my way down to the basement lair thinking of different ways to modify the implant. A filter would be awesome- omit some of the 'food' requests- but a language translator would be great too. It would save me from looking up the foreign words on the internet- that was, if I could even spell them in the first place.

The elevator doors opened to an empty room. I was hesitant to step off and make myself comfortable if no one was there, but I had nowhere else to hang while waiting for her. I sat for a few minutes, then tried to see anything through the giant Plexiglas that took up half of the wall. My face was pressed against the glass in a futile attempt to peer through it when Dr. Dubashi walked in from a side room. She cleared her voice, startling me. I spun around and must have turned five shades of red.

"You're here, good. We can get started." She had a smirk on her face, making me feel just a tad bit idiotic. I sat in my seat without being able to reply so promptly.

"Did you have any experiences with the device since yesterday?"

I went into the whole debacle at the holding center, leaving out my complete meltdown. As I explained the turmoil in my head, the more vivid the experience became, and I found myself growing angry and frustrated again. I stopped just shy of outrage, and switched gears to the story of the harbor seal and catfish. It was always good to end on a lighter note, anyway, I thought. It made for a good segue to my idea of a filter. I wasn't quite sure how to word it or describe it, and not

181

being able to make eye contact with Anoushka as I spoke wasn't helping her understand. I just didn't think I could make words come out if I turned in her direction.

"Are you asking if the device itself can be modified from where it currently is located?"

"Yes, that's exactly it." I was glad she could put it into words, if I couldn't.

"I'm afraid that's not possible, Dr. Wake." She was so final and resolved in her answer, I wasn't sure if I could or should try to explain it further.

"So, there's nothing we can do? Reprogram it or something, I'm not sure how it works, but..."

"No, the implant is a fixed mechanical structure, it cannot be altered without removing it."

I felt a slight shock run through my body. There was no way I wanted them back in my brain mucking around. If they were going to go in again, it would be to get that thing out. I felt a little deflated. Maybe I was too optimistic coming in here, but I was so hopeful for answers.

"We can work on how you use the device. It all comes down to training your brain. Think of it like a new appendage: Sensory information is coming through haphazardly, and your brain needs to learn how to interpret it. You no longer feel the constant sensation of a sleeve on your arm, yet it is there. It's the same concept, only in language."

It was starting to make sense to me, but I still felt deflated. My way was so much easier! Now I had a lot more work ahead of me, and there was no way of knowing how long that would take. Still, the upside was that I had a lot more sessions with Anoushka, and she was growing on me.

"I can alter the lessons to work on filtering the information coming in first, if you'd like? We can start by having you just focus on one thing at a time, and let the voices- the ones that you think have less important subjects- fade to the background." I nodded, still lost in my thoughts of how it was all going to work. Suddenly my ideas of fun for the weekend were slipping away, and I could only see the longer road ahead of me. I felt silly, really, having expected something easier to be available, and now to be feeling sorry for myself because it wasn't. I was just going to have to suck it up.

My next stop was to the holding facility to check on the zoo animals. I needed to check on their progress and make sure their medical treatment plans were working. Martin was in charge of making sure things ran smoothly, and I was glad I had him as a partner.

"What's the word?" I felt in a better mood by the end of the training session, and was hoping the rest of the day would run smoothly, despite the gloomy feeling that it started out with.

"The word of the day is...stable." Martin didn't even look up.

"That's always a good word to start the day." I stared at him for a minute to see what his body language was saying. I couldn't tell what kind of mood he was in. He finally looked up and smiled.

"Yes, stable, steady, the same, constant, no change....in other words, a little boring. But I'll take it." He went back to filling out paperwork, just a routine day.

I grabbed the giraffe's chart- I figured it was as good a place as any to start. Gathering the necessary supplies, I told Martin to meet me when he got a chance, just in case I needed a hand. We spent a good amount of time re-bandaging and reassessing its condition, agreeing that it was coming along nicely. I didn't hear anything from the giraffe, bolstering my confidence in the control I was learning.

The Capuchins were next. For having been in a private zoo without much contact, they were surprisingly docile. No injuries were noted on them, just the thin body conditions, and they seemed to be taking to their diet well. They were on a plan to slowly gain weight, as a food frenzy would just wreak havoc on their systems. A few 'food' demands were slipping through my newly formed mental filter, making me wonder if I truly had some control or if I was getting tired already.

183

The lemurs were in a similar state. These guys were friendlier, and the trouble was keeping them from climbing all over us while examining them. Weights were coming up slowly, as desired. Well, as desired by us, not so much by the lemurs who were fervently looking for grapes and other treats I commonly carried in my pockets for after the exams. A few more 'food' demands were heard, but much less so than the previous day. I tried not to look conspicuous when responding to their communications- I couldn't let Martin know anything about it.

We continued on the rounds over the next hour and a half, ending on the tiger. Again, without tranquilizing him, the exam was merely a visual inspection, but the swelling from the tooth root abscess was coming down, and he managed to get some food down now that he could do some chewing. His stools were loose, but to be expected with the diet change and the new medication. I made a note to keep an eye on it, to make sure he wasn't losing too much fluid from his body. Stool samples were run on everyone, as a routine, ensuring intestinal parasites weren't causing some of the observed emaciation.

I let Martin head off, back to the stack of paperwork awaiting him. Pulling up a chair, I sat just outside the tiger cage, wanting to communicate with him. It would be the first time since the incident in his cage that I felt secure enough to go through the experience again, and I was eager to see how it went.

"How are you feeling?" I looked around nervously at first, in case someone overheard me, but it wasn't uncommon for me to talk to my patients. I concentrated just on his voice, trying to push the other voices to the background.

"Food." I looked around again and back at the tiger to make sure it was his voice.

"How are you?" I tried again.

"Food. Thank you." I jumped back a little in my chair. Focusing again on just him, he seemed to smile, or maybe it was just my imagination.

"You're welcome. I'm glad you're feeling better." I had to cut it short as a zoo worker, still on loan, walked by and smiled at me. That's as far into crazy town that I could let them think I was, so I nodded to the tiger and headed back to the desk where Martin was set up.

"I have to head out for a bit," I told Martin. "I want to see if I can check on the birds that were taken in by the FBI. I didn't really get a chance to check them all out when I was in that basement before all hell broke loose."

"Really? You don't think you'd get flashbacks? You're now on three attempts on your life- all shootings- in the last couple of weeks!"

"I think I can handle it, we'll see. I might not even get into the facility. STAFE forbade me from working on another sting operation with the FBI. They may not want to have anything to do with me." In the back of my mind I was wondering how I'd get through the security if that were to occur. I guess I'd wing it, if it came to that.

"OK, good luck. Let me know if you need back up. Martini, at your service!"

"Seriously, who really calls you that?" I grinned and patted him on the back as I headed out.

I had to use some old ties to get in to see the confiscated birds. I knew that the U.S. Fish and Wildlife were housing the birds taken in by the FBI- Jon had dropped that bit of information when he was driving me home after the sting operation. I had a connection at the Humane Society that had a connection at the USFW, and, well, my name got bandied about a bit. I was allowed clearance as a courtesy, claiming that my role in the operation had some loose ends to tie up. It would have been legitimate if I weren't taken off the case- I mean the paperwork alone would have taken days. But, oh well, I didn't have to participate in that end of things now.

A couple of employees were walking around, finishing up with the cleaning and feeding detail. I tried to find a quiet

185

corner to start the process, without looking too out of place. The usual 'food' was being said by so many voices that I wasn't sure if I was going to get anything meaningful. I was hoping a name or detail would come through to help Jon and the rest of his team find the man in charge of the smuggling, not to mention the dog fighting ring.

Focusing on just one voice, one that wasn't saying 'food' or 'comida', I heard something that was at least out of the ordinary. The voice was saying "perro". I wasn't sure of its meaning, so I started writing down any words that I heard as best that I could. Spelling would be an issue, but I could work on that later when I put it into the computer. Google was good at guessing what I meant in English, maybe it would come in handy with Spanish as well.

I heard 'canino', which I was pretty sure meant canine, but I needed much more if Jon was going to move forward on the bust. I concentrated again, but all the chit chat was just that-chit chat.

"Does anyone know any details about the people who took you from your families?" I had to look around again to make sure no one was listening. I didn't think I'd get a response, it was rather a long and complicated sentence. I tried again.

"Bad people who stole you. Names?" It was an awkward attempt, even I felt stupid saying it, but if it got me anything I would be grateful. Looking around again, "Name of person who took you?"

I waited somewhat impatiently, as I felt like I didn't have a whole lot of time to spend there. I was sure one of the security agents would be coming around sooner than later. I tried to focus on an answer.

"Espinoza." It came through the noise a little fuzzy, but clear enough to hear it. I followed that voice as best I could to whoever was telling me that.

"Espinoza? Anything else?" I would have been locked up for sure if anyone was watching me.

"Espinoza. Espinoza, Mateo.....Mateo Espinoza." The bird looked proud of himself, as well he should. I shoveled on the praise and asked for anything else he could remember. The bird next to him noticed what was going on and jumped into the conversation.

"Mateo. Perro. Pelea de perros. Pelea de perros." I scribbled it down.

"Envio. Veinticinco. Veinticinco envio," the first bird offered up. I couldn't tell if they were both happy to help, or if they were now in competition with each other to share more details. Either way, I gladly welcomed all information offered.

"Domingo...Domingo...Domingo..." They were now arguing, and it was instigating others to join in the discussion- well, quarrel by now. I felt the thin wall holding back the other voices come crashing down. It was a jarring clamor of discord in my head. I felt woozy, and I knew I had to get out of there before I collapsed again.

I clung to the wall as I made my way back to the door. The security guard looked up and was about to say something, so I quickly said that I got a call from headquarters and had to rush out. I wasn't sure how I looked at that moment, but if I looked anything like I felt, then I was lucky to make it out of there without someone calling an ambulance for me.

I made it out the building to a bench down the street before I had to stop and collect myself. These events were becoming unbearable, and if I hadn't made any progress in the training I'd be clawing at my head to dig the device out myself. I caught my breath, and although my head was pounding, I was able to make it back to the metro and head home. I think I had all I could take for today.

Back at my apartment, I was happy to find little Uri napping. I wasn't up for even the smallest conversation right now. I rummaged through the cabinet to find the ibuprofen (why didn't I just keep it on the counter?), and swallowed a couple with a can of seltzer. A glass of wine would be welcomed right now, but not with the NSAID, and not before I translated these scribbles into something usable.

I turned on the computer and rubbed my temples while I waited for it to boot up. My notes didn't make sense to me, but I trusted that the Spanish-English dictionary online would assist with that. I assumed that Mateo was a name, probably

187

the first name of Espinoza? But the other words were alien to me. One by one I entered what I could for spellings, and got Domingo right on the first try, it meant Sunday. Envio took a couple of tries but came out to mean shipment, or close to that at least. Pelea de perros took a while, but it eventually came out to be dogfight. Veinticinco was the hard one. It took several spellings to get Google to spit out twenty-fifth, as in a date.

The birds had Mateo Espinoza together, and dogfight with dog, then shipment with the twenty-fifth. The word Sunday was last, so as far as I could decipher it all, some type of shipment was coming in on Sunday the twenty-fifth, whether it had anything to do with dog fighting, I didn't know for sure. They could have just been connecting Mateo Espinoza with dog fighting and the shipment. Maybe they were all spoken of in front of the birds at one time. Any case, Sunday the twenty-fifth was the day after tomorrow, and I had to tell Jon about it.

I reached for my phone, but stopped when I realized that I couldn't tell him how I found out the information. He had no idea about the implant, and I couldn't tell him. How would I get the information to him without telling him how? I had a wire on me during the sting, so it couldn't be anything anyone said to me. Something I read while at the Feathers and Fur? No, they would have found it on the scene. The only plausible way that I could come up with was that I overheard it in the stairwell. It was too faint to get picked up on the microphone, and I just remembered it now. It was a doozy of a story, but it would have to work.

Chapter 22

It was a slow start for a Saturday. Normally I would be up and out and about doing errands- things that I couldn't get done during the work week. But today I still had to train and check in on the zoo animals, so subconsciously, I felt the need to linger in bed longer than necessary.

Uri was in his usual state of cuteness, and I spent a little time trying to teach him the word and concept of love. He'd catch on, I was sure of it. Grocery shopping had to be somewhere on the list today, I told myself as I looked through the bare cupboards and mostly empty fridge for something to eat. "Coffee it is!" I said out loud.

As soon as I got off the metro, I hit a bagel shop in the L'Enfant Station area before heading over to headquarters for training. I slowed down before getting to the building. I wanted to finish breakfast, but I was also growing hesitant to continue these practice sessions. The last one went better than the first, but it was exhausting. Dr. Dubashi- Anoushka- instilled fear in me. Not as much as Dr. Aquene did, but enough to make me feel uneasy. It was bad enough that I got caught up in the sound of her accent, but sometimes I would completely miss what she said, leaving me looking (and feeling) like a moron.

Still, it had to be done, or so they said. I didn't want to think what would happen if I objected. I took the elevator down to the lair- as I referred to it in my head- and plopped down in the chair waiting for the doctor to make her entrance. She arrived through the side door, and away we went. At the end of the session I asked if we were going to work on other species, not that the pinnipeds on the other side of the glass were not great conversationalists, but I wondered how much variation was going to occur with different animals. I already had experience with birds, lemurs, Capuchins, tigers, fish, as well as seals and dolphins, and they all had their different degrees of verbal skills- not to mention language barriers! Anoushka wanted to stay in her laboratory, under fixed conditions, to measure my progress. That was fine, I supposed, but I was starting to feel more and more like a lab animal- just an experiment to my employers.

I left feeling kind of used, but happy for the small steps of progress I was making in training at the same time. A mixed bag of emotions, you'd think I would be used to that by now. I tried to shake it off and move on to the next thing- taking care of the zoo animals. At least their improvements could be seen and measured- that was enough to put a smile back on my face.

I once again caught the metro and walked the remaining distance to the holding area. I was glad that it was a Saturday, and once I got through the clan here, I had the afternoon to myself. I was also glad that it was a nice day, and I didn't have to hoof it all over town in the rain. I could smell the musky scent of the animal collection as I approached.

Martin was there and gave me the eye when I walked in. I think he was getting tired of being the first on scene. I smiled trying to diffuse and harsh feelings and asked how things were going. He half smiled, nodded, and then handed me the giraffe chart. I guess we were going to plow through the cases right off the bat. All the better to get out of there and on with our days.

"Did you have a rough night?" I tried to get him talking.

"You could say that. Ricky, the drummer I told you about? I was out watching his band last night. There's only so much 80's music a person can take. I really don't know how he does it....without killing someone." Martin looked exhausted, and I wasn't sure if he was tired of the band or of the drummer.

"Maybe you guys should get together when he's not working, you know like, away from the band?" I knew that he really didn't like me butting in to his personal life, but I was just trying to be helpful.

"Ya, well, he works all weekend, and I don't have time during the week to do much. I guess that's what you get when you date a musician."

I agreed, having dated a guitarist once myself, albeit quite a while ago, so I dropped the subject. We worked on the bandages in relative silence- at least as far as human communications went. The rest of the crowd had quite a bit to say. I mindlessly changed the dressings while I practiced blocking out the extraneous voices. Martin didn't say anything until we had moved on to the Capuchins.

"So have you heard from Jon, the FBI guy?" He said in a sassy fashion.

"As a matter of fact, I spoke with Jon, the FBI guy last night. I remembered some information that I overheard during the sting, and I wanted to make sure he knew about it. It sounded kind of important." I really wanted to tell him all about what was going on, but having been sworn to secrecy, with who-knows-what as a consequence, I kept the details to myself.

"Ooooh, sooooooo, are you going to see him again?"

"Maybe, I don't know. I would imagine. The case still hasn't been wrapped up, and there are a lot of details to go over. We hadn't set anything up yet, if that's what you're asking." I felt my cheeks warm with blush.

"Well, I think you ought to get on that pronto. I mean, on the setting things up thing." He smiled and blushed a bit himself with that comment.

We finished the rounds making innuendos and various snide comments to each other. Martin was definitely growing on me like a brother. It was good to have someone around that felt like family. I helped him fill out the paperwork for the day so we could both get out of there and on with our weekends.

Martin gave me a lift back to my apartment and came in for a few minutes to say hello to Uri. The little conure seemed to remember him and proceeded to cuddle and coo in his arms.

Maybe the bird should live with him, I thought, but then selfishly decided that I liked having him around. Besides, Martin could visit whenever he wanted- it wasn't like I was keeping them apart.

After Martin left, I went through my email and social media- bored with the results as usual. I toyed around a bit online, looking for something to do for the rest of the weekend, and oh yes, and I had to remember to go to the store. The phone rang, distracting me from my distractions. It was Jon.

"I just wanted to inform you of our plan. My partner and I have set up another sting, this time at the shipping yard. We think they are expecting a delivery from Mexico, probably drugs. There will be a few teams in on this one. It's all set up for Sunday, just like you said you overheard in the stairwell."

"What can I do? I want to help take them down." I really did want to take out those animal abusers.

"No, sorry, you can't be part of this. It's much too dangerous. We almost lost you the last time, and, well, your employer said it was out of the question. You'll have to sit this one out." We spoke about a few more things, and then we said our good byes. I was mad at STAFE again for forbidding me from participating in the sting, as if they had control over my life. Then I was mad because they DID have control over my life, my body, my brain. I was mad because I was worried for Jon and the rest of the FBI. The smugglers weren't the most stable people I had ever seen, and that threatening feeling from the other day was back and lingering around like the stink of day-old fish. Speaking of fish, it seemed like an excellent time for a certain road trip repeat. I gathered up my phone, some cash- what little of it I had around- and headed for the garage.

I managed to stop at a grocery store along the way as I headed out of town. I only purchased items that were not frozen or refrigerated, as I had no idea when I'd make it back to the apartment. At least I had food for the trip, which was the most important thing at that moment. I was sure come Monday morning, I'd be kicking myself for lack of variety of eating choices, but that was a couple of days away.

"Riders On The Storm" by The Doors was playing, the sky was already darkening, and I was heading out to the edge of the land. The trip seemed shorter this time. Whether it was my mood or the fact that I had done it before and knew where I was going, I wasn't sure, but it didn't matter. I was on a mission to let go of the week and embrace the weekend. And I was secretly hoping I could save another life- be the superhero that I couldn't tell anyone about.

It was a little bit more than a half moon and a beautiful clear night sky when I found my way back to the cove. I sat on the same rock as before, waiting to hear the critters of the night start in with their demands and requests. I had no pizza to offer this time, just a mostly eaten bag of chips, but I was happy to share it with whoever came along first. To my dismay, it was a skunk. Oh boy, I said in a quiet voice, trying my best not to provoke it. It was asking for food, as the rest of them always did, so I obliged. Sprinkling what was left of the bag a good distance from the rock- I didn't want to take any chances with "accidental" discharges- the skunk happily chowed down on the remnants and moved on.

I heard some peepers chatting away about looking for mates, and I let them have that conversation by themselves. No raccoons were hanging around today, and even the owl- looking for food, of course- was a good distance away. I felt alone, maybe the first time since the implant, really, and I wasn't sure I liked it or not. Maybe I was getting used to having the chatter in my head. I wasn't too sure I would go so far as to say that I liked having the chatter, just that I noticed it when it wasn't there.

I undressed and slipped into the coolish water, taking my time to acclimate to the temperature and the almost quiet of the cove. After a few minutes, I went under. The moonlight penetrated a little deeper than it did the other night, possibly from the lack of any clouds, and I could get a better look at the depth of the cove's water. It was considerably deeper than I had imagined, making me glad I hadn't realized it when I was out in the middle of the open water when the seal moved on.

"Hello? Does anyone need help tonight?" I said looking around, but only saw a few small fish swim by.

"Hello? Anyone?" No one answered. I felt dismayed. Surely someone would at least say hi. Maybe they all had hot dates on this Saturday night. I went up for air and swam around for a while. If I couldn't play superhero, at least I could get some relaxing 'spa' time in.

I was about to throw in the towel when I felt something swim past me. I submerged and took a look around. A familiar face popped up out of seemingly nowhere, surprising me. It was the harbor seal from Thursday night. It swam in circles around me, with no particular urgency.

"Hello! How is everything tonight?" Maybe it had something for me to help with.

"Hello! Hello!" At least it was in a good mood. "Bad stuff." It said and swam over to a mass of debris deeper than I wanted to dive down to.

"Bad stuff? You mean trash? Yes, it's bad stuff, I agree."

The seal swam around and repeated it a few times. I'm not sure what it wanted me to do about it, so I finally gave in and dove down to the pile of rubbish. I attempted to grab it and pull it up to the surface with the intent of removing it from the water, but it was far too heavy, and intertwined with too many rocks and barnacles.

"I'm sorry, but I can't move it. Did it hurt you or someone? Did someone get tangled in it, too?"

"Bad stuff. Bad stuff everywhere." I couldn't help it, but I felt like the seal was blaming me for it. I tried to explain that some bad people did bad things, and as a result, bad stuff ends up where it shouldn't. I'm not sure how much of it was understood. It circled around me a few more times, saying 'hello' and then swam off. Maybe that was its way of saying it knew it wasn't my fault, but it still didn't feel good.

I headed back to my car feeling more like a villain than a superhero. This road trip wasn't turning out like I had intended. I sat in my car for a few minutes, just to think.

Starting up the vehicle, I immediately turned the radio off. I didn't want any sound right now, I was feeling bad and it was starting to turn into a pity party. I drove slowly up the street heading home. The car seemed off somehow. It wasn't driving smoothly- it felt strange- so I pulled over. Getting out, I walked around it to look for anything obvious, and there it was.

I had a flat tire. Of course I did. Why wouldn't I? I went through the stages of pity and rage, finally landing on resolution. There was no spare to be found, so I reached for my phone. Certainly AAA could get me out of this. No signal. I took a deep breath. Pity and rage didn't help a minute ago, it wasn't going to help now. I locked up the car and headed out on foot in the direction of Route 2. At some point I'd get service, right?

Several miles up the road I heard a voice. Not now, I thought, I didn't have the time or patience to deal with that. It kept coming through the haze, and became clear as day, "help!"

Running in the direction of the voice, I headed through the woods to my left. I stumbled over several branches, almost taking one to the face, and then stopping to listen again. As best I could tell, I was running in the direction of Route 2, just through the forest instead of on pavement. The voice was closer. Again picking up the pace, I did my best to locate the source. I slowed as I was getting closer, it was coming from a low to the ground source. Then I found it.

It was a deer, and it looked like it was hit by a car. I could see blood coming from the corner of her mouth. She appeared to have a flail chest- when there was some type of crushing injury to the chest wall causing the ribs to break. That section of the chest wall goes inward when the deer take a breath in and outward when it exhales- the opposite of what it normally should do and opposite of what the rest of the ribcage was doing. I didn't have any medical equipment with me, and I had no real way to stabilize the flail chest, so I was left with applying pressure to it to keep it from causing more damage to the lung tissue by moving. The poor deer was in obvious pain and there was nothing I could do to alleviate it. I

195

thought of running for help, maybe getting to the road and flagging down a police officer. At the very least the officer could shoot it to put it out of its misery, but the deer answered that thought.

"No, stay." That was what she said. I wished she didn't, I pleaded for anything else. I looked at my phone, maybe there was service here, but there wasn't and the battery was getting low. She kept saying, "stay". So I did. I stayed with her, knowing that there was nothing I could do, knowing that she was in excruciating pain, knowing that she was going to die. I stayed.

It was just after dawn when she finally took her last breath. She was markedly too tired to say much during the hours that I sat with her leading up to that point. I didn't even have a way to bury her, making me feel useless once again. I could hear traffic not far off and assumed it was the road that I was originally headed for. I hiked my way out following the noise.

Flagging down an officer, I told him only about the flat tire, leaving out the details of the night, of the poor injured deer. He was kind enough to call triple A for me, and gave me a ride back to my car. There I sat and waited, trying not to listen, trying not to think. I had had enough of both.

I was back on the road several hours later, heading directly home. My phone was dead, so I couldn't call in to Martin to let him know I wouldn't be in any time soon to do a run through with the zoo animals. It was Sunday, so it didn't really matter, I supposed. I wasn't changing any medical directives, and any bandages Martin could handle alone. The drive home was a long one.

It was some time after two when I made it through my apartment door. Uri was mad, and hungry- so was I. I plugged in the phone after throwing what groceries that I hadn't eaten yet into the kitchen. Feeding Uri was next.

"Aaaah, what a great weekend it was- not. I hope you had some fun while I was out. I can't begin to tell you what went wrong since I saw you last." Uri just kept saying 'food' in between bites, and I kept thinking about sleep. Then the phone rang.

It was Jon's partner- there were complications with the sting. Jon was dead.

Chapter 23

Monday morning came and I was still in bed. I hadn't moved since I got the news yesterday. What was there to do? I couldn't eat, I couldn't work, and even though I spent most of the last sixteen hours in bed, I couldn't sleep. I had to call Martin, for a few reasons. He needed to know about my car issues and why I wasn't at the holding facility yesterday or this morning, and I now needed to tell him about Jon. It was hard to get the words out. Still, I went through the motions, surprising myself that I could relate the news with a stoic constitution, almost like I was dead as well. Martin said he'd cover for me at the facility, there really wasn't much to be done, anyway, and offered to stop by later. I wasn't in the mood for company.

Why did I tell Jon about the shipment? I shouldn't have even had that information. It was my fault that he was dead, and it was the fault of this stupid implant! I wasn't saving too many lives, but there were more than enough deaths surrounding me. I scratched at my head in a weak attempt to dig out the foreign object. I was crying again, but the tears were no longer flowing. I felt empty, like too many things had been taken away from me without my consent. I wasn't sure how much of this was about Jon, the deer from last night, or my current situation. Maybe it was all crumbling down around me.

The last thing that I wanted was to go to headquarters. I was expected to show up- as what was now usual- for morning training with Dr. Dubashi. There was no way that was happening today! They were the reason that everything was like this to begin with. In fact, maybe I was never going to go back there again. What would they do about it anyway? Sure they made veiled threats on my life before. But right at that moment, I didn't really care.

A road trip might be needed again. Back to the cove? That would probably only depress me more. I would want to find something to assist, to be the superhero again, but I was sure the opportunities would be lacking. Not that that would be a bad thing in general, it would be a good day if everyone and everything were copacetic. But it would be deflating for my ego that was in desperate need of a boost, to say the least.

I asked Uri what he thought. Guess what he said? Yup, 'food'. I took him out of his cage and snuggled with him a bit while I fed him. Even if he couldn't speak yet, he could be quite a comfort. "Warm, warm," he said while he nuzzled my neck. I agreed. We sat for a while on the sofa in the silence, for which I was grateful. I had no patience for the buzz of a thousand voices, each with their own demands. Somehow, everything was quiet and still. Then the phone rang.

"Dr. Wake?" It was Jaffey. I was so not in the mood.

"Jaffey, this really isn't a good time. What can I help you with?" I knew he wouldn't be calling unless it was something important, but if he was calling about blowing off training, I wasn't going to put up with it.

"Sorry to hear that. I, we, need your help again, I'm afraid. We are going to need your presence here. There's a flight..."

"Do you really need me there, or is this going to be like last time, and the first time, come to think of it. I'm not really in the mood for tough love and conviction, Jaffey. What is it that you 'need' me to do?" I could hear the disdain in my tone, and I felt bad. He wasn't the only one responsible for the implant and the resulting situation. But he was a part of it, and I didn't even know how much of a part. The leaving me out of the loop was also grating on my last nerve.

"You sound irritated. Has something happened? I heard training sessions were going well?"

I sighed, not wanting to have to explain once more what happened, so I gave him the short version. It was enough to

199

get my point across. Still, I felt bad and apologized for my mood. "What is it that you need me for?"

"It's Nkiru again, I'm afraid. New poachers have come around and tracked her to the Tanzanian border. There has been the biggest decline in elephant populations in Tanzania compared to other countries, and I'm worried that they'll be attacked by more than one group if they stay."

"What am I supposed to do about it? I'm a forensic veterinarian, I helped you track down where the poaching was coming from, but from there it's your specialty." I was frustrated and exhausted, and honestly couldn't see what he wanted me to do about yet another tragedy.

"Well, my dear Dr. Wake, this is precisely the reason why we introduced you to our technology, so to speak. We need you to communicate with Nkiru and her family, let them know the dangers they are approaching. We need to set up a plan to keep them safe."

I didn't really get it. I could hear thoughts of other animals, sometimes in several other languages, but I didn't have any special power to tell them anything. That part was the same, or so I thought. Voicing my concerns to Jaffey, he went on as if I was the one who didn't make any sense. It would be simple to say that maybe he knew something that I didn't. Clearly he knew a whole lot more that was being kept from me, and I was left to trust that this was the next step in my transformation. Well, why not, the present stage of metamorphosis wasn't proving to be the brilliant status that it had started out being. I reluctantly agreed to go.

Calling Martin back to let him know of the sudden change in plans, I offered him up Uri. Not so much as a demand for pet sitting, but as a friend for him. I knew how much the two of them got along, and I was feeling a little guilty for keeping them apart- just a little. Martin came by that afternoon, after rounds with the zoo critters, to pick up Uri and all his belongings. For a little bird new to the world, he was accumulating quite the load of goods. I was going to miss Uri, not just for the duration of the trip, but I wasn't deceiving myself about his long term residence. Uri was going to be

Martin's buddy from now on, I could tell. One more heartache to plague my mind on the long trip ahead.

The flight was long, as usual, but at least I managed to get some sleep. It wasn't enough, mind you, to deal with the emotions of the past couple of days, and certainly not enough to get me through what I was anticipating ahead, but it was better than nothing. Marcus met me at the Jomo Kenyatta International Airport, and we set out south to the border. Marcus was never much of a talker, and I could anticipate the answer to any question I had ever asked him- making conversation mute, literally. So I took in the scenery as we were jostled around on the uneven terrain.

Marcus pulled over along a generic looking section, and I wondered how he could tell where we were. Everything was covered in sand, a desert sprawling outward, with no visible ends or demarcations. We went off the road for a while, heading southeast, as far as I could tell, and I wasn't sure which country we had ended up in. Jaffey was there, at our stopping point, and offered me a hand out of the truck. There was no large tent, picnic table, or second vehicle, just a few rocks circled around under one of the only trees in the area. Whatever was going down, there apparently weren't going to be witnesses, and it made me nervous.

Marcus grabbed something out of the back of the truck, and I could only assume it was a weapon of some sort, he was quite proficient with implements of destruction. Jaffey and I headed for the rocks. Niceties aside, he started in with his concerns for the herd. Where Nkiru and her family were, it was questionable who had jurisdiction. Things were bad enough inside the lines when it came to rulings against poachers, and now it could all end up being awash in red tape. My level of nervousness went up another notch. I was fearful of taking another life, I had already killed once, and I had no desire to repeat such a horrific act. I could tolerate being the guinea pig, being the interpreter- for whatever it was worth-

201

but there was no way I was ready, willing, or able to murder again. I made it known to Jaffey what my intentions and reservations were, and he wasted no time mollifying my worries. How much trust did I have in this man?

However much it was, it was lessening by the minute. I no more believed that he would keep me safe, keep me from having to shoot another human being than I believed that he was on my side. He was one of them, one of the STAFE originals- or so I thought. He at least was far enough on the inside to know about the implant, and could have even suggested it when I was shot out here- out here with him to take care of me. It was high time we had a little discussion about this piece of technology in my head.

"How do you see this playing out? What exactly is my role, given this 'gift', as the doctors at headquarters call it? Am I supposed to just chit chat with them about where it's safe to go and they're supposed to know what I'm saying?" I wanted details, for once in this relationship.

"You have a lot of anger, I understand. We invaded your body without your knowledge..."

"Without my consent," I interjected.

"Without your consent, and now we are asking you to work with us, after what we did. I understand. But what you don't understand it the urgency under which we work. We have been doing this for many years, long before STAFE was created. This is a turning point- at least we hope it is. And you are the one that now holds the key. You are the one that can create a shift in the dynamics, a turn for the greater good."

I was lost in his rhetoric, it meant nothing to me. I wasn't on his journey- why was I to fight his fight? It didn't feel fair. It didn't feel like it should be my calling. "Why me? Was this planned from the beginning? Was I hired for this purpose, or was it an opportunity that arose when I was shot? I want to know how far back my involvement was decided. What choices do I have now, now that you all made me whatever it is that I am?"

"Dr. Wake, Alex, if I may, the device in your brain was put there because the opportunity presented itself, it wasn't planned, per se.   As for your involvement with the organization, well, that's another story to be told to you by someone else. It's not mine to tell."

I wanted to punch him in the face. Not his story to tell, my ass. He could tell me everything right now if he wanted to, but he didn't, and that pissed me off. My trust in Jaffey just plummeted to rock bottom. Part of me wanted to get up and walk back to the airport right then and there. But of course, there was the little thing of the desert being a desert and me being miles from my destination, so I thought better of it.

"I know it's frustrating," he continued, "but it's really for the best if you find out the rest of the story when you get back. Right now I need you focused on the task at hand. I need you focused on Nkiru and her herd. Their safety is the important issue. Don't you agree?"

Yup, wanted to hit him. Throwing the elephant's safety in my face, expecting my cooperation after all this- it was an insult, to say the least. I wondered where Marcus was, if I could get him to just take me back to where he picked me up earlier today.

"I would do this only for Nkiru and her family, but not for you. You have done nothing but lie and manipulate me, you deserve nothing from me." I couldn't believe I was caving in, but once a sucker, always a sucker. I couldn't leave knowing there was something that I could have done to help.

He looked at me apprehensively, as if judging if I were stable enough to continue. To be honest, I didn't know if I was, either, but we pressed on, detailing how we would cut off the herd before nightfall, herd them to an alternate course, and set up an ambush for the poachers. We were working on shaky ground, not just from a political and legal perspective, but these were some of the same poachers that Jaffey and Marcus crossed paths with before- so Jaffey thinks anyway- and they could know some of their tactics.

"Now explain to me how this device is supposed to help talk to the elephants. So far in training, we had only worked on listening, are you telling me it's somehow a two-way device?"

"In a way, yes. It's not something you need to train for, though. From what I understand- and I didn't create the thing, Dr. Dubashi did- she said that it amplifies thought patterns. So in a way, certain animals, not all, but certain ones can pick up on your thoughts. All you have to do is think, maybe a lot of thinking, but they should catch on to what you are trying to communicate. Have you not found this to be true yet? Maybe you haven't spent much time with the right species..."

I thought back to the incident in the tiger cage. Could he tell what I was thinking? He certainly knew that I was only there to help, but I always thought most animals could pick up on that.

"Anyway, that's the plan. Your job is to get them off their track. We think that the poachers can tell where the herd will end up by nightfall through estimating their route and direction. The rest will be up to Marcus and me. I would prefer it if you didn't arm yourself like you did last time." He sounded irked, like it was my fault the poachers had shot at us. I wanted revenge, yes, but I really didn't want to take another life.

"I would prefer it if I didn't have to arm myself, as well." With that, I got up and walked around. It would be dark soon, and we would need to be in motion before long.

Marcus came back with some small furry animal that he intended on cooking up, but I was far too anxious to eat. I watched the two of them partake, and wondered why we go to such lengths to protect one animal and have no issue with taking the life of another. The circle of life, part of the food chain- maybe it was all intent and need. All I could focus on was getting this night over with. As much as I wanted to get away from my life in DC, I wanted back in.

We headed out about an hour later. We were still a ways out from where we needed to be to intercede. Once we stopped, Marcus was up and gone. Jaffey held back until the herd was spotted, then left me to work out the details on my own. I had no idea how to do what was expected of me, so I just improvised.

I stood outside the truck and thought hard about shifting the pathway of the oncoming animals. They didn't respond. I tried again, and again, imagining all different scenarios that would result in the changing of their course. Frustrated and panicked, I headed right toward them, knowing it was a stupid move- you don't confront wild animals no matter what your intent was. I thought over and over to switch directions, until finally I said it out loud, "You have to go that way, the poachers are coming to kill you!"

Nkiru turned her head and looked directly at me and trumpeted. I was too scared to focus on what she said, only on what I was trying to tell her. "You have to go that way, away from the poachers!" And she trumpeted in response again. That time I caught it: She said, "Thank you."

I watched her lead the clan off to the north, back in the direction of the preserve, and it left me speechless. It was several minutes later, when the herd was a mere cloud in the distance, that I heard a shot ring out. It came from the same direction where I had seen Marcus head off when we first arrived. I didn't know all the details of their plan, I'm not sure I wanted to, but I was worried for Marcus's safety. Then I realized that we didn't have an exit plan. How was I to know if they were all right? I quickly ran back to the truck and waited behind it for someone to arrive, not knowing who it would be.

Chapter 24

Perhaps a gun would have been a good idea- not for offense but for defense. I didn't know who would be showing up. The truck was a good size, but it was apparently lacking any other weapons- a first, I think, for Marcus. Was that for my benefit? I heard footsteps coming, and could barely make out a figure. I hunkered down behind the truck, waiting for a better look. The face started to take shape in the minimal moonlight out tonight. It was an African man, perhaps in his teens. I thought they said the poachers weren't the same as last time, or were they all young? Maybe the poachers recruited another family member for this hunt, or maybe it was another group entirely out to illegally obtain ivory. Any fashion, I was in trouble.

As the person approached, a second body appeared from behind him. It was Marcus! He had a gun to the back of the pilferer, and was marching him back to the vehicle. I was surprised, I just assumed that he would have killed anyone he came across. I hesitated to step out from behind the truck into the open, but then I had no choice as they came closer. I called out to him, to ask if he was hurt at all. He gave a grunt leading me to believe that he was fine. I looked around for Jaffey.

Marcus was putting our guest into restraints and pushing him into the back of the truck when Jaffey came out of the darkness. He too was escorting a young male in our direction. I wondered what the plan was from there. This was new territory. Jaffey did the same to his prisoner as Marcus, and then proceeded to get into the front seat of the vehicle. I followed suit, not knowing what the game plan was. I got into the back seat, just in front of the captives. Marcus started up the vehicle and we headed back to where we were when I first arrived.

"So, what's next?" I was confused.

"I'm not exactly sure. I guess we'll find out," Jaffey replied and turned back around. That was all that was said for the whole ride. Maybe they really didn't have a plan, but it was more likely that they did and weren't sharing it with me. All I wanted to do was go home.

We pulled out a couple of tents from the truck when we reached the circle of rocks and made camp under the lonely tree. All four men stayed in the bigger tent, while I had a pup tent to myself. A sleeping bag would have been nice, but I guess you can't have everything. I imagined that the men weren't going to get much sleep that night- keeping one eye open on each other would get in the way of that. I wasn't sure I would get much shut eye, myself.

The next morning came, and apparently I was more tired than I had thought. I awoke to the sun coming up, and remembering where I was, I tried to listen for any voices or noises coming from the other tent or around me. Hearing nothing, I opened up the flap to find their tent gone, along with the truck. Did they leave me here? I couldn't believe that! I thought they must be nearby, perhaps finding food or something. I packed up the tent and waited. So many scenarios went through my head. But I kept coming back to STAFE saying to Jon that I was too important to them to be used in another sting operation, so I figured I was too important to just be left here in the middle of the desert- which brought me back to thinking about Jon.

Waiting turned fear into anger, and I decided I should walk it off. I had everything circling back in my head about Jon, the deer, the seal, Uri and the confiscated birds, the tiger, and most of all, this implant. At first, I tried to keep a mental note as to where I was and where I was headed, because the last thing I

207

needed was to be lost, but then I was too preoccupied and lost track of everything. I came across another clump of trees and wondered why we didn't camp there. It seemed much more protected. I sat down for a minute to rest, and took a frugal swig of water.

I had no way of knowing what time it was, save for looking at the sky, and right now the sun was much too bright to attempt that. I guesstimated it was only a few hours after sunrise, plenty of daylight to make my way back to the campsite, if for no other reason than using the tent again. I decided that if they left me out here for any longer than the day that I would try to hike back to the road, if I could find it, and hitch back to the airport. Not the safest thing for a woman to be doing, but if I had no other choice then that would be the plan. Then, of course, I would have to hunt down Jaffey and murder him. Maybe that's why they didn't want me to have a gun!

Through the din and buzzing of my ears, I could make out some sort of bubbling sound. I stood up and followed my ears. Only yards from where I had sat was a small brook, seemingly appearing out of nowhere. I certainly wasn't delirious and seeing a mirage, this was some sort of seasonal or transient water source. I sat down next to it, putting my feet in to cool off. The next thing I knew, the voices were back in my head. I looked around expecting to see a herd of animals with issues to discuss, but I found none. I waited.

One by one, a herd of kudu emerged from among the sparse trees. They approached slowly, not knowing what to expect from me. I sat quietly and made polite conversation. Soon they were gathered all around.

"Safe?" One had said. I replied that as far as I knew, it was safe. Many others followed suit in questioning the dangers around.

"Who are you hiding from?" I knew they were the dinner of choice for lions and leopards and anything fast enough to catch them.

"Fast cats," was the collective answer, and I felt sorry for their situation. I wasn't sure what they wanted from me, but we soon fell into an awkward conversation about predator and prey animals. I was considered one of the former, and their trust issues were well founded.

They asked why I was there, who I was hunting, and I tried to explain. At first I told them that I wasn't hunting anyone, I was waiting for others to come and take me away. But then we went into the whole poacher thing. They were curious as to why I wasn't hunting animals as well, so I took the time to explain how some of us were different. Why not, what else was I going to do while stuck in the middle of the desert?

I went on about the misadventures of the last two times I had visited the area and about Nkiru and her herd. They knew her, in fact, and had recently seen them. It felt like a long conversation, but there were many times of quiet contemplation, just gazing at each other. I think we were all amazed and taken aback a little by this most odd situation. I asked if there was anything that they wanted or needed me to do for them, but they had no urgencies, no requests. Then they asked the same of me. Surprised, I answered yes, only two. One was to stay safe, and the second was to talk with the other prey animals, set up a sort of communication line between the species, if possible. If they had the strength of many, they had a better chance at surviving, especially when it came to poachers. If you see humans with guns, tell another and so on. It might save a life, who in turn might save your life someday. I'm not sure they grasped the concept, but they agreed. Couldn't hurt, right?

I stood up and walked with them to the edge of the clump of trees, wondering what direction I had come in from. Understanding my dilemma, they pointed me to where I had pictured I came from. Could they see the pictures in my head, or was it somehow translated into words that they could understand? I had so many questions, and no one to give me answers, if there were any to give. I was the first with this implant, after all, or at least that's what they told me. For all I knew, they could have implanted hundreds of them, plotting some take over. I laughed to myself, but when I looked up, the kudu were staring at me. I could only tell them that I had no idea what was going on, I was in the dark. Maybe I was being paranoid, but it felt like they knew something that I didn't, giving a snicker as they headed back into the safety of the trees.

I had made it back to the campsite with still no sign of Jaffey or Marcus. Sitting on one of the rocks, I had another small sip of water, knowing that if necessary, there was a water source not too far away. Having conversations with animals was cool, I had to admit, but it was taxing. Maybe it will become easier, less straining, as I got used to it. But for now, it was a pain in my head. Was this really a 'gift'? I still had thoughts of it being a curse. Jon would still be alive if I hadn't given him the information. That deer would still be dead, and there were so many things I felt helpless about. How was knowing about more things that I couldn't fix going to help?

I heard them before I saw them, but from behind me came Nkiru and a few of her herd mates. I swung around quickly to ensure there were no poachers in pursuit before I said anything to them. Nkiru patted me on the head with her trunk. I didn't know how to take that.

"Hi, nice to see you again. Glad you are OK." I didn't know what else to say. They were majestic beasts, so quiet and almost graceful for their size.

"Hello, Alex. We have been waiting for your return." She knew my name! I was astounded, blown away by the idea.

"You were? How do you know who I am?"

"Your people have been out here for many years trying to help us, help my family. We have been waiting for you."

"Why me?" I was confused once again- more of my natural state of late- and I wondered what they were waiting for me to do.

"You are the one. The one we waited for, the one they promised us would come." Now I was scared. What did they expect from me? Once again I had more questions, and everyone around me seemed to know more than I did.

"Who promised you what? What am I to do for you?" I must have given off the air of sadness, because Nkiru reached out with her trunk again, patting me on the back. She went on to describe the interactions she has had with other species and other people from the organization who had come out here over the years, even before STAFE was started, and some of what they had promised they would do.

Apparently, this implant, now residing in my brain, had been in the works for many years. It was part of a plan to create a network, much like what I had just suggested to the herd of kudu. She kept saying that the first step was the communication network, but didn't know anything beyond that. I replied to them that they knew more than I was told so far.

We agreed to work together, to start on the network now, regardless of what the others might be planning. There really was no time to waste. The rest of the herd gathered around, and we started putting together the backbone of our communication tree. The kudu were to tell the other animals of prey- for they certainly couldn't have conversations with the predators- and the elephants were to attempt to let the leopards in on the plan. The leopards would have to tell the lions, and so on. Everyone was going to have to do their part if this was going to work.

I told them that I wouldn't be around a whole lot, but I could come out from time to time to work on any issues once the tree was established. We needed to work on some type of signal to let Jaffey know what was needed and by whom when I wasn't around. It was complicated, but I think it could be done. We spent the better part of what was left of the daylight hashing out the details.

Nkiru and her herd were just heading out when Jaffey and Marcus finally pulled up. I didn't know if I wanted to cry out of relief, or kill them both and leave their bodies. I settled for something in between.

"Where the hell were you?! You left me here in the middle of a desert with no real provisions and certainly no note of when or if you'd be back, I could kill you both! If only you let

211

me arm myself this time..." I was livid, but it was a controlled anger- or so I told myself. They didn't say much, as I expected, and I noticed that they were alone. "Where are the prisoners you captured from last night?" I wished I hadn't asked that the second it started coming out of my mouth. I really didn't want to know.

"We weren't sure where to take them, as I had mentioned it gets confusing along the borders as to jurisdiction. We finally decided to take care of it ourselves." I gave him a questioning look, and didn't ask about it any further.

"Nkiru and her family were just here." I tried to change the subject.

"I saw them just leave. Everyone all right this time I trust?" Jaffey spoke softly, but I think it was out of exhaustion. Marcus was busying himself with my tent, and I was glad to see that we weren't planning on staying another night.

"Yes, they are fine, well, for now anyway. We came up with a plan. I need to tell you about it, as you will be my go between when I'm not here." I spoke with authority, although none had officially been given to me. I decided it was time for me to take charge, not to sit back and wait for someone else to tell me the bits and piece of whatever web I was stuck in. It was time that I took control of my life. It was, after all, my brain that this highly anticipated device was attached to.

"I see." That's all he said. We spent the ride back up to Nairobi in the back seat discussing the plan while Marcus drove. I didn't know how much Marcus knew, but Jaffey wasn't being secretive around him. He had to be in on some of the basics, at least. Jaffey helped me fine tune the communication tree, trying to allow for missed information transfers, incomplete deliveries, and incomplete conversations that were bound to arise when one species was trying to talk to another. There were so many potential holes in the plan- I was growing more doubtful as we approached the airport.

"Do you think it could work?" I asked Jaffey, not wanting to seem weak, but truly wanting his opinion.

"That's exactly how we pictured it would start."

"Who, exactly, pictured it would start this way, and why am I always left in the dark?" I felt the anger start to rise again.

"Well, Dr. Dubashi, who created the device, Dr. Aquene, who helped her get the contacts together, myself, and of course, it was all originated by Dr. Ceta."

Dr. Ceta, I almost forgot all about her. she was the one who created the organization to begin with. She would be the one with all the answers. I wondered if Jaffey ever met her, and where she worked from. Could she be in DC at headquarters somewhere in the giant building?

"I have never met her. What is she like?" I did what I could to get any information out of Jaffey, but it was no good. He just smiled and said that I would meet her eventually.

That wasn't good enough, I thought. "So you've met her then?" I had to keep trying. But, he kept avoiding the answer. We had reached our destination, and I was about to head home with only a few answers, yet feeling somewhat satisfied with our future plan. It was hard to imagine any long term arrangement with people who were so deceptive, but I was slowly adapting to the accordance. I was still pissed, don't get me wrong, but I was adjusting to the new expectations they had of me. Maybe I could pull this off, be the superhero.

I was glad to be going home, back to the mess I left behind. I still worried about the implant, about my role in Jon's death, and about my future. But for now, I wanted to spend time on the flight home coming up with a plan to meet this illusive Dr. Ceta.

Chapter 25

Well, I didn't get my plan cemented together on the flight-in fact I had slept the entire way back to DC. Being an interspecies translator was taking its toll. Certainly having to adapt to all the changes as of late had also worn me thin. I was grateful for the time alone- even if I was crammed into a flying hunk of metal with a hundred or so others- and I was grateful to be home.

So I was left with no real plan of action, some residual hostility, and a whole lot of questions. When I took charge and told Jaffey what the plan was going to be, he seemed to accept it. Perhaps I could use the same approach at STAFE headquarters and demand to see Dr. Ceta, finally. I didn't see what the problem was. However elusive she was, and however otherwise occupied, it wouldn't seem outlandish for my request (or demand) for a meeting.

My apartment was empty and lonely without Uri there. I really didn't think it would make much of a difference, he had only been with me a short time, but walking through the door with no one there to greet me was a sad feeling. It brought back memories of my last dog, Moses. When he passed, the house was so noticeably empty then as well. I threw my bag into the corner of the bedroom- figuring I'd get to it at some point when I ran out of clothes again- and proceeded to fill up on caffeine.

It was Thursday morning, and I had no idea who would be at the organization. Maybe I should head over to the holding facility first- take care of business, get it out of the way. I decided to call Martin first, to see what was going on.

"Hey there, how's my bird?" It was the first thing on my mind, although I hated to sound all possessive of him.

"You can't have him back! Are you home now?" He sounded like he was in a good mood.

"Yes, just arrived. What's going on with work? Zoo animals doing well?" I figured everything was pretty much as I left it.

"Well, the Capuchins were transported to their new home at the Chicago Zoo, the ostriches went to the Bronx Zoo, the reptiles all went to Florida, and most of the rest were healthy enough to go to the National Zoo. It's just the tiger left, waiting on dental surgery. Depending on how things go, he's slated to go to San Diego. Are you planning on coming over today? There's really nothing left to do right now, I don't think."

I was elated that they were all able to settle into better establishments, places where they could move around and have decent medical care. I was saddened, in a way, though. I was already missing them all, particularly the lemurs. They were so playful when I worked with them. I was hesitant to ask about the dog fighting ring, how it was resolved, because I didn't want the details of Jon's death. Yet I had to know where our cases stood.

Martin replied, "Jon's partner arrested that Espinoza guy. I guess he was some drug boss from Mexico. He smuggled in illegally procured exotic animals- I guess parrots were his specialty- as well as drugs. Well, he owned that dog from the last crime scene that you went to in Maryland. He was also the guy that rented the other house in Maryland and owned the dogs whose remains were found there, the two full bodies. His partner said something about him killing a guy in a warehouse? This guy apparently had trained under Martinez of the Twentieth Street Gang. You know, the one that owned 'Darling Dan'? He had been a yard boy for him just after the guy that offed himself out in West Virginia- the one who owned the two skeletonized dogs without skulls. Anyway, they both worked for that Martinez guy around the same time, and moved out to Maryland to start their own gang and dog

215

fighting ring, only it didn't take off so well. The FBI thinks that the dog fighting was just a side thing, and they were more focused on pushing drugs through the area."

"So that guy in West Virginia really offed himself? I thought it was questionable if it was that or murder?"

"The FBI is still going with suicide, at least that's what they told me. He apparently killed his girlfriend- the body we found at the first scene- and was the one who was starting the drug ring out this way. I guess he could have been offed by Espinoza, wanting to take over the gang? I don't know, but you missed the service for Jon."

I didn't want to hear that part. "Did you go?" I had an involuntary response to pull the phone away from my ear, not wanting to hear anymore, but I pulled it back.

"No I didn't go. I thought about it- going for you, you know? But I couldn't bring myself to do it. I would have felt so out of place with all those FBI people."

"So how's my bird?" I desperately wanted to change the subject.

"You mean MY bird? He's just ducky, thank you very much." I knew that was coming, and I was OK with him keeping the little conure. Of course, being stolen property- evidence even- I was kind of glad it wasn't in my possession anymore.

He asked about the trip, but I had to be lean on the details. I wondered how long we would have to keep up this charade- was it forever? It was getting harder not to include Martin in on the whole picture. I really would have loved his input on my current plan to barge into headquarters and demand a meeting with the phantom Dr. Ceta. I'm sure he would have had something cheeky to say, or even have some double-O- seven advice. But I had to go it alone. I left it hanging whether or not I was expecting Uri back, knowing full well that he was Martin's for life now. Then I told him how pleased I was with his work with the zoo animals. He really was an asset.

I sat debating whether or not I should take headquarters by storm. I wondered if Dr. Dubashi was expecting me to train today. Did they know I was even back in town? Well of course they did, they knew everything about me, I answered myself. I wouldn't be surprised if they had a tracking device attached to the implant. They wouldn't want to lose track of such an important piece of equipment, would they? Sufficiently stewed in resentment, I headed downtown.

The metro was packed for a Thursday- blossoming cherry trees had that kind of impact on tourists. Everyone seemed happy that it was a beautiful spring day, but I had to stay focused on my outrage and resentment. I had to have the courage to demand this meeting. That is, if there was anyone there to demand it of.

I walked in the foyer looking around for security. There was just the usual guy at the inner door, and nodded me through. I pushed the button for the top floor inside the elevator and away I went, on to find my answers. The doors opened to the reception area, and there was no one there. I felt a sinking feeling in my chest. What if all this bravado was for nothing? I slowly walked in and looked around. The doors to the main office were closed. I had one more chance. Taking a deep breath, I barged my way in, ready to spout out my appeal. But, there was no one there either. I was fully deflated, out of options for the moment. I thought of going down to the lair below, but I would have a hard time being angry with Dr. Dubashi, at least if it was just her alone.

I walked out of the office and headed back to the elevator wondering what to do next when the door opened. There stood Dr. Dubashi and Dr. Aquene, and it took me off guard for a minute. Before I could speak my peace, however, Dr. Dubashi started in about missing training before I went to Africa. I started to get caught up in her chastisement, almost feeling bad for it, then I remembered why I was there in the first place.

"I want..."

217

"Did you think you could avoid us, avoid training, avoid your new position?" Dr. Dubashi cut me off.

"I need answers, and I am sick of..."

"You will get answers, dear doctor, when you are ready to hear them. I'm not sure this attitude will get you what you are looking for." Dr. Aquene interrupted this time. She was distinctly angrier than her comrade. I waited for them to talk themselves out- they obviously had objections to my behavior, and we weren't going to make it far with all the interruptions.

"Dr. Wake, this is serious business. STAFE has invested heavily in you, and your cooperation is, well, required." Dr. Dubashi was playing the good cop role, and it was wearing thin on me.

"Why was I picked for this role, anyway? I think I've been kept in the dark long enough. What exactly is my role here with STAFE, and what is their agenda?" My anger was coming back up just in time. I was on a roll.

"There are many things we need to tell you. We were waiting for you to get accustomed to your new role. It's complicated, why don't you come in and sit down." Dr. Dubashi escorted me to the big office with Dr. Aquene following behind. I felt queasy, and was once again wishing that I hadn't come here at all.

We settled in, with Dr. Aquene and Dr. Dubashi taking turns rehashing the beginnings of the organization. Most of it was old news to me- I had heard a lot of the bits and pieces along the way. Then Dr. Aquene paused- she had a flair for the dramatic, I thought- and went on with the more hidden side of the organization.

"Dr. Ceta started this operation out of extreme need. She contacted Dr. Dubashi, against the advisement of, well, we'll just say others, and the two of them built this group to what it is now. This is an international organization, you know, but it is far more reaching than you could imagine." I was picturing Nkiru while Dr. Aquene spoke, remembering what the elephant said to me about expecting me. She had been told that I would be coming soon, but I didn't know how long Nkiru had known about the plan.

"STAFE really stands for STop Animals From Extinction. Dr. Ceta was extremely worried that we had turned a corner from which we couldn't come back. She was desperate to find a solution, some way to keep the species alive." I could see a tear well up in her eye as she spoke, and then I started to wonder which species she was referring to.

"The organization has a few goals that drive the overall mission. Unfortunately, one of those goals is to, well, take care of those who harm and kill animals. That is, to intervene when the law is insufficient. I'm sure you already figured that one out. It's not something we wanted to do, but after years of attempting to do things by the law, Dr. Ceta decided that it wasn't working. There were many species going extinct, being wiped out for many reasons, most of which were caused by humans." She paused again, then stood to look out the window. I could tell she was getting emotional, and I worried what was going to follow.

"We really wanted to educate people, that was what all this was for. I thought that if we could educate and inform...people would change their ways. Clearly, I was wrong. Dr. Ceta knew that approach wouldn't work. I guess I was stubborn at first. I had faith once- faith that the human race could turn things around still- but we couldn't make it work. Things were deteriorating at an extreme rate. Dr. Ceta saw that, long before I could. We still have a huge educational department, don't get me wrong. It's still one of our main goals. You may have noticed that the building the lab is housed in is occupied primarily by the media group, ARM. It stands for Animal Rights Media- it's how we 'push our agenda', to paraphrase the opposition. We have infiltrated many segments of the media in several parts of the world, but we have to keep it covert. If anyone knew of our real agenda, well the backlash would be immense."

I had to think back to the time that Martin and I took a trip over to the lab and met Georgie- the ride from hell in that elevator, free-falling in the dark, the feeling of being watched. I knew that ARM was something more than it appeared. Were they trying to kill me back then, or were they just scare tactics-keeping me away from their secret endeavors? Some of the stranger details were starting to make sense to me.

"What do you mean by real agenda? Are you still talking about the part where you take the law into your own hands?" I tried not to sound judgmental, but they had included me when they put this device in my head and made me a part of their plan.

"Not exactly. Our agenda, our plan, is more complicated. It's much more extensive than just that. We like to think of it as an uprising, really."

"So you all want to take over the world??" I was floored. I had no idea how big their scope was. What exactly would be their endgame?

"Not so much a takeover. A new mutual understanding between the species." Dr. Dubashi interjected. She did have a way with words, but I wasn't sure that I was falling for it anymore.

"And is that where I come in? I'm the translator, the....negotiator?" I wasn't sure I wanted this role at all.

"I worked for years on a way to facilitate communication between species, Dr. Wake. Most of my work, my blood, sweat, and tears were tied up in the device that now occupies part of your brain..."

"Wait, wait, occupies PART of my brain?? I was under the assumption that it was a small device attached to one of my lobe-, an addition to my brain- not occupying part of my brain! What did you do to me?!" I flew out of my chair, as if to physically attack her, but I stopped short.

"You were greatly injured, Alex. You were...well, let's just say that you probably wouldn't be alive if we didn't interfere. The device is an integral part of your existence now. I'm afraid it will always be...while you're alive." She sounded sinister, almost threatening- a first for Dr. Dubashi.

I was at a loss for words. Maybe I would've died, but I wouldn't have been there in the first place if they didn't lie to me. All I could do was stare at her in disdain, show her my contempt for the whole situation.

"Dr. Wake, I assure you we did what had to be done, to save your life. Don't look at it as part of our plan, we didn't know for certain who would be the first." Dr. Aquene tried to break the tension.

"The first? so there are more or there will be more? Is this all part of the agenda as well?" I sunk back down in the chair. There was nothing that I could do about my own head, but I wanted more answers.

"There will need to be more, yes. You can't be everywhere at once. Communicators, translators, whatever you want to call them, they are the biggest part of our plan. Once we have more scientists on board- we are actively recruiting from some of the greatest universities and corporations- we can work on the next level."

"The next level? And what would that be? Taking over the government?" There was an extremely pregnant pause, and I flew out of my chair again.

"Calm down, Dr. Wake. It's not like we are planning on overthrowing the government. We just plan to influence decisions higher up. Laws and regulations will have to be changed, you are aware? It's appalling what people are allowed to do to animals- the way they're treated, abused, and killed. Laws most certainly will have to be changed, and the political pull we will need will be great. So yes, we are slowly acquiring those on the inside of government, in several parts of the world." Dr. Aquene sounded defensive, as if she wasn't quite sure it was the right move, but perhaps their backs were against the wall. Perhaps they felt as if they had run out of options.

"So I just happened along with a traumatic brain injury and you stuck this device in my brain- no, made it part of my brain. Now I have no option but to go along with your plan?"

"It was a little more calculated than that, Alex. We had our eye on you for a while. You had been very outspoken at the trials where you were an expert witness, and had a certain something. Well, Dr. Ceta noticed it first. She saw video of proceedings where you were testifying. She knew right away

221

that you needed to be on board- one of us. I wasn't as certain of your commitment, however. There were a few tests we performed along the way." Dr. Dubashi let me in a few more details, and I started to feel sick again.

"What else did you do to me? What other tests?" I thought about the shooting on my way home from work but couldn't see how that would test for anything, unless it was a way to cause a head trauma and gain access to my brain.

"We had to do a few minor things....we bugged your apartment." Dr. Dubashi said it with a questioning look on her face, waiting for me to put something together. I thought back to any awkward or telling moments, anything out of place. Then the clicking sound came to mind. Was it that? Why would it have made that sound? I looked up at her.

"Alex, I can't explain it to you now. I will in time, but for now, know that we just needed to find out, well, what your talents were. Some people have a sixth sense about things. Some people can hear or see things that others can't. We needed to know what, if any, your talents were. Dr. Ceta needed to know for sure." She said it so casually, like everyone went around with superpowers. It all sounded ridiculous.

"Did you have me shot at? Either on my way home or while I was in Africa? Was any of that you?"

"Not at all. As we have said, you presented with the brain injury. It was just excellent timing." Dr. Aquene answered.

I wasn't necessarily buying their answers, especially that last one. It was more than enough for me. "I want to see Dr. Ceta. I think it's about time that I meet the person who's responsible for all of this, the one that did this to me."

The two of them looked at each other and then looked at me. After a long pause, they answered in unison, "I'm afraid that's not possible."

Chapter 26

Why couldn't I meet with her, was she dead? I left the office in such an emotionally confused state. Anger was the dominant theme, but curiosity and strangely, optimism rounded out the field. They were still holding so much back, so much that I wanted to know, but had also given me quite a lot to digest.

I headed back toward the apartment, but never actually made it. Instead, I found myself continuing straight for the parking garage and taking out the car. If there was a time for a road trip, this was it. There was so much to think about, mostly things out of my control, but how I responded to it all was still under my rule.

I rolled down the windows- an odd thing to say seeing as no one really "rolls" them down anymore- cranked the radio, and headed east. "33 Degree" by Thievery Corporation was playing, and I was pondering the depth of infiltration the organization had. Scientists and political insiders from around the world were in on the secret. Hell, the elephants in Kenya knew about at least part of the plan. The drive felt short, mostly because I was so lost in thought. I was lucky the traffic wasn't too heavy.

I stopped for some pizza along the way. I hadn't eaten much in several days, and the last thing I needed was to feel weak from hunger- the jet lag was bad enough. I knew the coons wouldn't be around in the daytime to help me finish it off, but it would be night soon enough. I made my way down the embankment to my usual hangout by the cove.

I sat for a while, listening to the voices of the daytime animals as they prepared for the dark. Did they know what

223

was going on? Were they in on the uprising? The sun settled down in the trees, leaving fantastic oranges and reds behind. I worried about the future, now more than ever.

The doctors sounded convinced that this was the only way, the last option to save the species- which ever ones they were referring to. Maybe they meant all of them in general. I wondered if this Dr. Ceta had brainwashed them or otherwise convinced them of this plan. Surely circumstances weren't so dire that taking things into their own hands was the only option?

Most of the noise in my head was coming from me, my thoughts, but the results were the same. I had an excruciating headache, and all I wanted at that moment was to get relief. I slipped off my clothes and dove in. The water felt colder today for some reason- maybe it was because the air was so warm. I submerged to get used to the temperature, and I was thankful that it slowly alleviated the throbbing pain in my head.

Part of my brain was preoccupied with putting all the pieces together- the strange happenings in the building where the lab was, the strange clicking sounds in my apartment- which had yet to be adequately explained to me- and the need for me to repeatedly travel to Africa. How long had they been watching me before I joined their organization? I certainly didn't believe that putting the implant into my brain was just a stroke of good timing.

Feeling daring, I swam out of the safety of the nook and into the open waters. Hey if a shark came along, maybe I could just talk my way out of him eating me. I wasn't sure I had much regard for my life. It was apparent that I was a pawn for STAFE, and few things were under my control. I worried that there was a Lo-Jack system in my head, maybe even something to take over my thoughts or actions at some point. I really had no idea what I was dealing with.

I went under water again, looking for something to get my mind off of the madness. It may have been a while before it came around again, but it did- the harbor seal from previous encounters found me floating in its neighborhood. I felt the usual swirling sensation as it swam circles around my body, so

I went down and said hello. The seal was kind enough to come to the surface, so we could have an exchange with the presence of air- always helpful for longer conversations, especially for us humans.

I asked how its friend was doing, it turns out that it was her offspring, and she was a female, details that I didn't catch the first time around. We had a long, if not bizarre, conversation about pollution. She couldn't comprehend the notion of dumping so much useless, dangerous debris in the waters, and I didn't understand it enough to explain to her the reasons why.

She had other concerns as well. Ones that were totally our fault and ones that weren't. Noise pollution was a big one. So many animals down here use sound to find each other, find food, and to listen for predators. Not to mention, sound was also crucial for migration and echolocation. The booming depth charges, engines, and drilling were causing havoc under the seas. Over-fishing had caused the loss of many species and the scarcity of food sources for others. Then there was the issue with all the traffic. Why were so many boats necessary? Their oil discharge, propellers, and noise were creating even more problems for the lives that lived under water.

I had little to say. Mostly I just agreed. There wasn't much that I could do, by myself, to alleviate the stresses of sub-aquatic life. Maybe we were so far along with the destruction and perils of human interference that something drastic needed to be done. Perhaps Dr. Ceta was correct, it was time. This brought me back to thinking about her- Dr. Ceta. Was she still alive, and why couldn't I meet with her? I was getting upset again when the seal dipped under the surface. She came up suddenly and seemed alarmed.

"What's the matter?" I couldn't hear anything that sounded injured or crying for help, but the seal obviously did when she submerged.

"Someone's in trouble!" She said and went back under.

I went under to listen, but still there was nothing. The seal grew panicked. Someone desperately needed help. She swam out a ways, with me lumbering behind. One thing my body

225

wasn't made for was swimming, at least at decent speeds. The seal came back even more alarmed than before. We had to go, and go fast. She told me to grab on to her flipper and we would go faster, so I did.

At first it was clumsy, her balance was off, and I was catching waves in my face. Ultimately we managed to do it in a series of shorter distances all under water. I wasn't sure how long I could hold my breath, so the lengths were short at the beginning, but then I grew more confident, and we covered more ground.

We were far out to sea when we came up close to the voice calling for help. By this time, I could hear it as well. Some animal was trapped and couldn't breathe. There was a large vessel sitting in the open water, but no engine was running. I couldn't see anyone on board from the low position I was in at the water's surface. I felt the panic now as we swam around looking for the source of the voice. It was coming from below- way below, much further than I thought I could dive safely. The seal had made the depth to scout.

She surfaced and indicated that a dolphin had been trapped in a fishing net and it looked hopeless. I tried to gear myself up for the dive- there was no other option now. I had to find a way to get the animal free. I took an initial look, but the net was dragging so far behind and deep. Even if I made it down, I wasn't sure I could make it back up.

I had to do it, I had no choice. Taking a deep breath, I went down, but again wasn't able to make the journey. I panicked and came back up. The harbor seal had an idea- I would grab hold of her flipper again, getting down to the net as fast as possible. Once again I took a deep breath and we flew through the water. I grabbed hold of the net, looking for a hole or some way in. The netting itself consisted of thick rope and was covered with seaweed. It had been dragged behind the boat in an attempt to catch other fish, but unfortunately caught the dolphin as well. I couldn't see a way to help it.

The seal brought me back to the surface, a little too fast, but in enough time not to pass out. I had to come up with another plan quickly. I didn't have any tools with which to cut the netting- it was the only way to get the dolphin out. I wanted to yell to the boat to get someone's attention. Maybe they could release the net or something. But I was too afraid that they would just pull away with the dolphin in tow. The commercial fishermen weren't usually so obliging to give up their catch- it was their livelihood.

Maybe I could sneak up to the boat and release the net myself. I looked around the sides in an attempt to find a way up. How did people get back into their boats when they fell in? The only way up I could find was the fishing line itself. Pulling on the line, I checked to see what kind of tension it held. It was tight enough to hold my weight, but I wasn't sure I was strong enough to hold on as I climbed up. It was my only opportunity to get on board.

It was a struggle, I won't lie. I had slipped back several times, even crying out once. I feared that those on the boat would hear me, but I got lucky. When I made it to the top, it was all I could do to pull my body over and fall to the floor of the vessel. I tried to lay still- to listen for voices. I was sure that someone would have spotted me by now. Creeping along the rail, I could make out the tops of the heads of two men. They appeared to be sharing stories, laughing about something, completely unaware of my presence, for now anyway.

The controls for the net were in the compartment with the fishermen, and I had no way to get in without being caught. What if I threw something to the other end of the boat? They would hear it and go check it out, right? No such luck. Whatever tale was being orated had them engrossed. There had to be some other way.

Feeling distraught, I snuck around back to the rear of the boat. What if I could cut the line, or the netting? There was a seat with hinges, enclosing a storage area. I made sure that the men couldn't see as I opened the hold. A few screwdrivers, a hammer, a life jacket that looked like it never got worn, and a roll of duct tape were all heaped together. None of those

227

provisions would help me out. I rummaged around, digging through the contents for something more. Something cut my hand and I almost cried out. I knocked some boots over as I pulled out my arm so fast. There was some movement in the compartment- the men had heard the commotion.

There was no time, I had to get out of there. Sticking my hand back into the bin, I found the knife that had cut me, and I grabbed it. The footsteps were almost at the corner, I had to do something fast. It was too late to throw a distraction the other way, and there was nowhere to run. There was no recourse, I had to jump.

I knew that the fishermen would hear the splash and be watching for something to surface, so I had to hold my breath for a long time. I could make out their outlines as I peered up through the water. At last I had to swim under the boat to the other side to go up for air. I hoped they would give up the search, sooner than later- there was work to be done.

The harbor seal met me on the far side of the watercraft and indicated that we were out of time. I inhaled deeply and took hold of its flipper again. The submerging was rougher this time, the seal was going faster and in a more chaotic fashion. Her panic was getting to her, but we didn't have time to regroup. I had the knife in my mouth- it seemed logical at the time with one hand being occupied by a flipper and the other hemorrhaging from the cut. I supposed that sharks would be coming soon, but I didn't have time to worry about that.

The descent ended abruptly, and I immediately went to task cutting the net. I struggled at first- it was slippery having been in the water for so long and covered in algae and seaweed- but I quickly made progress. Some of the fish that were still alive had swarmed the opening I was creating, making it difficult to continue. I had no breath to waste on admonishing them for their plights to free themselves. All I could do was cut as fast as possible.

I had to forcefully assist the mass of exiting creatures to get to the dolphin. It was weak by now, on its last leg, so to speak, and I needed to pull it out of the netting manually. I was on

Chapter 27

That night held some of the best sleep that I had gotten in quite a while. I somehow felt relieved, that the reason for all of this was becoming clear- although I didn't have all the answers yet. The dreams about the clicking crickets also faded away now that I knew it was somehow all related to STAFE. I was going to get my answers, whether it was going to be through the organization directly, or out of those animals around me who were in on it all.

I still had the instinct to get up and feed Uri, even though he had moved on to his new digs. Maybe I should think about getting another dog. I took my time getting up that morning, I had nothing dire to tend to, although I was probably expected at the lair to train. I was still deciding on that one.

Bach was on the radio- the Lute Suites- setting the mood for a relaxing Friday. If only I had food in the house for breakfast. Once again coffee was the meal by default, but that was OK. I was feeling oddly at peace. I thought that it might be a good time to demand another meeting, while I was in such good mood, but that could wait for later.

Dr. Dubashi had said that my apartment had been bugged- were the devices still here? I took a look around. My mind went back to our visit to the lab that day, seeing all the surveillance equipment in the far room. Was that for me? No devices were found, but my armoire had been messed with. The clothes were disheveled, leaving a space big enough for a person to stand. Was I being watched as well? Just what lengths had they gone to? Maybe if I did my laundry more often I would have realized their infiltration. Good housekeeping had its merits.

The phone rang but I didn't want to answer it, not while I was still in a good mood. Nothing beneficial would come from it. I let it go to voicemail, and poured another cup. A shower would be a distraction- a reason not to answer if they called back. So I took my time basking in the steam. After getting water logged last night, standing under a shower head spewing more water wasn't the first thing on my to-do list, I'd admit, but it felt good.

Bach had transitioned into Handel by the time I got out, keeping it a morning of Baroque. That was fine with me. If it wasn't the soundtrack to a peaceful Friday morning, I didn't know what was. The phone rang again, and this time I picked it up. It was Carrie, and I didn't want to hear what she had to say.

"Dr. Dubashi and Dr. Aquene would like to meet with you this morning." She was short and to the point. I had to admit that I was expecting it to be about training, so I was a little intrigued.

"Could it wait?" I knew they were used to getting what they wanted, and I was risking a lot just suggesting that I wasn't agreeing to it, but I couldn't help myself.

"I believe you'll want to take this meeting, trust me," Carrie said and hung up. Well, I didn't trust her for sure, but it piqued my interest. What could they have possibly done now, and why did I need to be a part of it?

The metro was packed, something that was common for a Friday- the government buildings and sightseeing destinations were usually busy, some with waiting lines already. I had stopped at Universal Donuts on my way to the train, so I had to elbow my way to get some room to fine dine on my way in. Nothing like a few carbs to get your day going.

Headquarters was strangely desolate, with even the one guard absent from his post. I assumed the meeting would take place in the penthouse suite- I was getting used to the awkward visits to the over-sized room. Carrie was there to meet me at the elevator doors. She escorted me to the office, where the doctors had already made themselves comfortable waiting for my arrival. I felt like I was going to the shark tank, and it reminded me of the cut on my hand. I looked down at it as they heralded their salutations. Then I looked up.

Dr. Aquene was actually smiling- a stiff, forced smile- but a smile just the same. My stomach dropped, and suddenly I regretted having had that donut. Dr. Dubashi was sporting the same facial wear, but on her it looked real. I side stepped any actual contact with the two, opting for the winged arm chair to the side. I didn't know what they were up to, but I was sure I didn't want any part of it.

"Dr. Wake, I'm glad you could make it." It was Dr. Aquene who started out the conversation as she walked back behind the massive desk. I wondered why she needed the seat of empowerment, the boss's chair, for this discussion. It was a gauche blend of mixed messages, and it had me worried.

"Did I have a choice? These days I wasn't aware anything was really under my control anymore." I said it more to tease a response- I didn't have the anger this time as I did before, although I'm sure it would've come back in a snap.

"Alex, I know you don't understand the whole picture, yet. We haven't been forthcoming in the details." It was Dr. Dubashi who spoke, and it made me chuckle. She wasn't quite sure how to take my response.

"You will get your answers, but it has to be on our terms, in our way. You do understand?" Dr. Aquene took over again.

"I understand that you like control, in more ways than one." I was to the point, and I was too confident to back down today.

Dr. Dubashi took on a more subtle demeanor. "We are grateful to you for your recent actions. It has been brought to our attention that you rescued someone critical to our work last night."

I wondered how much that dolphin knew. He took off right after telling me about his awareness of STAFE. He must have been more involved with the group than I figured. I felt a tinge of pride well inside.

233

"That dolphin had been working very close with Dr. Ceta and me. I don't know what would have happened if we lost him. We owe you the truth for what you've done, even if you're not quite as prepared for it as we hoped you would be when the time came." Dr. Dubashi sounded cryptic, but I was elated that I would finally get some answers.

"As you know now, our agenda here at STAFE is to save all species from extinction, in whatever fashion necessary. We aren't proud of some of the steps we are forced to take, but we were left with no other valid options. You also now know that you are our first- our prototype, if you will- interspecies translator. We didn't know it would work, but Anoushka has labored relentlessly for many years to develop this technology. We think this is the time- the most critical time- to initiate the next phase of our project, and we need you on board." Dr. Aquene sounded more like she was asking rather than ordering, a first between us.

I stood and walked to the window behind her. It wasn't a power move, although I supposed it could have been taken as such. Staring out at the city on such a busy morning while its future was being decided in that room was overwhelming. None of it felt real.

"At this point, we need you to decide your future. As the only translator, your well-being is of utmost importance. You took quite a risk last night, jeopardizing your life. You have proven to us your commitment to the welfare of others, and for that we commend you." Dr. Aquene said from her chair, although she wasn't turned to face me. I felt that acquiescing power to another was not a strong point of hers.

"I didn't really do anything. You people were the ones that put this device in my head- without my knowledge or permission." I spoke to the window, not knowing how I really felt about the whole situation. I didn't want any emotion to show on my face.

"No, that's where you are wrong, Alex," Dr. Dubashi said. "We only gave you a device that converts words and in some cases, thoughts into understandable messages. It has no power over your actions or will. You were the one who decided to swim out there and risk your life to save another. That was completely under your control. It was you who chose to be the protector."

I turned to look at her even though I felt the tears start to well up, then I had to turn back. It was a ploy to get me to join ranks with them, I knew it. All this talk was crazy, wasn't it? They were the ones that bugged my apartment- no, had someone IN my apartment. I wasn't about to forget all that. I still wanted answers.

"You had someone stake out my apartment, inside my armoire. Are you going to tell me about that?"

"There are many things left to tell you. I think the best way would be to show you." Dr. Aquene got up from her chair and offered me her hand.

They took me down to the lair, but we didn't stop in the main room, the one where I practiced my new skill with Dr. Dubashi and the water creatures. We went to the back room- the room that the doctor would emerge from as I waited for our lessons to start. It wasn't elaborate, nothing out of the science fiction literature by far. It housed nearly identical equipment as the main room, up to and including the large Plexiglas window on the side. Only this window was facing a different direction.

Dr. Dubashi offered me a chair. I felt odd being the only one seated, but I waited patiently while they put on their performance. I half expected a light show to be cued- some sort of carnival extravaganza. Instead, the lights were dimmed and I was offered a set of headphones. We usually started out the training that way, so my focus turned to the other side of the glass. From the murk of the water I could make out the form of an approaching pinniped or dolphin. As it swam closer it spoke.

"Good morning, Dr. Wake. We meet again." It was the dolphin from last night.

235

"Hello again. How are you today? We both had a scare last night, didn't we?" I wasn't sure what was going on, how he got to the building, or how involved he was with the organization.

"I wanted to thank you once again. And to introduce you to someone." I watched as he swam away, only to return with another dolphin by his side. "May I introduce you to Dr. Ceta."

I was once again speechless. Never in a million years had I imagined- Dr. Ceta was a dolphin. A dolphin. This whole organization was created by a cetacean. How did this all happen? I was too dumbfounded for words, so I just nodded my acknowledgment. What was going on? Memories came flooding back from being shot, from almost dying, and I wondered if I actually did. Dr. Dubashi brought me out of my stupor.

"Ceta and I, well Dr. Ceta as we have referred to her for obvious reasons, have been working together for years. When I started to decode their language, we found that our species had much in common. It was a natural progression of our ideas, really. We decided to start STAFE to protect all those who were being wronged in our society."

"Dr. Ceta?" I was having a hard time wrapping my brain around this. "So you refer to the dolphin as doctor?" I was now addressing Dr. Dubashi, trying to put the pieces together.

"Yes, we felt a more formal title would be useful, for professional reasons. The organization was held in the highest regards by many in the scientific community, and we needed to be fully accepted. I'm sure you will need some time for all this to sink in."

That was the understatement of the year. I worked for an organization that was run by a dolphin. That happens to a lot of people, right? "How did she... how did the dolphins get here? Aren't we several miles from the ocean?" I was glad that I was sitting, I was sure that my legs would have given out by now.

"We created extensive tunnels running under the city. Some go out to the ocean, some go out even further. We needed a way to get all our members gathered together. The

District of Columbia is actually sinking due to what's called a forebulge collapse, created during the ice age, and it's dropping as the sea level in the Chesapeake Bay is rising from climate change. Put the two together, and you have a perfect storm for aquatic infiltration." She sounded proud of her endeavors, proud of her accomplishments. I supposed I would have been as well.

"How extensive is the organization? I know some elephants in Kenya are part of it."

"It's quite remarkable, really." Dr. Aquene was jumping in to the conversation while Dr. Dubashi was enamored with her water bound friends. "We have called on the cetaceans and pinnipeds by ocean, the corvids by air, and a multitude of animals by land. Some of the Capuchins you had in custody were originally part of the network. That was before they were illegally captured and sold on the black market. We have been organizing collectives around the world."

"That's why now is the time." It was Dr. Ceta interjecting. "I have been witnessing the demise of many species and now it must stop. We are about to move into phase two, with your help, Alex."

"...You need a translator."

"That is correct. We, unfortunately, had to spy on you, to test you, to ensure you were the one."

That reminded me of the armoire and the clicking noises in my apartment. "Who was in my place? What were those noises?"

Dr. Aquene answered, "I had an operative inside. He informed me of your activities by walkie-talkie. What you heard were the clickings of Dr. Ceta and her associates when we were discussing you. She needed to know if you could understand any of her communications. She sensed there was something different about you from the beginning.

"Well, all it gave me were creepy dreams. The clicks translated into the chirpings of giant crickets, and then joined by several other animals. They all wanted to tell me something."

237

Dr. Dubashi smiled and nodded to the window. The dolphins had mimicked the gesture back.

"That is what I thought," Dr. Ceta replied. "You already had the ability to understand to some degree, you just needed a little help."

They were all looking at me as if I had done something to be proud about. Dr. Dubashi sat down in a chair next to me and held my hand. "You now have a choice to make. It wasn't a coincidence that you and Martin are without families, we chose only those who could easily slip through society, to disappear if necessary, and not really be missed. You now have the choice to disappear, to work for us underground, so to speak. Or, we could keep you on in the same role as our forensic veterinarian while working covertly on our secret agenda. It's up to you."

It was the first time in weeks that I had choices, that I was in control. My mind reeled over the possibilities. Whichever choice I made, I knew that I wanted Martin by my side- I needed my right hand man. I felt like I was at the brink of a new life, waiting to cross over the threshold on to new discoveries. There certainly were a lot of things to think about.

———————————————————————

THANK YOU!

Thank you for reading! If you would be so kind as to give a review on Amazon, I'd most appreciate it! And if you enjoyed it, please tell your friends!

www.amazon.com/author/a.davis

And rate it on **Goodreads** and **BookBub** too!

Other books available by A. Davis:

The Undertaker's Revenge- A Love Story
Keys To The Coffins
Cryptic Notes
The House That Death Forgot

Visit: **adavisworks.com**

Facebook: **www.facebook.com/adavisworks**

Twitter: **@adavisworks**

Made in the USA
Las Vegas, NV
18 July 2022